SAD

Opposites Ignite

Cover design by Wicked Smart Designs

Editing by Music City Freelance Editor

QUALITY CONTROL: I strive to produce error-free books, but even with all the critique partners, beta readers, and editors, sometimes an error slips through. Pretty please, if you find a typo or formatting issue, let me know at sadirastoneauthor@gmail.com so I may correct it. Thank you!

For up-to-date information about Sadira Stone's books, giveaways, and more, please sign up for Sadira's mailing list at www.sadirastone.com.

First edition

ISBN: 978-1-7357856-3-9

This book was professionally typeset on Reedsy.
Find out more at reedsy.com

To Duncan, my HEA

Foreword

Dear Reader: I began writing this series before the Pandemic of 2020 hit. After much careful thought, I decided not to include references to Covid-19 and our current political turmoil. My purpose in writing this series is to provide myself and my readers an escape from harsh reality, so I've set the Bangers Tavern series in a pandemic-free, alternate contemporary time. My best wishes for the health of my readers as we adapt to our new normal and strive for a more just society.

Chapter One

"Ow ow ow, Turn off the damn light." Eddie Volkov groaned and threw an arm over his eyes to block the blazing sunshine streaming through the skylight above his bed. December mornings should be mercifully dim and gray, not sharp enough to stab his bleary eyeballs.

The hangover kettledrums in his skull pounded him fully awake. *Not December. January first.*

He held his breath and turned his head. Beside him, soft curves undulated beneath the quilt. A blaze of electric blue hair fanned over his spare pillow. As he wound a curl around his trembling finger, images solidified—hot breath, scorching kisses, moans and pleas and silky tattooed skin. Cloud-soft breasts filling his hands, cushy thighs gripping his hips, pulling him closer, tighter. Bright, dark eyes that saw past his awkwardness and right into his defenseless soul. Those same eyes squinched tight as her sweet, fiery pussy clenched around his cock again and again, his name tumbling from her lips.

Rosie. Here. In my bed. After a year of silent pining, his wish had been granted.

He hadn't dared hope she meant anything by it when she kissed him beneath the mistletoe at work. After all, she flirted with all her customers at Bangers Tavern. But more mistletoe kisses followed in the weeks leading up to Christmas, just quick smooches as if she were sampling him, deciding if he was worth a tumble. He put everything he had into those kisses—not too handsy, not too wet, carefully angling his hips away to hide his insistent erection. Each time, she broke away with an enigmatic smile. Never asked for more, never lingered to chat after work.

Yesterday he arrived at Bangers to find the Christmas decorations replaced by New Year's streamers and balloons. No more mistletoe. And that, he figured, that was that. Time to surrender his stupid hopes and get on with his life.

But after closing time, the whole Bangers crew stayed to toast the new year. River, their head bartender, poured a round of champagne sparklers, and then another. Maybe two more. Who knows? Kiara cranked up the music, and they all danced in a giddy, exhausted scrum, kicking up streamers and half-deflated balloons. One by one, his work family took their leave until only he and Rosie remained, swaying and laughing under the spinning disco ball. With his arms around her lush curves, Eddie forgot his awkwardness and asked for one more kiss. Nothing would come of it, right?

Never in his twenty-eight years was he happier to be wrong.

And here she lay, sleeping peacefully beside him, every glorious, tattooed inch of her heating his bed and sparking new hope. *She spent the night. That means she wants more than a one-night stand, right?* Tickly warmth spread from his chest all the way to his fingers and toes. Burying his mile-wide grin in the pillow, he whispered, "Yessss."

Fearful of waking her, he scooted closer. His painfully hard cock throbbed inside his—check that, no shorts. *I just slept naked beside the most beautiful girl on the planet. Happy New Year to me.* His inner caveman begged to grasp her tight and bury himself inside her. But no, that would be creepy. He needed her wide awake before asking for another round. And maybe she didn't even like morning sex. Maybe she'd want to pee first, or brush her teeth, or unsnarl her hair. Did he have a spare toothbrush? Should he make coffee? Pancakes? Eggs?

Shit and double shit—his parents expected him for New Year's brunch. What time? He twisted to reach for his notebook. Not there, on the corner of his nightstand where he always left it. Had he dropped it somewhere? Left it at the bar? The hangover drumline kicked up the tempo as he searched his fuzzy brain.

Whose idea had it been to come back to his place? Memories dissolved and ran like watercolors, leaving a blurred puddle of sensations—breathless whispers, giddy laughter, lingering gazes, tracing the swirls and lines of her tattoos with his lips and tongue. Glorious. Heavenly. Perfect.

Totally worth losing the notebook. He turned back to Rosie's sleepy-soft body, gingerly slid his arm around her middle, and nestled his chin into the sweet-scented crook of her neck. For the first time in as long as he remembered, he didn't give a damn about checking his morning to-do list. Who needs daily goals and affirmations when you have a goddess snoring softly in your ear? He pressed his lips to her temple and surrendered to sleep.

* * *

"Ow." Something sharp and scratchy poked the crook of Rosie's neck. She yawned and stretched, and the pointy thing withdrew with a raspy mumble. *What the...?* Her eyes flew open, then squinted against the piercing sunlight. A warm hand closed on her breast.

Where am I? She sucked in a deep breath and scanned the room. The bed smelled foresty, like cedar and moss. Light streamed through a window in the slanted ceiling. Atop the old-fashioned brass bed, a blue and red quilt covered her and—she bit her lip and turned her head. *Eddie.*

The rotten-sock taste in her mouth and the throbbing behind her eyes left no doubt. Definitely too much booze last night. Nothing wrong with partying on New Year's Eve, but she'd partied herself right into a sweet, shy co-worker's bed. That's why she seldom drank much—more than two drinks, and buh-bye inhibitions. Now what?

Shame tightened her queasy belly. Dawn, her boss at Bangers Tavern, had warned her, after their first mistletoe smooch, "Eddie's got it bad, kiddo. Tread carefully, okay?"

"Got it bad? Is he sick?" Sure, Eddie was skinny, but with a wiry muscularity that reminded her of Michelangelo's David, and bright chestnut eyes that held hers for long, heart-thumping moments. At work, she'd sneak glances at his shoulders and biceps and crunchy little butt as he hefted beer kegs. No taller than her, he seemed strong enough to lift a car.

"Eddie's tender-hearted," Dawn had told her. "I got no problem with you flirting with customers. Carpe diem, I always say. But workplace romance screws with my staff.

4

Don't toy with Eddie."

But why did Dawn hang mistletoe from the bar's ceiling if she didn't want people to kiss? Eddie would wait until the boss was in her office, then find some excuse to linger beneath that clump of green, his eyebrows flicking up in a flirtatious question. *You wanna?*

Damn it, she did wanna. His crooked smile was so tempting. And his lips were so soft, his kisses so sweet—unlike the slobbery mauling she got from most guys she dated. Desire simmered under his cool surface, making her want to dive deeper.

New Year's Eve served up the perfect excuse. When the bar staff toasted the new year, it was so easy to land in Eddie's arms. So easy to keep dancing as their coworkers filed out, leaving them alone beneath the kitschy disco ball, its dizzy sparkle whirling them around and around.

And now he slept beside her, sunlight glinting off his wavy brown hair, glossy lashes fanned across his cheekbones, dark scruff shadowing his razor-sharp jaw. So pretty, so vulnerable, so one hundred percent wrong for her. Clean-cut guys like Eddie never stuck around with girls like her. God knows she'd bashed her head against that brick wall enough times to learn her lesson.

Breath held, she gingerly removed his hand from her breast and wriggled toward the edge of the bed. Eddie sighed and squirmed into the space she'd vacated, nuzzling her pillow. *No*, she corrected herself, *his pillow. Gotta get out of here.*

Rising on unsteady legs, she turned back for a final look. Sleep melted his solemn daytime expression into peaceful sweetness. His bare shoulders rose on a shiver. As she bent to tuck the quilt around him, her boob brushed his arm.

"Huh?" His eyes fluttered open. His brow rumpled, then smoothed as a bleary smile spread across his pillow-creased face. "Good morning," he croaked and pushed up on his elbow. His gaze sharpened as it raked over her naked body. "Wow."

"Yeah. Wow." She waved a limp hand over the bed. "Last night was, uh—really something." She shuffled backward, stifling the impulse to cover her bits. After all, he'd seen every inch of her. He'd sampled it all, too. Twice, if she recalled correctly. The details were still kind of blurry, but she remembered lots of giggling, Eddie's silky hair tickling her inner thighs, the slap of flesh on flesh, and a climax so powerful she nearly blacked out.

Eddie's gaze held hers. "Last night was spectacular." The quilt slipped down, baring his lean chest, tight little pecs dusted with chocolate brown hair, and ab muscles that bunched as he sat up.

She stepped back and bonked into the bookcase, which rattled.

"Easy now." He sprang from the bed, dashed to her side, and reached past her to steady the wobbling shelves. His arm brushed her shoulder.

She was a sucker for muscular forearms, and Eddie's were superb. She bit the inside of her cheek. *God help me.*

He shuffled closer until his hard belly brushed her soft one. In bare feet, they stood eye to eye. His fingertips skimmed down her sides before he wrapped his arms around her and pressed his forehead to hers. "I can't believe you're here."

His cock pulsed against her thigh, firm and getting harder, raising goose bumps on her skin.

"You cold?" He snatched up the bedspread and wrapped it around her shoulders. "Babka's quilt," he said, tucking it

6

under her chin. "Warm you right up."

"Babka?"

"Short for Babushka. Russian for grandma." His fingertip traced a bird design that reminded her of the Chinese phoenix her own Maa Maa Chu embroidered on the pillowcases she gave Rosie. "For your trousseau," she'd said with a hand-pat. Fat chance of that.

"It's beautiful." Rosie clutched the quilt, fighting the urge to wrap it around both of them like a horny burrito. How tempting to tumble back into bed, fully awake and aware. Just one more time before she put a gentle end to this delicious mistake. But that would just increase the chances of hurting Eddie. Better to rip off the Band-aid.

She cleared her throat. "Listen, I'd better go. I've got a family thing." *Total lie.*

"Yeah, me too. Brunch with the fam." His eyebrows flicked up, his lips parted, and for a moment she was sure he'd ask her to join him. But he only tilted his head and surveyed her as if searching for something—maybe the words to give her a polite brush-off.

Which was fine. Perfect, even. Never mind that sinking feeling in her stomach. If Eddie saw this as just a casual thing between friends, then she had nothing to worry about.

"Better get dressed." Pretending confidence she didn't feel, she handed him the quilt and set off in search of her clothes. It felt weird bumbling around his pristine apartment in her birthday suit, but the low whistle behind her proved he liked what he saw. Funny how many skinny guys went for big, curvy girls like her. Despite fashionista propaganda, she never found herself without male admirers for long. Still, those first naked moments could be awkward, especially since they'd also be their last naked moments.

Soft footsteps padded behind her, and a fingertip traced the spiral tattooed on her hip. "So much artwork on your skin. I could look at you all day, Rosie."

She snatched up her sweater and held it to her chest like a shield. Eddie faced her, eyes hooded, his thick, ruddy cock pointing skyward. Her gut clenched like a fist as she forced the words out. "Look, Eddie. You're sweet."

His face crumpled in slow motion.

A sickly rush of regret forced the words out faster. "And hot. Any girl would be lucky to call you hers."

His chest rose and fell on a shuddering breath. Damn it, couldn't he make this easier on her?

"But I can't. I'm sorry."

Merciless, his dark gaze. His lips pressed into a thin line. "Why not?"

Okay then, honesty it is. "Because we work together. And if... *when* this falls apart, we'll have to face each other every day." She cleared her throat to chase away a wobble in her voice. "The Bangers crew is like family to me. I need work to be a place where I'm safe, you know? Where I can just be myself and do my job and not have anyone hammering at me to be something else, someone else."

"I don't want you to change, Rosie." His palms stroked down her sides. "I just want you."

"Yeah, now. But later when things go south?" She stepped out of his embrace. "That's how it works, you know. At first, it's all, 'Baby, you're perfect just as you are.' Later, it's 'Why can't you be more this? Do more that? Not be so damn... much?' " She raked her fingers into her hair—or tried to. Last night's romp had left a huge snarl on the back of her head—and in her gut.

His hands dropped limply to his sides, then tightened into white-knuckled fists. "It's because of my size, isn't it?"

Woah, where did that come from? "Eddie, I—"

His brows drew together. "I've seen you at work, flirting with those guys."

"What guys?"

"Huge, all of them. Guess I'm just not your type, huh?" His erection bobbing, he trudged past her and around the bookcase that served as a room divider.

Heart hammering, she stood rooted to the floor. Did she go for big guys? She'd never really noticed. At five-seven, she was taller than some guys, shorter than others, wider than most. So what? Life was hard enough without beating herself up over her size.

Apparently, she'd just triggered a flare-up of Eddie's comparisonitis. *Shit on a flaming stick.* "Eddie, look." She stepped around the bookcase and bonked right into him, his face red, his arms full of her discarded clothing.

He pushed the bundle into her arms. "Save it. Better this way. Let's just chalk this up to a drunk mistake and go back to the way things were." Turning away, he muttered, "Dawn was right."

She dropped the clothing and planted her fists on her hips. "Wait, she talked to you too?"

Arms crossed, he nodded. "Shoulda listened. Now, would you please put your damn clothes on? Hard to talk sensibly when you're all…" His gaze raked her from head to toe, then he groaned and turned his back.

"Fine." She yanked her tights up one leg, then nearly toppled over when she lifted the other foot. "You didn't mind looking last night."

"Goddammit, I always like looking at you, Rosie." He huffed. "Should've kept that to myself."

So much for sparing his feelings. She was no damn good at this emotional tippy-toe stuff. She zipped up her short skirt, wiggled into her sweater, and stuffed her panties and bra into the pocket of her coat. Hopeless to comb out her sex-snarled hair, so she tugged her knit beanie over the mess. "For the record, Eddie, I like looking at you too. Don't try to hijack this discussion, okay? We both know that messing around with a coworker is stupid."

"Tell that to Charlie and River." Brushing past her, he threw open his closet and pulled out a perfectly pressed T-shirt and flannel pajama pants.

"That's different."

He whirled on her and glared. "How, exactly?"

Good question. Charlie came back to Tacoma in December to care for her dad, whose leg was mashed in a car crash. She stepped in to cover for their absent head server and ended up staying. Now she and River, Bangers' hot blond bartender, were a giddy, giggly couple, despite the occasional squabble at work.

"Here's how." She ticked off on her fingers. "Charlie does website design, so she doesn't need her job at Bangers to survive. And River's a fantastic bartender, so if they break up, any bar would be glad to have him." Whereas she would never find another boss like Dawn, who let her schedule shifts around her search for a tattoo apprenticeship. She needed all of that—her work family, her flexibility, and the damn good tips she earned at Bangers. She couldn't afford to screw this up.

Eddie's chin dipped, and his voice lost its sharp edge. "You're a fantastic server. Any bar would be glad to have you."

This was so hard! She should've listened to Dawn. But she had plenty of time to kick herself later. Right now, she needed to extricate herself from Eddie's apartment.

"Thank you, Eddie. And I'm really sorry. I acted without thinking—my specialty. I never meant to hurt you." *Or myself.*

He tilted his head and regarded her like some tricky puzzle he was determined to solve. "Why did you?"

"Hook up with you?" She shrugged. "I wanted to. I was a little drunk. You're so cute and quiet, and I wanted to see what's behind that brick wall you carry around."

"But you didn't like what you found?"

Her hand twitched toward his. She forced it back down. "I did, actually. A lot. But now isn't the time for me to be starting something with a new guy."

"With me, you mean."

She stomped her foot. "With anyone, Eddie!" She pointed from her chest to his. "See, this is why we could never work. You're so closed off and suspicious. I'm telling you the truth, okay? I like you, just—"

"Just not enough." He raised both palms. "Okay. If that's how you feel, I won't bother you anymore." His voice rasped like a rusty hinge.

Tears blurred her vision. "I'm so sorry, Eddie."

He squared his shoulders and flashed a wry half-grin. "Don't be. Last night was more fun than I've had in a long time. But I really do have brunch with my parents, so let's end this." He lifted his chin and thrust out his hand. "Friends?"

A hot tear dribbled down her cheek. "Friends." She clasped his hand tight, knowing if he pulled her in for a comforting hug, she'd lose it. She'd take back everything she said and dive in with both feet.

But he just walked her to the door, pecked her cheek, and let her go.

* * *

Rather than watch Rosie walk out his door, Eddie turned his back and started washing their dirty glasses. The front door clicked open, then she squeaked like a dog's chew toy. He whirled. "Rosie? You okay?"

She'd frozen in the door frame, clutching her coat to her chest. On the landing stood his grandmother holding a tray.

"Babka!" He rushed to the doorway and stepped in front of Rosie. "What are you—"

"Surprise, lapochka!" With her ample hip, she nudged him aside and strode through the door, a woman on a mission. "You missed the big family party in Seattle last night, so Dedka and I came down to toast the new year with you." She set the tray on his kitchen counter and pinched his cheek. "My hard-working boy." Leaning past him, she winked at Rosie. "Always working, this one. But I guess you know that, Miss... ?"

Rosie croaked as if she'd swallowed her tongue.

Babka poked his ribs with her sharp elbow. "Why didn't you tell us about your new girlfriend?" In his grandparents' old-school world, overnight guest equaled serious relationship, not one-shot misadventure. What a freakin' disaster.

"Babka, this is Rosie Chu, my friend from work." A

truthful statement, sort of. Hopefully, he and Rosie could get back to being friends someday, once they moved past this awkwardness—maybe in a few months, when the memories of their dead-end passion faded.

Right, like that's gonna happen.

Beaming, Babka flung her arms around Rosie's middle and squeezed tight. "Such a gorgeous girl. Welcome to the family, sweetheart."

Rosie's mouth opened and closed like a startled goldfish. "I, er…" Her wide-eyed gaze met his over the top of Babka's snow-white head.

"Please," he silently mouthed, then raised his voice. "Rosie was just leaving. She has a family thing."

Babka grabbed Rosie's hand and patted it. "Family is so important, especially on the holidays. You're what, Korean? How does your family celebrate the new year, darling?"

Great. Let the interrogation begin.

"I'm half Chinese," Rosie said, "but we just have a normal American brunch—eggs, hash browns…"

Babka gave a conspiratorial wink. "To tell you the truth, not many of us Volkovs even speak Russian anymore. But we still like our Russian traditions. I made pelmenyi—little meat dumplings. Chinese people love dumplings, right? Come try one before you go."

"Babka—"

With a dismissive wave, she trotted to the door. "Oh, I almost forgot." She pulled his little moleskin notebook from her skirt pocket. "Found this on the landing."

Relief duked it out with panic as he tucked the notebook into his pocket. If his sharp-eyed grandmother looked between the covers, she'd have questions about his lists of bar equipment, cocktail recipes, sketches of floor plans...

"Both of you, downstairs. Everyone's waiting." Babka flashed a grin over her shoulder. "Hurry before Dedka gobbles all the herring." The door closed behind her with a bang.

Rosie clapped a hand to her mouth. "Herring?"

"With sour cream. Good for a hangover." No doubt his grandmother was already telling the rest of the family about his new girlfriend. His single status was the source of much consternation at family gatherings, as if he were nearing his expiration date.

He clasped Rosie's arms. "Look, I know it's a lot to ask, but could you come down to my parents' house for just a few minutes?" When her jaw dropped, he added, "They're really old-fashioned. If they think I've had a one-night stand, they'll be so disappointed in me." Panic forced his rusty brain wheels into motion. "Please, Rosie, just let them think we're dating for now. Later, I'll tell them we broke up."

Rosie nibbled her bottom lip, a distractingly sexy gesture. Finally, she sighed. "Well, I guess I'm partly to blame for this mess. If a few dumplings will get you out of it, I'm game."

Relief whooshed through him as he slid his hands into hers and squeezed. "Thank you. Half an hour tops, I swear. You won't be late for your family thing?"

A grimace flickered over her features. "No big deal. I'll call them." She patted her tangled hair. "But I would like to clean up first."

He gestured toward the bathroom. "All yours. Want a Raf coffee?"

"A what now?"

"Russian style. Kick-ass espresso with vanilla and foamed cream."

"Yes please."

He poured her a generous cup from the thermos Babka brought, dug out a spare toothbrush and fresh towels, and left her to her ablutions while he plated a serving of Babka's coffee cake.

She emerged fresh-faced, her heavy eyeliner gone, her scarlet lipstick replaced by pale pink gloss. She'd pulled her hair into a low ponytail, too. He'd never seen her looking so subdued. She'd even tied a scarf around her neck to hide her tattooed cleavage. Shrugging, she gave him a sheepish grin. "Best meet-the-parents look I can do on short notice."

"You look great," he assured her. "Coffee cake on the counter. Helps shield your stomach from the coffee. And the vodka."

She blinked rapidly. "The which?"

"Just one shot." He grinned before shutting the bathroom door. "Like Babka said, we Volkovs are big on tradition."

He blasted himself fully awake with the world's fastest shower, brushed his teeth, and neatened up his almost-beard, all the while rehearsing what he'd say to his family—if Rosie hadn't already come to her senses and fled. But no, once he dressed in pressed khakis, a button-down shirt, and shiny loafers, he found her standing at the counter, a fork in her hand and her phone to her ear. "Ma, seriously, don't wait for me. I won't be long. Just grabbing a coffee with a friend."

She ended the call and gave him a head-to-toe glance. "Are you going to church?"

He straightened his tie. "Just saving myself a lecture. Russian tradition, gotta wear new clothes on New Year's Day. I'm not screwing up your plans, am I?"

"Nah. It's just Mom and me, my sister and her boyfriend. Nice guy, but insecure. Always sucking up to Mom." She curled her lip and adopted an oily tone. "Oh, Ms. Callas, your spanakopita is divine."

"Spana— Isn't that Greek?"

"Yeah. Ma's family came over from Rhodes." She shrugged into her coat. "So, your parents live downstairs?"

"Pretty pathetic, huh? Twenty-eight and still living over my parents' garage."

She snorted. "Not as pathetic as me. I'm twenty-five and still in my childhood bedroom. I could never afford my own place without a thousand roommates."

He took her hand. "I really appreciate this. I'll do my best to block their questions. Like I told Babka, we're just friends from work."

Another snort—a very sexy sound, coming from her. "C'mon, Eddie. Your grandma just saw me braless with a huge nest of fuck hair. She knows." She reached for the door. "Shall we?"

Chapter Two

Rosie followed Eddie down the stairs and across the driveway to a pretty two-story bungalow with river stone pillars on the porch. He opened the side door. "Brace yourself."

What have I got myself into? She gulped and nodded.

He led her through a yellow-painted kitchen with a strong 1970s vibe, counters loaded with foil trays, Tupperware, and crumpled wrappings. Eddie whistled. "Thought I'd be spared the traditional year-end force-feeding. Looks like they brought the leftovers."

He tugged her forward. TV sounds and laughter rang out from the next room. Stomach wobbling, she planted her feet. "I don't know, Eddie. I feel bad lying to your family."

Grasping her hand in both of his, he whispered, "I said we're work friends, and that's what we are." When she balked, he raised her hand to his lips and kissed her knuckles. "Half an hour, tops. I promise. A few dumplings, a toast to the new year, and we're out of here." The soft brush of his lips did funny things to her core—warm, tickly things. If she had the sense God gave mud, she'd back out now. But Eddie's grandma already thought Rosie was his girlfriend. What could it hurt to play along for a few minutes more?

She nodded, and Eddie broke into a sweet, crooked smile that made her feel even more guilty. Eddie wasn't the kind of guy who indulged in meaningless hookups. Should've considered that before plastering herself to him on the dance floor last night.

Hand in hand, they entered the dining room. The red and gold floral tablecloth caught her eye—hard to see clearly under the load of dishes and platters. Too bad. Its intricate, old-country design would be a great addition to her sketchbook of tattoo ideas.

Caught in mid-scoop, a petite, fifty-ish woman with Eddie's dark hair and bright eyes dropped her serving spoon into a cut-glass bowl of potato salad. "Eduard, you brought a friend!" She spread her arms, and Eddie stepped into them and pecked her cheeks—left, right, left.

"Mama, this is my work friend Rosie Chu."

Mama scrunched her lips to the side, clearly not buying the "work friend" bit, then smiled broadly. "Welcome, Rosie. Happy New Year. S Novim Godom." She elbowed her son. "Tell her what to say."

Eddie rolled his eyes. "You answer with i vas takzhe. Means 'And you too.'"

She did her best to wrap her lips around the slippery sounds. Who knew Russian sounded so sexy?

"Pleased to meet you, Mrs. Volkov."

His mom flapped her hand. "Oh please, it's Alina. Come." She clamped her arm through Rosie's and towed her to the sofa where a short, handsome man in a shiny shirt and pinstripe slacks sat between Babka and a white-haired gent, also short and dapper. The old guy's attention was focused on the TV, some old comedy in Russian with English subtitles.

"Look, everybody. Meet Eddie's new sweetheart!" Alina beamed.

Behind her, Eddie scraped a hand down his face, then mouthed, "Sorry."

Well, shit. This whole scenario itched like a steel-wool sweater, but playing along assuaged her guilt over giving Eddie the wham-bam-thank-you-sir treatment. She forced a toothy smile and waggled her fingers. "Hello. Happy New Year."

Babka poked her son, who lifted the remote and paused the movie before standing to shake her hand. "Sorry, miss. We always watch this movie on New Year's Day. *The Irony of Fate.*"

"Sounds grim."

"Bah." Babka flicked her fingers. "It's hilarious. You see, this guy gets drunk and ends up in the wrong apartment. A beautiful lady lives there, and—"

Eddie cut in. "She doesn't need the whole story, Babka. Rosie has to go meet her family."

"Of course, of course." With a grunt, Babka launched herself to her feet. "But first, try my dumplings, eh? And a few blini with scrambled eggs and caviar. And Alina's pickled beets." She nudged the old guy with her foot. "Alexi, get up. Say hello to Eddie's *devushka.*"

"Excuse me, dear. Lost in my thoughts." He rose, clasped Rosie's hand in his broad, warm palm, then turned to his son. "I have decided. We will try that eco-solvent."

"Dad," Alina scolded. "We have company. No one wants to hear about the dry-cleaning business."

The grandfather pointed a knuckly finger at Alina. "The dry-cleaning business paid for all of this. Dry-cleaning is in our blood." He turned to Rosie, whose hand he still held. "Tell me, miss, wouldn't you rather have this beautiful sweater cleaned with organic products?"

"Um, sure?"

Grandpa grinned widely, and Rosie noticed the strong family resemblance to Eddie. Age had softened his jaw, but the sharp cheekbones, bright eyes, and slim, sturdy build were the same. "Now, our Eddie," he continued, releasing Rosie to clap his grandson on the back, "he knows the importance of keeping up with the times, eh? He'll do us proud."

Eddie's gaze slid to hers, and his grin turned brittle and fake. "Sure, Dedka."

"Of course he will." Babka hooked her arm through Rosie's and tugged her toward the overflowing table. "Now, come try my dumplings."

The juicy meat-filled dumplings were delicious, and so were the blinis—little buckwheat pancakes topped with scrambled eggs, smoked salmon, caviar, and dill. Eddie's mom loaded her plate with pickled herring in beet-tinted sour cream sauce, potato salad studded with veggies and chicken, and a generous slice of walnut cake topped with plum jam. She knew she should save room for brunch with her family, but everything was so scrumptious. While she and Eddie ate, squashed together on the little loveseat, she caught his grandma whispering something about "good, sturdy hips" to his grandfather. She glanced up, and the woman gave her a thumbs-up.

Alina settled onto the couch and cleared her throat. "So, Rosie, tell us about yourself. You like working at the bar with our Eduard?"

She wiped sour cream from her lips and glanced at Eddie, who wrinkled his brow in an apologetic gesture. No problem, this one she could answer truthfully. "I do. Bangers is a fun place. We're like family."

Eddie's dad grunted. "Our son doesn't tell us much about his night job, besides how much he loves the tater tots." He lifted a slice of salami to his lips. "No reason he should work in a bar when we need him in the shop."

Alina elbowed him. "Hush, Papa. A young man needs to be around other young people. Besides, he's only working at the bar until he finishes his business degree."

That explained why he was forever scribbling in a little notebook he carried in his hip pocket. Must be doing his homework.

Eddie set his plate down. "Dad, could we not talk about this today?"

His father opened his mouth but shut it when Alina elbowed him again. "Time for a toast." She gathered empty plates from the coffee table. "Eddie, you choose."

He followed her to the dining room and returned with a tray of shot glasses and an oddly-shaped bottle, slim, white and bent to one side. "From Siberia. The bottle's supposed to look like a mammoth's tusk." He poured them each an ice-cold shot, nudging the smallest pour toward Rosie.

Babka rubbed her hands together. "Our Eddie knows the good stuff."

Grandpa stood and raised his glass. With a solemn expression, he intoned, "We raise our glasses to Ded Moroz, Grandfather Frost, and his granddaughter. To the new year. Za nó–vij god."

Rosie mumbled her best approximation of the phrase and swallowed her shot. It burned pleasantly. "Excellent," she muttered to Eddie.

"Like Babka says, I know the good stuff." He bumped his shoulder against hers before downing his shot, then added, "I'm here with you, aren't I?"

She clenched her fist in her lap so hard her nails dug into her palm. *Don't get attached to him.*

Oblivious to Rosie's stiff posture, Alina continued her interrogation. "So, Rosie, you're going to spend the day with your family? That's good. Family is what holds us together, right, son?"

"Sure, Mama." He leaned his head onto Rosie's shoulder and whispered, "Take me with you."

"Aww," Babka cooed. "Look how in love they are. You've been hiding her from us, lapochka. Are you a student too, dear?"

"Sort of. I study art." Good thing her scarf, long sleeves, and thick tights covered her tattoos. Except for her blue hair, she presented a pretty conservative picture this morning. Though colorful people like her were a common sight in Tacoma, she bet Eddie's family wouldn't be quite so welcoming if they saw the tattoos covered by her winter clothes.

Eddie's dad leaned forward and fixed her with a sharp-eyed gaze. "What is your family's business, Rosie?"

"I—uh—pardon?"

"Your parents have a restaurant? An import store?"

Eddie shot to his feet. "For Chrissake, Dad, could you be more offensive?"

Babka clucked. "Don't be racist, my son. You need to get woke."

For Eddie's sake, Rosie kept her voice steady. "My mom is a history teacher."

Undeterred, the older man pressed on. "And your father?"

"He died when I was small."

Alina and Babka glared at Eddie's dad as if he'd personally caused said death.

*And on that awkward note...*She pushed to her feet. "It was lovely to meet you all." *Except you, Dad.* "Thank you for the delicious food, but I really have to go. My family's waiting." *And will give me shit when I show up in last night's clothes.*

"I'll walk you out." Eddie shot another glare at his dad, then clasped Rosie's hand and walked her back up to his place where she'd left her bag and coat. "Listen, I'm sorry about all that."

"Don't be. Your grandma's adorable. Your mom too." Already, sharp-toothed guilt gnawed her for deceiving two such welcoming women. But it was for the best. Strait-laced, serious Eddie would never fit into her crazy life, and his family's warmth would cool if they found out his supposed girlfriend was a college dropout tattoo artist wannabe who used their son for a quick, selfish thrill.

"Well, I appreciate the act. I know you didn't want to stay. I'll call you a ride." Eddie pulled on a jacket and lifted his phone.

After making the call, he waited beside her on the sidewalk, shoulders hunched against the cold. Tiny snowflakes swirled around them and stuck to his hair like sparkly confetti. He stared up the empty street and sighed.

She fought the urge to slip one arm from her coat and enfold him in its poufy warmth. Whispers of sensory memory swirled with the snow, snippets of pleasure from last night, smooth skin beneath her lips, lean hips rolling against hers, driving his heat into her again and again…

Her sharp exhalation clouded the air. A red Prius rolled toward them.

"Here's your driver," Eddie muttered. He averted his gaze as he opened the passenger door and waited while she climbed in, then closed it gently and turned away. No word of good-bye, no crooked grin, just a thin, lone figure out in the cold.

She twisted in her seat to watch him until the driver rounded the corner, then let her aching head thunk back against the seat. So much for remaining friends. She'd be lucky if he even spoke her at work.

Voices echoed in her memory. Accusing fingers pointed. *Rosie, when will you learn to think before you act?*

Chapter Three

"There you are." Mom's tone held an edge of impatience as Rosie stepped into the overheated kitchen. "We'd nearly given up on you. Fix yourself a plate." She gestured to the stove, where skillets of scrambled eggs, supermarket hash browns, and dry turkey sausage waited. You'd never know it was a holiday by Mom's outfit. With her dark hair pulled back in a short ponytail and her crisp blouse and slacks, she looked ready for work at Stadium High School. The leopard-print lounging PJs Rosie bought her for Christmas were probably still in their wrapper, tucked away to be regifted.

Rosie shed her coat and scarf. "It's like an oven in here."

"Because you just stepped in from outside," her younger sister quipped. Early in life, Amara developed the annoying habit of parroting Mom's favorite sayings. Rosie should be used to it by now, but it still grated her nerves.

"Happy New Year, Rosie." David, Amara's brown-nosing boyfriend, at least had the decency to treat this like the special occasion it supposedly was, even though the menu here was much less inspiring than the Russian spread at Eddie's place.

A vision swam into focus: Eddie at her side, holding her hand as she faced her family's nitpicking. She gave her head a shake and pushed that thought away. *Just friends. If I'm lucky.*

"Make yourself a plate, dear." Without asking, Mom filled a champagne flute nearly to the rim with Prosecco before adding the tiniest splash of orange juice and setting it beside Rosie's empty plate.

"I really don't want any more alcohol, Ma." She scooped up a tiny portion of too-dry eggs and slid bread into the toaster. The coffee carafe wafted a burnt-grounds scent, but a big glug of Mom's too-sweet, plastic-tasting creamer would cover the bitterness.

"Nonsense," Amara chirped. "We always toast the new year with mimosas. It's a family tradition."

Mom clucked. "Perhaps our Rosie had too much alcohol last night?"

Yeah, and a shot of killer vodka this morning. "I work in a bar, Ma. Of course we toasted the new year. River made these delicious champagne sparklers with raspberry liqueur and—"

"That's nice, dear. Come tell us about your evening."

Ugh. She sat and lifted her glass. "To the new year." Clinks all around. Hopefully, no one noticed her spit her mouthful back into her glass.

Mom pushed the jam jar toward Rosie. "Did you have fun last night?"

"Meet any cute guys?" Amara added.

"Lots of fun." She crunched her toast and kept them waiting while she chewed. "We had games at the bar, and karaoke. By midnight, it was one big singalong. Then everyone went out onto Sixth Ave to yell Happy New Year." In the jostling crowd, Eddie managed to position himself at her elbow, so when it was time for a midnight kiss, there he was. It was unlucky to greet the new year without smooching someone, right?

David forked up a mouthful of bland, crumbly eggs. "Nothing like a good ol' dive bar."

Rosie bristled. "Bangers is not a dive bar, it's a neighborhood tavern."

"Isn't your specialty tater tots?" Amara sniffed. "Sounds like a dive bar to me."

"Oh, hush." Mom gave her youngest a dismissive wave. "Your dad and I used to go to Bangers back before you were born. Arnie, the former owner, was a real character."

Why hadn't Mom shared this before? "You should come sometime, Mom. Diego makes the best daily specials. Last night it was tater tots topped with sour cream, smoked salmon, and chives. Sooo good."

Mom patted her hip. "No thanks. I'm big enough as it is."

And I'm bigger. Rosie sighed and braced herself. Would Amara let Mom's comment pass? Little sis inherited her bird bones from their dad's family, whereas Rosie got her wide hips and big boobs from Mom's.

Sure enough, Amara shot Rosie a squinty glance as she smeared butter on her toast. "Honestly, Rosie, if you'd just pay more attention to your diet—"

Mom rapped the table with her knuckles. "Enough. Don't spoil our morning with your squabbling."

Amara huffed and pushed away her plate. "Hey, Rosie, are you done with those earrings you borrowed? I need them for a work party next weekend."

Rosie's throat constricted, nearly sending a mouthful of

coffee in the wrong direction. Hadn't she worn Amara's sparkly earrings last night? The details were still blurred by her hangover fog. "Um, I might've left them at my friend's house."

Amara's eyebrows shot up.

Mom deployed her full-on teacher voice, honey covering sharp steel. "I'm sure Rosie will return them in time, won't you dear?"

"Of course," she muttered, eyes on her plate.

Glancing anxiously between the three women, David cleared his throat. "So, ah, what's new, Rosie? You still taking art classes at TCC?"

"Nope." She'd already aced every art class Tacoma Community College offered. She was damn proud of that, but when faced with the math classes required to finish her associate's degree, she'd dropped out. Why torture herself? She didn't need a degree to become a tattoo artist, just an apprenticeship—and those were hard to come by, especially in a tattoo-addicted town like Tacoma. Building her portfolio and introducing herself at studio after studio took all her daytime hours, and serving at Bangers filled her nights. She was working her ass off—but try telling that to her grad-student sister and her privileged boyfriend.

"I'm working on my portfolio," Rosie grumbled.

"Is that what you call your skin?" Amara asked, lip curled.

"Enough!" When Mom barked commands in her teacher voice, both sisters knew well enough to back off.

After a long silence, David cleared his throat. "So, we had fun last night." When no one spoke, he added, "My friend's parents hosted a party at their house on Capitol Hill. Great view of the city. We watched the fireworks."

Must be nice to be rolling in dough while we peasants toil in obscurity.

Rosie sucked in a breath and blew it out. David wasn't a snob, just clueless. After all, he happily trailed after Amara whenever she visited her humble Tacoma home. Turning down the Chu's offer to relocate the family to Bellevue after Dad died was a huge bone of contention in their extended family. Like her eldest daughter, Mom preferred to make her own way.

Amara poked at her congealed eggs. "U Dub has a good art program. Yeh Yeh and Maa Maa would pay your tuition, you know."

"I know. Not interested." Her paternal grandparents didn't approve of her career path either, but at least they didn't pester her about it the way Amara did. Besides, lack of tuition money wasn't the point.

Amara opened her mouth, then caught Mom's warning glare and snapped it shut.

Rosie nibbled her toast. "I actually got some cool ideas at my friend's house this morning. His grandma made this beautiful Russian quilt with a phoenix design, like—" *Ahh, shit. Just admitted I was in some guy's bedroom.*

Mom shot her a sharp look but refrained from quizzing her. "The phoenix is a popular image in many cultures. Greek, Chinese, Russian…"

"You've got a Russian boyfriend now?" Amara elbowed David and grinned.

"I have an American *friend* whose family came from Russia—I dunno—a long time ago. Even his grandparents don't speak with an accent." *But they sure cook with one.*

Mom's eyebrows rose. "You've met his family already?

29

Interesting."

Rosie winced. "Eddie is a friend from work. That's all. He invited me over for breakfast." Not the whole truth, but close enough.

"You partied all night, then?" Amara smirked.

Rosie shot her a dead-eyed stare. "That's what people do on New Year's Eve." Young people who don't have a stick up their ass, anyway. So what if a significant portion of said partying played out under Eddie's phoenix quilt?

She pushed her chair back. "Now, if you'll excuse me, I need a shower and a nap." She kissed the top of Mom's head. "Thanks for brunch, Ma. Leave the dishes. I'll wash up later. Nice to see you, David."

She scraped her barely touched food into the trash can, then climbed the stairs to her room, grumbling with every step. Ever since Amara got accepted into the University of Washington's Asian Studies graduate program, Rosie had endured her nagging about the importance of higher education—especially when Mom was there to witness said nagging. For God's sake, didn't the family's shining academic star get enough praise without rubbing Rosie's face in her success?

With cement-shod feet, she trudged into her room, stripped off her clothes, and wrapped up in her satin robe. A steaming shower eased some of the tension from her shoulders, but also refreshed her memory of last night's steamy moments in Eddie's arms—soft lips skimming over her collarbone while he kneaded her breasts and teased her nipples to tingling peaks. Whispers and moans and rumbling laughter. Lean hips rolling against hers, that lovely thick cock nudging between her thighs.

Such a sweet guy, and a fiercely good lover, unhurried and

thorough. Under other circumstances, they could maybe share something real.

"Don't kid yourself," she grumbled. "Guys like him don't want girls like me for anything more than a fuck buddy." Someday she'd find someone who fit—someone just as messy and impulsive as her. Not some neat-freak, tradition-minded, family guy like Eddie.

She dumped shampoo on her head and dug in with her fingertips, trying to scrub away the ache. Too late. All her frustration and self-recrimination came spilling out in messy, snotty sobs. Once again, she'd let an impulse knock her sideways—and this time she'd hurt a really decent guy. Lying to his adorable mom and grandma filled her with guilt, but what could she do?

She rinsed the last of the shampoo from her tear-stung eyes and cranked the faucet to icy cold.

Chapter Four

The next day, everything was back to normal at Bangers Tavern, the customers as thirsty as ever. In the storage room, Eddie hustled through his restocking duties.

"Looks like our Eddie had a happy new year, am I right?" Jojo, Bangers' mammoth bouncer, dropped his huge palm onto Eddie's shoulder. "Good job, little man."

Eddie stifled a groan and shrugged off Jojo's grip. "Nothing happened. We're just friends." *Not my choice, but there's not a damn thing I can do about it.*

"Gotcha." Jojo smirked and cocked his forefinger like a pistol. "A gentleman never kisses and tells." He leaned against the storage room door while Eddie unfolded the step ladder and fetched bottles from the top shelf. "Why you still schlepping bottles? You been workin' here a year. Shouldn't you be bartender by now?"

"Not trying to become a bartender. I'm learning the business." He loaded a selection of vodkas and gins into a plastic crate. "Besides, we got two good bartenders. Dawn doesn't need a third."

"So you're gonna, what, open your own place?"

Eddie scooped ice from the big machine into a seven-gallon bucket. "That's the plan. Do me a favor?" He set the bucket at Jojo's feet, then lifted the crate of bottles.

Jojo hefted the bucket and followed him to the bar, where Kiara and River were busy slinging drinks. The New Year's Eve streamers and balloons were gone, replaced by the usual Seahawks helmet cutouts and blue and green streamers.

No matter the time of year, there was always something colorful fluttering or sparkling from the ceiling at Bangers, holiday decorations or sports bling or both. Sports on TV, beer signs on the walls, loud music and raucous laughter, greasy bar snacks galore, plus pool tables, dartboards, and a few elderly pinball machines. Customers showed up in jeans and hoodies, ready to wash away the day's stress with craft beer and squash it under a mountain of tater tots. Though his shifts as barback left Eddie with sore shoulders and aching feet, Bangers felt less like work and more like home. That is, until Rosie.

She still hadn't shown up for her shift. Five minutes late—not that he'd say anything. He filled the ice bin, then placed the liquor bottles on shelves in the huge, antique back bar. Salvaged from an Alaska saloon, its polished columns and curlicues gleamed in the low light, oddly elegant against all the sports bling. Atop the center, a carved cherub spread its chubby arms as if blessing the booze. Its dumpling-cheeked smile reminded him of Rosie's.

His stomach tightened. There was no avoiding her at work. His best hope was to keep his head down and his eyes off her tempting curves until the sting faded.

A bell dinged at the pass-through window, and Diego's curly head appeared, topped with a Bangers' ballcap. "Bacon barbeque burger for Jojo, extra jalapeños."

"Thanks, dude." Jojo collected his dinner and returned to his stool at the entrance, where he checked IDs. The bar was hopping tonight, typical for a Saturday. You'd think after the New Year's bash the crowd would be thinner, but all the regulars turned out, including grumpy old Gus, perched as always on the last barstool near the back wall.

Gus waved him over. "Happy New Year, kiddo. Get me a Rainier, will ya?" As new co-owner of the bar after gifting Dawn enough money to buy the building from their landlord, the old fart delighted in issuing orders.

"Sure thing, Gus." Eddie pulled a pilsner glass from the shelf. While it filled, he let his imagination carry him on a little side trip, picturing the furnishings he'd pick for his own bar. Better lighting, for sure—not bright, but golden, maybe those beaded lampshades like his grandparents inherited from the old country, and—

Kiara's hip-bump sloshed beer across his hand. "How's it going, stud muffin?" She'd had her braids redone since he saw her last—blue and green strands woven among the black ones. She reached across him to fill a tall glass with winter IPA. "You and Rosie had a fun time?"

"Sure." He schooled his features into a bland expression. No way would he let her tease any details out of him. He just prayed that Rosie would be as discreet. "Dawn's not coming in tonight?"

"She's not supposed to, but she'll probably stop by." Their boss fell from a ladder while hanging mistletoe shortly before Christmas. The doc diagnosed a dislocated shoulder and minor concussion and ordered her to stay home for two weeks. But as far as Dawn was concerned, the bar was home.

He delivered Gus's beer, then ran a quick inventory. The keg of porter was running low. As he headed for the back room, a flash of electric blue caught his eye. There she stood at the server station, dressed in a silvery top cut low to display the bouquet of pink and red roses tattooed across her lush cleavage. Jeans shorts hugged her plump hips. Black tights and sturdy knee-high boots—sexy, earthy, gorgeous. While she waited for her drink order, she bunched her sapphire curls into a topknot and shoved a pencil through to anchor it, revealing the slender vine tattooed behind her right ear. Less than forty-eight hours ago, he'd traced that vine with his tongue. His stupid dick inched upward at the sight.

She's not for me. He forced his gaze downward as he approached. He couldn't ignore her, or people would talk. He couldn't greet her too warmly, or people would talk. What the fuck was he supposed to do, then?

"Hey, Eddie." Instead of her usual husky warmth, her voice sounded flat, tired.

"You feeling all right?" She did seem a little pale. "You want a coffee or something?"

Her smile flickered and died. "Nah, I'm good. You?"

He shrugged. *Don't pout. Be a man about it.* "Okay, I guess. Babka says hello."

There it was again, that sad almost-smile. "Tell her I said hi." She swiped a palm down her face, leaned onto the bar, and whispered, "This sucks."

"Yeah, it does." Knowing he wasn't suffering alone lightened the load just a tiny bit. He laid his hand over hers. "Hang in there, beautiful. We'll get past this."

"Well, well, well." Charlie stepped up and set down her tray. Her glossy brown ponytail swung as she looked from Eddie to Rosie, grinning. "How are the lovebirds this evening?"

"Look—" Rosie started.

"Listen—" Eddie said at the same time.

They exchanged wry grins. Rosie lifted her chin slightly, a silent signal. *You're up.*

"We're just friends. Right, Rosie?"

"Right," she chirped with a fake, wide-eyed smile. "You and River are the only lovebirds here." She loaded her drink order onto her tray and sailed into the crowd.

With a shaky exhale, he returned to his duties: trekking from storage room to bar, with side trips to pick up empties and to the kitchen to help Diego and Chelsey when food orders got backed up. He restocked glasses, tapped beer kegs, and kept his eyes on his work and off Rosie.

By his mid-shift break at nine, Eddie was feeling better—not good, exactly, but almost okay. He ducked into the kitchen to collect a burger and carried it to the break room, settling onto a folding chair. His eyes strayed to his locker, where a small package wrapped in shiny green paper hid inside his parka. He'd dithered at his apartment doorway, tucking the thing into his coat pocket, then removing it, over and over. Finally he stuffed it in, telling himself he'd decide once he saw how it went with Rosie at work. What better way to prove to himself that he was getting over her than to give her his gift? At least he wouldn't have to see it on his bookshelf anymore, a reminder of the love affair that wasn't.

The break room door banged open, and Rosie stepped through holding a chili dog in a paper boat. "Oh!" She froze in place, her gaze darting from him to the door. "I was just going to…" She lifted her snack.

"It's cool. Come in."

She sat in a folding chair and stared at the hotdog in her lap. Finally, she raised her gaze. "I hate how awkward this feels."

"Yeah, well—it's going to feel weird for a while. We'll move past it." Though he wished like hell they didn't have to. Maybe a peace offering would help. He retrieved the package from his locker. "Russian custom, you give gifts for New Year's Day. I didn't get the chance, so…here."

Her lashes fluttered. "For me?"

"It's no big deal. Just—take it."

She set the hotdog aside and unwrapped the bright blue notebook. Small enough to fit in her pocket, it held creamy blank pages between its peacock-print covers. She flipped through, then held it to her chest. "It's beautiful."

"Yeah, well—" He shuffled his feet on the cement floor. "Saw it in that gift shop up the street, and I thought of you. You're always sketching on napkins, right? Maybe you can use this instead. If you want." *Say something, please, or I'll just keep blathering like a moron.*

She raised her huge, dark eyes to his. "You bought this today?"

"No, no—before we…" He sighed. "Anyway, I wanted you to have it. You know, as a friend."

She clutched it tight. "Eddie, this is so thoughtful. Thank you."

Her silent stare made him so itchy he backed toward the door. "No big deal." He turned away, but she wasn't finished with him.

"You like notebooks, huh? I see you writing in yours all the time. What do you write about?"

Damn, he thought he'd been discreet. "Just stuff I need to remember."

"For your classes?"

"Sometimes." Let her think his obsessive list-making and list-checking was for school. Seemed less weird than admitting to his neurotic need for control, the nagging fear of forgetting some crucial part of his plan. His daily to-do list and monthly goals made him feel like he was making progress—reassurance that even though it would take years, he'd eventually grasp his dream. But someone as spontaneous and free as Rosie wouldn't understand.

"You go to U Dub?"

"Just one of those online colleges." No way could he afford the tuition at the University of Washington. And no way would he bury himself in student loan debt, either. The business degree he was slowly plugging away at was just a tool, one more step in his plan.

"Getting your business degree, right? Gonna revolutionize the dry-cleaning business?"

"No." He dreaded the day when he'd finally deliver that news to his parents. They wouldn't understand.

"Okaaay." She tucked the notebook in her hip pocket, took a bite of her hotdog, and chewed slowly, eyes down.

Great, now we're back to awkward. "Sorry. Didn't mean to bark at you. It's just—that's a sore subject."

She lifted a shoulder. "None of my business, anyway."

It could be, though.

She rose and dumped the uneaten half of her hotdog in the trash. Her eyes were glossy when she faced him again. "I'm sorry, Eddie."

He reached for her hand. "You don't have to keep saying

that."

She squeezed his palm. "I'm gonna keep on saying it until you believe me."

Damn it, he was trying to give her what she wanted. How to make her see that? "I don't blame, you, Rosie. You're not a bad person, you're just—impulsive, I guess."

Her posture stiffened. "And you never are? Or do you always have a plan in that little notebook of yours. Guess you didn't plan on me." She whirled and strode through the door, letting it thud closed behind her.

Mouth agape, he stared after her. How did she know? Had she peered over his shoulder while he was writing? With a sigh that emptied him from toes to aching head, he pulled out his notebook, crossed off "Ask Rosie out," then wrote "Get over Rosie" and underlined it three times.

* * *

Before returning to the bar floor, Rosie leaned against the hallway wall and massaged her aching temples. You'd think, after Eddie just poked her most sensitive sore spot, she'd be able to let go of feeling so damn sorry for him. But his gift rested in her pocket, pressing against her ass the way his hands had just two nights ago. She imagined them standing hip to hip in the bar, hands tucked into each other's back pockets, not bothering to hide their attraction. But that was never gonna happen. Might as well let go of pointless dreams.

She fluffed her hair, lifted her chest, and strutted to the bar. "Back from break."

At the servers' station, Lana tapped her fingers on the bar

while Kiara filled her order. Jojo hovered behind Lana, toying with the tips of her two long pigtails, a sappy grin on his face. She tugged them from his grip and shooed him like a pesky puppy. "Cut it out, Jojo. Don't you have work to do?"

Poor giant, he looked so dejected as he trudged back to his workstation. Rosie nudged her friend. "He's totally crushing on you."

"Pffsh. He's just being annoying. Does that to all the girls, right?" Lana nodded toward Rosie's section. "That high-top wants three Coronas and six tequila shots. And there's two ladies asking for you by the pool tables."

"That's Charlie's section."

Lana shrugged. "They asked for you, though. Charlie won't mind."

"Thanks, doll." Rosie patted her best friend's ass, delivered the beers and tequilas, then swung by the pool tables in search of the two mystery ladies. Spotting them, she sucked in a breath, whispered, "Holy shit," then pasted on a smile. "Ma, what are you doing here?"

Her mother angled her head and tapped her cheek. "Is that any way to greet your mother?"

Rosie pecked as ordered. "I'm glad to see you, of course, just surprised."

"You remember my friend Betty from school?"

The fifty-something woman in a Stadium High School hoodie extended her hand. "My goodness, Rosie. Haven't seen you in ages."

"Hi, Ms. Watson." Rosie glanced around nervously. No sign of Eddie—not that he had any idea what her mom looked like. And it wasn't unusual to see patrons her mom's age in Bangers, especially for trivia night, karaoke, and sports games on TV.

None of those were happening tonight, though.

Her former English teacher patted Rosie's shoulder. "You're looking well, hon'. Still making art?"

"Absolutely. What can I get you?"

"Cider for me." Betty's head snapped to the right. "Scuze me a minute, girls. Gotta say hi to my neighbor's son." She hopped off her stool and disappeared into the crowd.

Rosie propped her tray on her hip. "Seriously, Ma, what are you doing here?"

She shifted on her stool. "Listen, I felt bad about yesterday. I should've cut your sister off as soon as she started bad-mouthing this place."

And my tattoos? And my career plans? And my life in general? Rosie forced her scowl into a neutral expression. "That would've been nice."

Ma's soft hand grasped hers. "It's hard to see your kid go in a direction you fear may bite her in the ass. But you're a grown woman, and it's not my place to—"

"Rosie, is that you?"

She spun and came face to chest with Eddie's mom, a fuzzy knit beret twisted in her hands, her head tilted like a worried puppy. *What is this, Moms' night out?* She'd never seen Alina Volkov in the bar. Then again, tiny as she was, Alina was easy to overlook in the crowd.

"My goodness," Alina squeaked, her nervous fingers tapping her own chest. "Such a big tattoo."

Ma snorted. "That's just the tip of the iceberg. How many now, Rosie?"

"Mama?" a strangled voice called from the bar, followed by a crash.

"Eddie!" With remarkable speed, Alina darted toward the

bar, her long coat flapping behind her, Rosie hot on her heels.

At the end of the bar, a red-faced Eddie clutched the jagged remains of a half-gallon bottle. A puddle of clear liquid spread among the glass shards at his feet. Gin, by the smell of it. Scarlet drops fell from his fist and plopped into the puddle.

"My boy, you're hurt," Alina wailed. She unwound her scarf and lunged for Eddie's wounded hand.

"Mama, stop. You'll ruin your nice scarf."

"Here." Rosie's mom chugged up and pulled a packet of tissues from her purse. "Apply pressure."

"Thank you, thank you." Alina patted Mom's shoulder. "Baby, do what she says."

By now, a crowd had gathered, drawn by the commotion.

"Okay, okay, let's back off, folks."

Rosie exchanged a panicked glance with Eddie. Of all the shitty times for the boss to make an appearance. Dawn must've been working in her office, since the doc forbade her from working behind the bar, her usual spot on a busy Saturday night.

"Go on, now." Dawn shooed the customers away, then planted her fists on her well-padded hips. "Holy cow, Eddie. You trying to stab someone?" She pried the jagged remains of the bottle from his hand, then opened his fist. "There now, that's not so bad. Fingertips bleed like a mother, don't they? Go wash it up, kiddo."

Eddie groaned. "Sorry, boss. I heard my mother's voice, and when I turned to look, I must've hit that." He pointed a bloody finger to the iron railing that kept customers from crowding the server's station.

"This is your mama?" Dawn removed her Seahawks cap and patted her short gray locs. Her wide smile bunched her tawny, freckled cheeks. "Pleased to meet you, Mrs. Volkov. Welcome to Bangers. We'll get Eddie bandaged up. Let me find you a table."

"She can sit with me." Rosie's mother hooked her arm through Alina's and tugged her away, throwing a sharp backward glance at Rosie.

River popped around the corner holding a string mop and bucket. "I'll take care of this."

"That's my job," Eddie protested.

"Shut up and wash up," Dawn snapped. "First aid kit's in the staff bathroom." She softened her tone and patted his shoulder. "Then go comfort your mother. Looks like you 'bout scared her to death."

While Eddie hurried off to do Dawn's bidding, she turned to Rosie. "Both the mamas here? You two making an announcement tonight?"

Rosie's heart stuttered to a standstill. "What? No! We're just—"

"Don't give me that 'just friends' bullshit." Dawn snorted. "Must be something in the water here. First Charlie and River, now you two."

"I swear, Dawn, there's nothing going on between Eddie and me. Yesterday, my mom was telling me about how she loved coming here back in the day, and tonight she just showed up with her work friend."

"Feels like I'm the captain of the freakin' Love Boat." She waved Rosie off. "Go on, get to your customers. Hopefully, they don't want any gin."

Biting her lip, she returned to her station, sending Charlie to take care of her mom's table.

"They okay over there?" Rosie asked when Charlie returned

to the server station.

Charlie flashed a wry grin. "Real chummy. Your mom didn't know you were dating Eddie. Mrs. Volkov cleared that right up. Seems real fond of you but a little freaked out about your ink."

"God help me."

An hour later, the moms were still chatting and laughing, though Ms. Watson had left.

Lana passed, her tray filled with empties. "Where's Eddie? These tables are a mess."

Good question. He must be hiding out from his overprotective mom—not that she blamed him. She glanced around. No sign of him, but—*oh crap*. Dawn had joined the moms at their table. She waved her ball cap and hollered, "Rosie."

Rosie gulped and made her way toward them, her mind racing from stupid explanation to pointless excuse. Her lies had come home to roost.

Dawn rose from her bar stool and thumped Rosie's back. "Darlin', get these fine ladies a plate of tots on the house." She slung her arm around Rosie's shoulders and towed her toward the bar. "Those two are getting pretty tiddly on gimlets. Some greasy carbs will stop the slide. And you better get your man over there and answer some questions. The longer you wait, the worse it'll be."

"Dawn, I swear—"

"Get your stories straight."

Like a wide-eyed prairie dog, Eddie popped up from behind the bar, spotted the boss and Rosie whispering, and ducked back down.

Dawn clucked her tongue. "Eddie, get your skinny ass over

here."

Shoulders hunched, he shuffled toward them.

Dawn slung her other arm over his shoulders and drew the two of them into the hallway. "Listen, you two, you're grown-ass adults and responsible for your own decisions. But I do not appreciate being lied to." She drilled each of them with a stern glare. "You're more than employees, you're family. And while I don't approve of coworkers dating, I'm not going to fire you for it. Unless it gets in the way of your work. When you're here, minds on the customers. No drama. Got it?"

They both nodded.

"Now go sort things out with your mamas before they get so drunk they fall off their barstools."

Eddie croaked, "But you just said—"

"Get the tots and go." Dawn strode back to her office.

"Now what?" Eddie clutched his head as if trying to keep his skull from exploding.

"We tell them the truth?"

"What truth—that we spent one drunk night together?"

Her chili dog curdled in her stomach. "Well, that is the truth, I guess."

He grasped her shoulders. "Rosie, my parents are old-fashioned. They won't understand." The plea in his chestnut eyes plucked hard at her guilt strings.

"So, what—we pretend to be dating? For how long?"

"I dunno. A few weeks? Long enough for me to think up a good reason for us to break up."

"You mean, like how we're as different as two people could possibly be?"

"Something like that." He grasped her hands and wove his fingers between hers, filling her chest with happy, buzzing bumblebees—totally inappropriate, and not at all helpful. When would her body catch up with her brain and realize Eddie was not the guy for her?

"Come on, Rosie, my grandmother saw us together in my apartment. If we break up now, she'll think I used you for a one-night stand. She'll lose all respect for me. Please, just play along a little longer."

She untangled her fingers from his and huffed, "Okay, okay. I helped caused this mess. I'll help clean it up."

Grinning, he pecked her cheek. "It'll work out. Now, what'll we tell them?"

After a moment of strategizing, they linked hands and made their way across the bar floor. As they passed the front door, Jojo snorted. "Just friends, huh?"

Rosie's mom slapped the table when she caught sight of them. "Here they are, our sweet babies."

Dawn wasn't kidding—these women were well sauced. Empty glasses littered the table. She hadn't seen her mom this plastered since the last presidential election.

"Shh, Ma. No need to yell." She squeezed Eddie's hand for good luck. "This is Eddie. We're, uh, kind of—"

"In love!" Alina hooted. She lifted her glass, hooked her heels on the rungs of her barstool, and rose, wobbling precariously. "A toast, to young love."

"Mama, sit down!" Eddie hissed through clenched jaws.

Too late. All around them, customers raised glasses in a toast to their make-believe love affair.

Rosie groaned and dropped her head onto Eddie's shoulder. "We are in deep shit," she murmured.

"Leave it to me," he whispered, then extended his hand. "Mrs. Chu, it's an honor to meet you."

She waved away his formality. "It's Diana. And I go by Callas, much to the dismay of my in-laws."

Alina nodded. "Why not? Nothing wrong with a woman using her own name. It's the twenty-first century, right?"

Diana leaned an elbow onto the table. "What's your family name, Alina?"

"Preobrazhensky." She hiccupped, then giggled. "Volkov is easier. So, Miss Rosie, tell me about all these tattoos."

"Oh, I, uh—"

Mom sighed. "I told her to keep them in places she could cover up, but did she listen?" Her speech had developed a distinct slur. "Baby girl, people are gonna get the wrong idea about you. They'll think you're some kind of—"

Rosie felt her jaw tighten. "Some kind of what, Ma? Criminal? Drug addict?"

Eddie wrapped his arm around her shoulder. "I think they're beautiful. Rosie is an artist, and her tattoos express that."

Alina's eyes widened. "You tattooed yourself?"

Actually, she'd tried that back in high school, a shooting star inside her forearm. The results were blurry and lopsided. She'd since had a professional clean it up.

"No, these are all done by professionals." Might as well throw it out there—her career plans might provide the fuel Eddie needed to stage their breakup. "But I hope to become a tattoo artist one day."

Alina pursed her lips. "In the old country, tattoos were for criminals, mafia. Bad dudes, you know?"

"You see?" Ma spread her palms wide.

"But not here." Alina grasped Ma's hand. "The young generation, they like to be colorful. I say, more power to them." She leaned closer and examined the roses blooming across Rosie's cleavage. "I wish I could be so daring."

"You can start small." Rosie winked. "Maybe a tiny flower on your ankle. Very delicate and feminine." She'd tried to talk her mom into a mini tattoo, to no avail.

"So," Ma fixed them with a stern teacher look. "How long have you been seeing each other?"

"Well, we—" She bit her lip. Already, she'd forgotten an important part of their cover story.

Eddie squeezed her shoulder. "I've been mooning over Rosie ever since she came to work here." His gaze softened. "It wasn't until last month she finally agreed to go out with me."

That last bit was technically true, clever boy, since New Year's Eve was just a few days ago. But had he really been crushing on her that long? Or was that just a face-saving lie?

"We've been getting to know each other at work," she added. Mostly, she'd been getting to know how it felt to kiss him under the mistletoe. Really, she didn't know much about Eddie at all.

"Well, Eddie." Ma slapped the table. "Now that I've met your charming mother, we'll have to get the families together. How about dinner on Saturday?"

Rosie shot Eddie a silent *help me* glance.

"We work on Saturday, Ms. Callas."

"Lunch, then?"

Alina sighed. "Saturday is our busiest day, I'm afraid. We need Eddie at the shop."

"Oh." Ma frowned, then brightened and raised a finger. "How about—"

"Tell you what, Ma. Eddie and I will work out a time, okay?" *How about never? Does never work for you?*

Alina grinned. "Young people today, so independent. They

don't want their mamas interfering."

Eddie wrapped his arms around Rosie from behind and murmured in her ear, "Great. Now our moms are BFFs."

"They'll forget about it once they sober up," she whispered. "Okay, Ma, we have to get back to work. Let me call you a ride."

"Nonsense," Alina's emphatic gesture nearly knocked their glasses to the floor. "Vadim will drop you at home. He's coming to get me in—" She glanced at her watch. "Oh my goodness, he must be outside now." She pulled her phone from her purse. "Yes, he's here. Let's go, Diana."

Ma dropped two twenties on the table, and the two women shrugged into their coats.

"Mama, wait a minute," Eddie called. "You never told me why you came to the bar."

Alina's forehead rumpled. "Why did I come to the bar? Ah yes, your cousin Irina is getting married next month. February sixth. Very sudden, you know?" She winked. "Tell your boss you need the day off. Rosie too."

Out they went, giggling into the night.

Rosie gathered the empties onto her tray. "Guess we have to break up before the sixth of February."

"Are you kidding? My cousin's wedding will be a blast. Just hang in there until February seventh, okay?" He pecked her lips and trotted back toward the bar.

Rosie brought a shaky hand to her suddenly damp forehead. Make-believe dating a guy she never should have messed with? And their moms were drinking buddies now? And a wedding invitation? Just one hot, drunken night with Eddie had sent her life was spinning out of control.

Damned mistletoe.

Chapter Five

This midweek workout was either going to save Eddie's sanity, or else kill him. Either outcome was better than the lovesick funk he'd marinated in since last weekend.

Jojo growled into Eddie's ear. "You got this, little man. Gimme ten more."

Despite the chilly temperature in Jojo's garage, sweat soaked Eddie's T-shirt as he dangled from the homemade pull-up bar. He shifted his grip and, with a grunt, heaved his legs up to chest level. His abs burned with well-earned, energizing pain, the kind that cut through the bullshit and anchored him in the moment.

Jojo, his equally mammoth brother Kai, and River chanted, "Six, five, four, three..."

With a grunt worthy of the beast he smelled like, Eddie powered out two more leg-lifts before dropping to the cement floor. Hands on knees, he gulped air.

Jojo pounded his back. "Feels good, don't it? River, you're

up."

Their self-appointed personal trainer put his brother and co-workers through this grueling workout twice a week, an hour of sweat and pain before Jojo's shift as a phlebotomist at Tacoma General. Eddie loved the camaraderie of their makeshift gym, plus the bone-rattling death metal blasting from the ancient speakers, and the good-natured teasing. He couldn't match Jojo and Kai's hulking muscularity or River's GQ physique, but the guys respected his determination. Not since high school wrestling had he enjoyed using his body this hard.

Well, except for New Year's Eve, but he wasn't going to think about that.

With a pained screech, River finished his set and dropped to the floor. "That's what I'm talkin' about." He flexed and grunted. "Gotta keep in shape for our ladies. Right, peanut?"

"Don't call him that." Kai handed them smoothies the color of pond scum. "Pound for pound, Eddie's stronger than all of us." He slurped his drink, then raised an eyebrow. "You ever think about boxing, Eddie? You'd make a kick-ass welterweight."

He chuckled grimly. "My parents would kill me."

"Man, you're too old to worry about that shit," River swiped his sopping face on his Bangers' hoodie.

"Shut up." Jojo pitched a wadded-up towel at River's head. "Some of us honor our parents."

"Yeah," Eddie grumbled. "Especially us only children. I don't have a meathead brother to help carry the weight. It's all on me."

Kai grinned and nudged his brother. "Which one of us is the meathead?"

"S'a matter, Eddie?" River emptied his glass. "All is not well in the dry-cleaning business?"

He curled his lip. "A lifetime of chemicals and wire hangers isn't my idea of paradise."

River squeezed him in a sweaty side-hug. "You gotta tell 'em, man. Take a stand. You'll feel better once you do. Took me too long to finally tell my parents no way was I joining their real estate firm."

"How'd they take it?"

River's laugh held an edge. "Not great at first. But they accepted it eventually, and now they're scouting properties for my future bar." He snorted. "With their taste, I'd end up with one of those cookie-cutter gastro-pubs."

Eddie knew just the kind of place he was talking about. Edison bulbs, uncomfortable metal chairs, metro tiles on the walls—all that clichéd, trendy shit. His place would have a dark, old-school vibe, with a cool name like Dacha. Russian bar food, a huge selection of vodka, Soviet-era posters...

"River's right, ya know." Jojo sat on a weight bench which creaked dangerously. "Keeping secrets from family? Bad idea. They know you better than anyone. They'll figure it out."

So far, they hadn't, maybe because they assumed Eddie wanted what they wanted for him. He'd tell them eventually, after he had all his action steps lined up, his degree completed, a small business loan secured, a year or two managing a bar...

"Speaking of keeping secrets from family," River waggled his eyebrows. "How long you been hooking up with our Rosie?"

Kai's jaw dropped. "That hot fat chick with the tattoos?"

Eddie punched his arm. "She's not fat, meathead."

Kai scowled and rubbed the sore spot. "No disrespect. Like I said, she's hot. She's with you now?" He whistled. "I'm impressed."

"So's Rosie, I bet." Jojo knuckled the top of Eddie's head. "Little muscle man's got stamina."

Eddie extricated himself and raised his palms. "Look, Rosie and I, we're just—"

"Just friends, right?" River looked at the other two guys, and they all burst into guffaws.

Rolling his eyes, Eddie waited them out. "I was gonna say we're taking it slow. So I'd appreciate it if you don't give us shit about it at work." His strategy: keep as close to the truth as possible. Since Saturday's momapalooza, he'd dodged his parents' pointed questions, offering excuses about busy schedules and reassuring them he saw Rosie plenty at work—and after. That last part was a lie. Lately, their only physical contact was a quick hand squeeze when he gave her his cousin's ostentatious wedding invitation. God, there was so much more he wanted to squeeze, but that was his problem, not Rosie's. She was being fuckin' generous to help him cover for his stupidity. He couldn't ask for more, no matter how much he wanted to.

Besides, she was right. These guys' friendship was too important to risk over a stupid crush. Bad enough to limp through this pretend dating bullshit for his parents' sake. He had to keep things light and breezy, so when they stopped pretending, their friends wouldn't feel moved to take sides. He'd need to lean on his work family during the real family drama to come.

"Rosie's good for you," Jojo said with a sage nod of his shaved head. "You're coming out of your shell."

I am? He hadn't noticed. Probably just their imagination.

Jojo clapped his ginormous hands. "Okay, boys and girls,

Bulgarian death squats."

Gritting his teeth, Eddie attacked the one-legged torture. He welcomed the pain because it gave him a reprieve from obsessing over Rosie. Well, mostly. Okay, a little. "Twenty-three, twenty-four, twenty-five…"

An hour later, he climbed the steps to his apartment on limp-noodle legs. He had just enough time to squeeze in a hot shower and an hour of study for his Psychology of Marketing class before reporting to duty at his parents' dry-cleaning shop. This hectic pace was getting to him lately, along with the winter darkness, the constant icy rain, and—who was he kidding? He'd handled his responsibilities just fine before New Year's Eve. Rosie's rejection sucked all the energy from his routine. Before that damn mistletoe sent him into a tailspin, he'd kept his head above water by sticking to his daily to-do list, his affirmations, and a nightly meditation on his vision board. Now, he marched like an automaton through his days, joyless and glum.

"Quit being such a wuss," he grumbled as he peeled off his sodden workout clothes. "Everyone gets dumped. You'll survive."

He cranked up the hot water and stepped into the shower stall he'd installed with his grandfather's help when they renovated this attic space. "It's the little joys in life, lapochka," Dedka told him with a clap on the shoulder. "Good water pressure, good vodka, and a good woman."

"Well, shit." Too early for vodka, and even though he still craved her with every cell in his exhausted body, Rosie was clearly not the right woman for him. What was he thinking, lusting after someone so fuckin' hot and bohemian when he was this boring, workaday schlub?

He filled his palm with shampoo and dumped it over his head, then dug into his scalp while bubbles made their tickling way down his torso.

Just like Rosie's hair had tickled—soft, thrilling, like the brush of her lips over his skin. He glopped shower gel onto a washcloth and scrubbed it across his tired shoulders. If he turned his back to the mirror, would he still see the purple half-moons she'd left there when she came, her soft thighs gripping his hips?

His cock stiffened at the memory. Just a few feet away, he'd taken her. And she begged him for more, sobbing his name as her sweet pussy clenched on his shaft. Powerless to resist, he took himself in hand and stroked, head thrown back against the cool tiles, sunk in memory and want and pain.

* * *

Freshly cleared by her doc, Dawn stood on the low stage, mic in hand. "Welcome to Bangers' Trivia Madness! Tonight's prizes are from Galloping Gertie Brewing Company. Be sure and try their winter porter—deeelish."

Eddie chuckled as he sealed the last envelope of trivia questions. The boss rarely drank alcohol, but she sure as shit knew how to sell it.

Dawn continued reciting the rules. "Our beautiful servers will hand out the questions for each round. If you open the envelope before I call Start, your team is disqualified. And no Googling!"

"Aww, Dawn, Google is our friend," some guy called out.

His chucklehead buddies hooted and clapped.

Dawn lowered her reading glasses. "This ain't the Jeopardy Championship, son, just a fun charity game. But if you need a T-shirt that bad, you can have mine." Waggling her eyebrows, she tugged the hem upward, flashing a swath of round belly.

Laughter filled the bar.

"Tonight's proceeds go to the Tacoma Rescue Mission. We ready?"

Back at the bar, Rosie's fingers brushed Eddie's as she collected the envelopes for her section. Tingles danced up his arm from the point of contact. Too hell with common sense. He grasped her hand and held it for a moment.

Her eyebrows shot up. "What?"

He shrugged. "I miss you."

And I want you more than I want oxygen. And I can't believe you don't want me anymore, after the way you fell apart in my arms.

Snippets of memory tormented him: Rosie peeling off her sparkly red sweater to reveal a galaxy of images adorning her silky skin. The teasing brush of her bright blue curls on his bare chest and belly as she slid down, down...the liquid heat of her pussy as he drove into her body...the sting of her teeth nipping his shoulder...

Rosie's gaze dropped. She slid her hand from his and backed away. "I, uh, gotta do this." She waved the stack of envelopes.

He watched her slide through the crowd, flirtatious and funny and not his. It fuckin' hurt.

"On your mark, get set, trivia!" Dawn's shout popped his lovesick bubble. After restocking glassware, cutting fresh lemons and limes, and wiping up spills, he paused to suck down a cola and search the crowd for Rosie.

There she was at a high-top by the window, tray propped on her hip, chatting with a tattooed dude nearly as big as Jojo. Despite the icy weather, the guy wore a sleeveless T-shirt beneath his leather vest. Elaborate tattoos covered both beefy arms and wound up his thick neck. Shaved head, bushy red beard, probably had a Harley parked outside. He leaned in close to say something to Rosie, who tossed her head back and laughed.

Icicles stabbed Eddie's gut. Who was he kidding, with his sappy "I miss you" and lame gift? This guy was Rosie's type: big, buff, badass. Eddie rubbed his own skinny, ink-free arm. Maybe if he got a tattoo…

Don't be stupid. Needles make me puke. But man, what he'd give to see Rosie light up for him the way she lit up for Harley Dude over there. Her smile shone so bright, strong enough to fan the tiny flame he carried inside and build it into…

He shook his head. Whatever lame metaphor he was reaching for crumbled under the weight of cruel reality. Rosie wasn't for him. Later, once he accomplished his goals, he'd look for a nice woman, someone more like himself—serious, goal-oriented, methodical. Someone to help run the bar he dreamed of, maybe even start a family.

He pulled out his notebook and traced a finger over that day's bullet-point list. There was plenty in here to keep his mind off regrets—a Marketing project due next Monday and a paper for Business Ethics due Friday. And a suit fitting for his cousin's wedding.

Someone rapped on the bar, pulling his attention back to the task at hand. "Time for round two, Eddie." Lana twirled one of her long black pigtails, braided with ribbons in Seahawks blue and green.

He handed over the next stack of envelopes.

Lana fanned herself with them and tilted her head. "You and Rosie fighting already?"

Heat rushed to his cheeks. "What? No." He grabbed a bar towel and scrubbed at an imaginary smudge. "Why do you ask?"

"You guys stay on opposite sides of the room. Not like Charlie and River."

Sure enough, Charlie was behind the bar again. While River garnished a trio of tall fruity cocktails with mint and orange slices, she grabbed a handful of his ass.

"Get a room," Lana called.

"What?" Charlie batted her lashes. "I'm just helping with this drink order."

"Ain't no one ordered a River-ass-tini," Lana parried before turning back to Eddie and lowering her voice. "Everything okay? Want me to talk to Rosie?"

"I do not."

She would anyway, though. Lana and Rosie were tight, which meant their fake dating secret wouldn't last long under Lana's BFF scrutiny. Eddie beckoned her closer. "The thing is, we're both kind of cautious about the co-workers dating thing. Dawn's not a fan, and—"

"Gotcha." She patted his arm. "Smart of you, unlike those two horndogs." She tilted her head toward Charlie and River. "I mean, what'll we do if they break up? I love them both, but I'd have to pick Team Charlie."

"Why?"

"Sisterhood, silly boy." She loaded up her tray and sailed off to distribute booze and trivia questions.

The crowd gradually thinned as teams were eliminated from

the competition. On a pass through the main seating area to collect empties, Eddie stopped at the doorway where Jojo checked IDs and monitored for dust-ups. "Need anything?"

"Just the love of a good woman." He lifted his square chin toward the pool tables, where Rosie leaned against a column, scribbling in the blue notebook he'd given her. "Never seen anyone draw so fast. She's got talent, your girl."

Not my girl. The reminder stung. Why had he never seen her artwork? Time to fix that.

He loaded up his bus tray with empties, slowly working his way toward Rosie, still intent on her drawing. But before he reached her, Dawn called, "You done with your break, Rosie?"

"Yes ma'am." She snapped the notebook shut and hustled to the stage. Dawn handed over the mic and hopped down. Passing Eddie, she chuckled. "Can't hold it as long as I used to."

I did not need to hear that.

Rosie's husky voice rang out through the mic. "One minute left to finish your answers, people."

"I love you, Rosie," some guy hollered from a table in the back.

"Rosie's taken," Jojo called.

Eddie shot him a glare.

So did Rosie, before checking the Seahawks wall clock. "Five, four, three, two, time's up." Rosie caught Eddie's eye and beckoned.

He pushed through the crowd to the stage. "Something wrong?"

She extended her hand and tugged him up beside her. "Help me score these? We're running late, and I need to start the next round."

"Umm, I..." If there was anything he hated more than needles, it was public speaking.

Rosie spoke into the mic. "My lovely assistant Eddie will help score the answers."

"We love you, Eddie," squawked some drunk chick from the far end of the bar.

"Eddie's taken," Jojo called. "By Rosie."

His stomach tilted as he and Rosie exchanged frozen, wide-eyed smiles. So much for keeping their pretend-dating scheme on the downlow.

"Awww," a woman squealed, "Rosie's got a little pocket boyfriend."

Jaw clenched, Eddie scanned the stage floor. Just his luck, no trap door.

Rosie switched off the mic, turned her back to the audience and hiss-whispered, "What the fuck, Eddie? I agreed to pretend to your family, not to the whole damn world."

He whispered back, "Jojo saw us with the moms."

Squeezing her eyes shut, she blew out a breath. "Let's just ignore him. Five minutes from now, people will find something more interesting to talk about." She faced the audience with a phony smile. "Eddie will verify the answers, and—"

Ting, ting, ting. Someone tapped a glass with a fork. Others joined in, and soon the bar rang with tinkly din.

"Question one," Rosie shouted into the mic.

"Kiss!" someone called. Tipsy customers picked up the refrain. "Kiss, kiss, kiss."

Rosie's panicked gaze darted from him to the chanting mob. "Make them stop."

Only one way to do that. Eddie faced the crowd and raised

his forefinger. Like a prizefighter warming up, he rolled his head and shoulders, blew out a breath, then raked his fingers into her hair and mashed his lips to hers.

She squeaked. "Damn, Eddie."

"Hang on." He crooked his leg behind her knees and dipped her in a kitschy movie clinch. Giggling, she kissed him back.

What the hell, this may be my last chance. When she parted her lips to draw a breath, he swept his tongue inside.

For a long, sweet moment, the crowd dissolved, the noise faded, and the whole world contracted to the circle of their arms around each other, their mingled breath, the slide of her velvet tongue over his. Then something hard and cold pinged off his head.

"Jesus H. Christ on a pogo stick. Can't leave you two alone for two seconds." Dawn fished another ice cube from her glass and chucked it at them. It hit Rosie's chest and slid into her cleavage.

Eyes bugging out, she popped upright, nearly dumping Eddie on his ass.

"Steady now." He held her elbow while she fished the ice out of her bra.

Dawn was right, there must be something in the water—or something about touching Rosie that knocked him off center and released his fearless evil twin—because he snatched the ice from her hand and popped it into his mouth. The crowd roared with laughter.

"Go on, get back to work." Dawn gave his shoulder a shove. Was she smiling or grimacing? Hard to tell.

"My lady?" He extended his hand. When Rosie just gaped at him, he clasped her clenched fist and pulled her off the stage.

They made it as far as the bar before she smacked him upside his buzzing head. "What the hell were you thinking?"

His giddy mood popped like a soap bubble. "You said to make them stop."

Rosie stomped in a circle, muttering some very creative curses—which only made him want her more—so hot and fiery, with her heaving chest and blazing eyes.

Dawn's voice rang out. "Winner of round two is, drumroll please..." she paused for the customers to bang on their tabletops. "Kappa Alpha Theta!"

A quartet of girls in Puget Sound University hoodies hooted and clapped.

"Round three, coming up."

"Thanks a motherfuckin' lot, Eddie." She stamped to the bar, snatched the next batch of envelopes from Kiara, and moved off to distribute them.

Eddie slunk behind the bar and took out his frustration hacking up lemons and limes.

River's hand fell onto his shoulder. "Trouble in paradise?"

He shrugged. "Note to self: ask before kissing." But she kissed him back, damn it. He hadn't imagined her fingers tightening on his shoulders, her soft sigh as their lips connected, her hungry little moan when his tongue swept inside her.

"Don't worry, Eddie." Kiara gave him a side hug. "She still likes you."

"How can you tell?" he grumbled, his eyes on the mangled fruit.

"Because she keeps looking at you."

He glanced up. Rosie glowered and jerked her gaze away. *Yeah, she looks at me like she wants to roast me alive.*

62

Chapter Six

By quitting time, Rosie had calmed down enough to realize how wrong she was for biting Eddie's head off. Tonight's kiss fiasco had filled her pockets with extra tips—and dampened her panties something fierce. What really pissed her off was how much she enjoyed kissing him. A persistent tingle flared every time she glanced his way. And now she had to say sorry, weasel her way back into his apartment, and keep her stupid, horny hands to herself.

When the servers gathered at the bar to divvy up tips, she tucked an extra twenty into Eddie's jar.

Charlie snort-laughed. "You don't have to buy his affection, Rosie. He's already yours."

At the far end of the bar, Eddie dropped the plastic crate he'd just emptied. The clatter yanked everyone's focus to his scowling face. "Look." He waved toward the empty stage. "That kiss was just to get the crowd to shut up, like Rosie asked me to, right?" He pinned her with a glare, and her stomach dropped three stories.

"Er—right. We were just—kidding around."

"Is that what you kids call it?" Dawn hooked her thumbs through her belt loops like an old West gunslinger. "In my day, we called it fooling around."

Awkward! Rosie squelched the urge to cut and run, instead adopting a breezy tone. "Just a little fun. No big deal." Eddie's glare softened into a glum pout. A very kissable pout.

Dawn turned back to the register, and everyone else said their good-nights and drifted toward the exits. Apparently, the boss was done chewing them out for now.

"Hang on, you two."

Or not.

"Sit down." Her jaw set, Dawn gestured toward the bar stools. Eddie sat beside Rosie, casting nervous glances between her and the boss.

"Look, kids. I've already had this conversation with River and Charlie. Now it's your turn." She swiped a palm down her face. "I'm not trying to stick my nose in your private business, but there's a reason big companies have HR policies against dating coworkers."

Eddie spoke up. "It's just that Jojo—"

"I already talked to him. He's not gonna tease you in front of customers anymore. The big lunk means well, but he needs to think before he speaks." She pointed to Eddie's sternum. "And you need to think before you act. I can't have the appearance of sexual harassment in my business."

Eddie blanched and clutched the edge of the bar.

Mayday! She couldn't let him lose his job over something she started. "There was no harassment, Dawn. Just a joke between friends that went a little sideways."

Dawn crossed her arms. "You say that now, but what about next time? My customers saw you arguing. Someone's gonna get the wrong idea, and it'll be my butt on the line." She leaned closer, eyebrows lowered. "And my livelihood. So consider this your final warning. No relationship drama at work, or you're both outta here."

Rosie's heart skipped a beat. Then another one. "Understood."

Dawn's expression softened into weariness. "Now go on home. And I suggest you talk this mess out. In private."

Eddie slid from his stool and trudged to the locker room. Rosie followed.

Without a word, without a glance her way, he pulled on his jacket, scarf, and hat. She did the same, gulping deep breaths to push back threatening tears. She'd come to terms with Mom's disappointment, but knowing she'd let her work mom down left her hollow and queasy. And she'd hurt Eddie in the bargain—a sweet guy who didn't deserve the chaos she'd dumped on him.

"Eddie, I—"

He raised a hand but didn't meet her eye. "If you don't mind, I've reached my limit for tonight."

"But I—"

"Sorry I kissed you. It was stupid. I should've asked first, and—"

"—lost my earring in your place. My sister's earring, actually, and she'll skin me alive if I don't bring it back."

He glanced up, blinking rapidly. "Oh. You want me to look for it?"

"Could I just—easier for me to retrace my steps." Or stumbles. To tell the truth, her memory of falling into Eddie's bed was pretty blurry, though her memory of what transpired in that bed was solidifying more each day. Lots of steamy details that made it harder and harder to look Eddie in the eye.

He bit his lip and stared at the floor.

"Just two minutes. In and out, I promise."

He heaved a huge sigh. "Sure. Okay." A wry grin twisted his lips. "You know the way."

Silently, side by side, they walked to the parking lot. She climbed into her little Honda and followed Eddie to his place on Mason Ave. Lights still shone from his parents' house. *Marvelous.*

Eddie rapped on her car window. "You coming or what?"

She pointed to the house and raised her eyebrows in a silent question.

"I'm sure they're in bed. Mom feels more secure with the lights on."

She closed her car door as quietly as she could and followed him up the stairs. Halfway up, a blinding motion-sensor lamp flashed on. She froze, back pressed against the wall.

"God, you're jumpy." Eddie tugged her sleeve. "That goes off all night. Raccoons, deer, cats..." He unlocked the door and waved her through.

Eddie's apartment smelled of coffee, his herbal shower soap, and his woodsy cologne—a homey, welcoming scent that took her right back to New Year's Day, to the split second of happiness between waking in his warm bed and panicking over her stupid mistake.

She gave her head a sharp shake, but the memory clung. This time, Eddie wasn't wearing that heartstring-plucking, sleepy, sated smile. Eyes narrowed, arms folded, he stood with his back to the wall as if prepared for an attack.

She cleared her throat. "So, we, uh—went over there first, right?" She pointed to the sofa opposite his tiny kitchenette. "I was pretty wobbly at that point." No surprise, after downing three of River's champagne sparklers at the Bangers' crew afterparty. She checked the couch, digging into folds in the fabric, then squatted to scan beneath.

"Here." He kneeled beside her and switched on his phone's flashlight.

"Nothing." The floor was spotless. Weren't single guys supposed to be slobs? Anyone looking beneath her own furniture would find dust bunnies big enough to double as pets.

Eddie pulled her to her feet.

"Thanks." She shoved a hand through her hair. "So, as I recall, we—uh—made out here for a while. But we were still dressed at that point, right?"

Scarlet bloomed across Eddie's sharp cheekbones. "Yeah. The clothes came off later."

Steamy memories coalesced. The sensual scrape of his short beard at the crook of her neck. His clever fingers unhooking her bra and stroking her breasts reverently.

Eddie flexed his fingers, then clenched them as his gaze rose from her chest to her face and held for a long, tense moment.

Hoo boy. Move along. Resisting the impulse to fan herself, she stepped toward the TV. "I think we were standing when my sweater came off. That's probably what knocked the earring loose."

There'd been music playing, slow and smoky. He'd pulled her into his arms and swayed her in slow circles, his hips pressed to hers. And then he tugged her sweater up and off, tossing it—where?

She bit her lip and glanced around. "Eddie, do you remember?"

His heated gaze settled on her mouth. "I remember every detail, Rosie. Doubt I'll ever forget."

She clucked her tongue. "I mean, where were we when my sweater came off?"

His gaze skimmed her body, then he sighed and pointed. "I found it draped over the TV."

"Great," she chirped, her voice too loud and bright.

She knelt and peered behind the TV cabinet. "I can't see. There's something in the way." A poster board covered with magazine clippings, drawings, and words stood sandwiched between the TV and the bookcase. She slid it out. "Here."

Eddie snatched the cardboard and held it to his chest like a shield. A cutout image of a barstool fluttered to the floor. She reached for it, but he stomped on it as if a sudden gust might whisk it away.

Touchy, aren't you? Ass in the air, she shined her phone light into the void. "Project for your business classes?"

"Sort of." His footsteps crossed the room, then a cabinet door closed.

"Top secret, huh?" She glanced over her shoulder. His gaze was riveted to her butt.

"Find anything?" he asked in a strangled voice.

"No, damn it." She sat back on her heels and formed an O with her finger and thumb. "It's about this big, a gold hoop with tiny diamond dangly bits."

Their eyes met and held. Eddie giggled first. "Dangly bits?"

Her cheeks heated as she scrambled to her feet. "I can't help it. I'm searching the place where we—you know. My mind goes to naughty places. I have ADD, so I tend to blurt out whatever's on my mind."

He hooked his thumbs into his belt, framing his own dangly bits. "Convenient excuse."

An icy wave swamped her. No way could she let that remark slide—not if they had any shot at friendship. Jaw tense, she pushed to her feet and planted her fists on her hips. "You know, all my life people have called my condition an excuse. It's not. It's the way my brain is wired." She peered around the bedroom side of the bookshelves. If she focused on her search, maybe he wouldn't see the anger and disappointment twisting her features.

His hand fell on her shoulder. "Hey."

She shook him off. "Maybe it's under the bed."

"Rosie, come on. Look at me. Please."

Swallowing a jagged lump, she turned to face him. *Curse those sad puppy eyes.*

He spread his hands. "I'm sorry. I didn't know." He shuffled closer. "For the record, I like the way your brain is wired."

Her eyes misted over. *Damn it to hell and back.*

He stroked her arms from shoulder to elbow. "You're bold, and funny, and brave. And apparently, you're a great artist, though I've never seen your work. Why is that?"

Because my art is everything, and if you don't like it, I can't like you anymore.

She knew she was being silly and way too sensitive. After all, he was just a work friend—aside from one steamy night she'd never forget. Her future didn't hang on his opinion.

She squared her shoulders. "I'll show you mine if you show me yours."

Expressions chased each other across his face: confusion,

understanding, devilish delight. Taking her elbows, he drew her closer, until their bellies brushed. "I thought you didn't want to, but Rosie—"

She placed her lips beside his ear and whispered, "My artwork for whatever you're hiding in that cabinet." She gave his chest a playful shove. "But first, help me find my sister's earring. Otherwise, I'm a dead woman."

He slumped for a moment, then straightened and pasted on a nonchalant grin. "On it." He searched beneath the bookshelf while she checked the bathroom.

"Nothing?"

"Nothing." She scratched her head and glanced at his bed. "Guess there's just one last place to look."

His Adam's apple bobbed. "Right. Here we go." He stripped off the beautiful red and blue quilt and shook it out before folding it and setting it on the antique cedar chest.

Bit by bit, they stripped off the bedclothes. Nothing. Ditto underneath the bed. Rosie sank onto the bare mattress and dropped her head into her hands. "The family fuck-up strikes again. I'm gonna have to eat so much shit over this."

The mattress dipped as Eddie sat beside her and rubbed soothing circles on her back. "You're not a fuck-up, Rosie. You're amazing. And if your family kicks you out over an earring, you can come live with us." He leaned his cheek onto her shoulder. "Babka would love that."

"Must be great to have such a supportive family."

He didn't answer, just slid his arm around her waist and sighed. For a long, irresponsible moment, she soaked in his warmth.

Suddenly, he bounced to his feet. "Wait a minute. I once lost a book here. Grab that corner." He pointed to the foot of the mattress.

They yanked the mattress down, then dashed to the gap between the box spring and the headboard. A glint of gold winked.

"Oh, thank God!" Rosie snatched it up, threw her arms around Eddie's neck, and peppered his face with kisses.

"Hey now. Let's take a breath." He grasped her hands and stepped out of her embrace. "I thought we were aiming for just friends."

Disappointment feels just like needles. She'd never thought of it that way until this moment—not the buzzing sting of tattoo needles, but those big-ass needles they use for flu shots—a sharp pinch, followed by a dull ache. All she wanted to do was kiss Eddie silly then tumble onto his naked bed and re-enact their New Year's surprise. But she was the one who erected that boundary, and he was honoring it. Like a real friend.

Breathe. Let it go.

Eddie squeezed her hands before dropping them. "Look, I know I'm not your type."

Did she even have a type? A quick mental scan of her dating history didn't reveal any particular pattern. There were tall guys and short guys, buff guys and skinny guys, younger, older, even a few girls. None of them had ever lasted more than a couple months. And that was just fine with her. After her first clichéd heartbreak in her senior year of high school—dumped the night before prom, for God's sake—she filed boyfriends under F for Fun Only.

"Eddie, I don't have a type. What are you talking about?"

"You know, like that Harley dude you were talking to tonight."

"Harley? I don't know anyone named Harley."

Eddie rolled his eyes. "Shaved head. Red beard. Muscles. Tattoos."

"Ahh. That's Bruno." Holy cow, Eddie was jealous of a guy twice his age who smelled like a wet horse. She grasped his shoulders. "I'm not trying to get into his pants. I'm trying to get into his tattoo shop."

Adorable, the way Eddie's nose wrinkled. "Another tattoo? Where will you put it?"

She should let that opening go, but who could blame her? The setup was too perfect. She hooked a finger in the neckline of her shirt and tugged. "Oh, I've still got lots of un-inked skin. Didn't you notice?"

His eyes widened and darkened.

She punched his shoulder playfully. "I'm trying to get an apprenticeship. You know, on-the-job training."

"You need that?"

"No decent shop will hire me without one."

He nodded slowly. "Makes sense. I wouldn't want to be anyone's test case for something so permanent."

"Too bad." She grinned. "I have the perfect idea for your tattoo. Wanna see?" When he just goggled, she added, "Don't worry. It'll be years before I'm allowed to ink anything this elaborate on someone's skin."

Looking pale and queasy, he nodded. "Okay, show me."

He followed her back to the sofa, where she pulled her notebook from her bag and flipped to the design she'd worked on tonight, a double-headed eagle clutching a royal orb and some kind of scepter. "Best I could do without a closer look."

His jaw relaxed open as he traced the design with his fingertip. "This is my belt buckle?" He caressed the worn silver oval. "It was my great grandfather's. He fled Soviet

Russia in '38. Chemistry professor. Too vocal about his views, nearly got himself killed. He landed in Seattle and went into the laundry business."

"And your family's been doing that ever since?"

"Yeah." His chuckle rang dry and dusty. "Until me."

"I don't understand. You work for your parents, right?"

"For now." His thin-lipped expression told her to drop it. She might be tactless, but she could take a hint.

"Can I take a picture?"

Her pulse sprinted when he started to undo his belt. "Not necessary. I'll just—" She pushed the coffee table back, knelt between his knees, and snapped several photos. Flipping through the images, she grinned up at him. "Perfect."

There it was again, that funny choking sound. She patted his knee and pushed to her feet, then plopped down beside him. "Tell me about the design."

He blew out a breath. "Russian Imperial seal. Military officers wore it. Great-granddad's father was one. Killed in the Stalinist purges. Ugly business." He chuckled. "That's all Dedka will say about it—'It was an ugly business.' " He lifted the book and examined her rough sketch. "You're really talented, Rosie. Will you show me when you finish this?"

"Sure." Hard to speak through her wide grin. "Now show me yours."

His eyes widened, then crinkled in laughter. "Ah, my—" He pointed to the kitchen cabinets. "Okay. Fair's fair."

He went to fetch the posterboard. Even though his back was turned, she caught him adjusting himself inside his jeans. Immediately, her mind spun away to memories of his thick, heavy cock. She shifted on her seat to ease the sudden tingling heat between her thighs.

He removed a stack of books from the coffee table and lay the poster board there. "Feels like show and tell time."

She examined the patchwork of magazine clippings, computer printouts, and floor plans. Most of the images were bar and restaurant interiors—plush stools and booths, bar layouts, lighting fixtures, plus lots of bottles, mostly vodka. Here and there, images of people—bow-tied bartenders, a server or hostess in a sleek black dress, and in the top left corner, Eddie smoldering in a dark suit, arms crossed like some mafia badass.

She pointed. "Hot stuff, Eddie. I've never seen you in a suit."

"Well, you know…" He shrugged and dipped his head to hide a sheepish grin. "Bangers isn't that kind of place."

Understanding dawned. "But your dream bar is. And you're the boss."

"Someday."

"This is why you're studying business?"

With a wry grin, he ran his fingertip along the red arrow connecting words among the images: *Learn—Plan—Entrepreneur—Dreams don't work unless you do—Stand out—Simply the best.* "I have never felt like a bigger dork than I do right now. And I have a lot of years of dorkdom behind me."

She scooted closer and put her hand on his knee. "Eddie, you're not a dork. You're a man with a vision." Her eyebrows shot up. "This a vision board, right? We made these my senior year. Mine was covered with tattoos."

"Like you?" He nudged her with his shoulder.

"Well, back then I only had a few. They're expensive, you know." She nudged him back. "Do your parents know?"

He bit his lip.

"Right—that's why you hide it behind the TV." She squeezed

his knee. "Oh, Eddie. This must be so hard for you."

"It's—yeah." He slouched back on the couch. "They expect me to take over their dry-cleaning business."

"Can't someone else do it?"

"Only child. Family business. Tradition." He leaned his head onto her shoulder, and his soft hair tickled her neck. "To hear them tell it, our family crest is made up of wire coat hangers and plastic garment bags." He slid into a Russian accent. "Dry cleanink has been wery, wery good to our family."

"Very sexy accent, Boris." She ruffled his hair. "Vehr is Moose and Sqvirrel?"

He chuckled and laced his fingers through hers. "They've always been so proud of me. They even keep all my wrestling trophies in my old room, like some kind of shrine."

"Saint Eddie of Tacoma, patron saint of barbacks. At least they're proud of you, though. Beats being the black sheep no one expects anything from, especially when you have an over-achieving sister."

Back and forth, they talked into the wee hours about family, future, and the loneliness of taking a different path. Eddie fetched pillows and made chamomile tea with honey, "Babka's favorite." Her eyelids grew heavy, and Eddie's words faded into a pleasant baritone rumble washing over her exhausted body and mind—soft, warm, cozy.

* * *

An icy draft woke her. "Huh?" She rubbed her bleary eyes and rose onto her elbows. Eddie lay bent at a right angle, feet on the coffee table, his head in her lap, so peaceful and pretty with his long lashes brushing his cheek. He was dreaming, eyes darting beneath closed lids. He muttered gibberish and kneaded her thigh as if adjusting a pillow.

His sigh twisted her heart in a spasm of something dangerously close to love. Time to extricate herself. Too tempting to stay like this all night, even though her back ached from sleeping at an odd angle, her right leg was asleep, and—it wasn't night anymore.

"Eddie." She poked his shoulder.

He buried his face between her thighs. "Five more minutes."

"Eddie!" She shook him. "It's light out. And someone brought us breakfast."

He bolted upright. "What?" he croaked, his gaze whipping from her face to the kitchen counter.

"There." Rosie pointed to the table by the door, where someone had set a tray holding a thermos and something sweet-smelling covered with a kitchen towel. "Does your mom usually bring you breakfast?"

"Uh, no." He lurched to his feet and knuckled his eyes. "What day is it?"

Laughing, she hauled herself upright. "Thursday."

He pulled his phone from his pocket. "Eight-thirty. Holy shit. Did we?—" He gestured to the couch.

"Talked through the night, I guess. Or most of it. Is that coffee cake?" The memory of his babka's cinnamon swirl cake made her stomach rumble.

He crossed to the door and lifted the napkin. "Blueberry muffins." Grinning sheepishly, he held up the plate. "Breakfast for two."

She groaned. "Busted again."

Chapter Seven

The dry-cleaning shop's doorbell chimed, pulling Eddie from his Advanced Marketing homework back into his daily grind. A middle-aged woman bustled through with a pink gown draped over her arm and a panicked look on her face. Since his parents were in back arguing with the repair guy over a malfunctioning trouser press, it was his turn to deal with customers. *Oh joy.*

"Please tell me you can fix this. My daughter's winter formal is tomorrow night."

He pasted on a smile. "What's the problem, ma'am?"

"My brilliant child wanted to post her dress on Instagram in the middle of a pizza party." She pointed to a splotch across the bodice. "Any hope?"

"Well, grease is tough."

"Noooo," the customer wailed, fists clenched. "Do you know how long it took to get this dress?"

"Mrs. Rodriguez, so lovely to see you." Dad bustled from the back room, hands extended as if greeting a long-lost relative. "Such a beautiful gown. When do you need it?"

"Photographer's coming tomorrow at four."

Dad scrunched his lips to one side, then the other. "I can do that." He held up a finger. "I must warn you, though, we may lose a few sequins."

"Fine." She sagged with relief. "I'll get more at the craft shop. Hell, I'll glue-gun them on if I have to.

Mama popped through the swinging doors. "One-day service costs extra for formals. Such a lovely gown." She glanced at Eddie, then leaned toward the customer and winked. "Kids, right? Always making messes."

Eddie bristled. Compared to his mother, whose cooking involved flinging ingredients like Jackson Pollock, he was neatness personified. And Dad left a trail of papers around the house *and* the shop. More than once, he'd had to sleuth his way through piles of Dad's discards in search of a crucial receipt.

"Tag, son." Dad slid the gown to Eddie, who typed in the customer's information, then attached a bar code label to the hem.

"My son, the MBA." Dad beamed. "He is so smart with all these computer things."

Eddie suppressed a snort. Because he could only pay for a few classes at a time, he was still a year away from earning his bachelor's degree.

After the grateful customer left, Dad held up the gown. "What fabric? No peeking."

Eddie huffed. "Dad, it's right there on the tag."

"A dry cleaner must know his fibers. Touch it. Smell it. What's it made of?"

He rolled his eyes and gave a sniff. "Polyester and pizza."

Dad smacked his shoulder. "Rayon and elastane. You better take this seriously, son. One day, all this will be yours." He grabbed the dress and bustled into the back room, pale pink cloth fluttering behind him like a battle flag.

Mama sighed. "You could at least pretend to be interested. Dry cleaning puts food on your table and clothes on your back."

And pollution in the air and water. No matter how his parents encouraged and chided, he just couldn't work up any enthusiasm for the wonderful world of textiles. Rosie was right—he had to tell his parents, and soon, while they still had a chance to find and train someone to take over the shop. But they were so proud of their business, and of him. Striking out on his own might break something that couldn't be repaired.

Mama sprayed the front counter with lemon-scented disinfectant. "Did you and Miss Rosie enjoy the muffins?"

"Yes, Mama. Thank you." He pecked her cheek.

"Interesting girl. Colorful. Not your usual type, but I like her."

Did he have a type? A hard-core introvert, he was attracted to outgoing women who found his shyness cute at first, then quickly grew bored when he couldn't match their energy. And he was small, so of course he was attracted to big, voluptuous women who seldom gave him a second glance. In the past year, he'd been on a handful of dates with women he met at Bangers or his parents' shop, but no one really clicked until Rosie.

"I'm glad you're getting serious with someone. We want grandchildren one day, you know?"

While Mama hummed and spritzed, he allowed himself to

sink into daydreams of Rosie's sexy alto voice. She was the first person he'd ever showed his vision board to, and she hadn't laughed. Instead, she'd asked questions and made suggestions as if they were discussing a concrete plan and not some silly pipe dream. What would it be like to have someone like her at his side, her softness to curl up with every night, her bubbly energy to propel him forward, her confidence to prop him up?

Perfect, that's what it would be. But how to convince her? For now, his best shot was to be the friend she wanted and make sure she knew he was interested in more. But he couldn't be pushy. No more surprise kisses, especially in front of an audience. Maybe...

The door chimed again, jarring him back to soul-sucking reality.

* * *

Rosie pulled into the last parking space at the sad little strip mall. Flanked by a tidy Pho shop and the Hallelujah Christian Bookstore, Screaming Eagle Tattoo was definitely the black sheep of the family with its peeling window paint and half-lit neon sign.

"I got this, I got this, I got this." Tucking her portfolio under her arm, she rose, popped the collar on her leather bomber jacket, and humming "Whole Lotta Rosie," strode across the lot.

Typical tattoo studio, with flash sheets and photos of tattoos plastered on the walls and metalcore blasting from the speakers. The buzz of tattoo machines and the rumble of conversation drifted through saloon doors behind the front desk. A bored-looking receptionist held up a finger and continued her phone conversation. "Swollen? Does it smell bad? Well, smell it."

It was pure luck that brought this studio's owner into Bangers last week. They got to talking, he complimented her on her ink, and voilà, an invitation to bring her portfolio.

"Eew." The receptionist screwed up her face. "Definitely see a doctor. That's totally not normal." She hung up and rolled her eyes. "We hand out aftercare instructions. Not our fault if they don't follow 'em." She tossed Rosie a half-assed grin. "What's up?"

"I have an appointment with Bruno."

"Really?" Wrinkling her pointy nose, she flipped through an appointment book. "'Cause he's got the whole afternoon slotted for his brother-in-law."

Had she screwed up the time? She checked the text he sent yesterday, then showed her phone to the receptionist, who shrugged.

"Go on back, I guess."

Rosie pushed through the swinging doors to the studio floor. It was even more colorful back here. Each of the eight artists' stations was painted a different bright shade, barely visible behind the artwork covering walls and cabinets. Bruno's shop had all the bases covered, from Polynesian to Japanese, new school cartoons, American classics, watercolor, and at one station, biomechanical tattoos that made the wearers look like cyborgs with skin peeled back to reveal mechanical joints and gears. Except for the girl up front, all the artists were male.

Rosie inhaled the familiar tang of green soap and bleach,

clutched her portfolio tighter, and approached the bald, ginger-bearded behemoth.

Bruno straddled his stool, its chest support creaking under his bulk as he shaded a storm cloud on his customer's left shoulder. She knew better than to interrupt, so she carefully leaned in to watch him layer blue over gray, adding depth and a sense of roiling motion. Good stuff.

The skinny dude lying face down opened his eyes and poked Bruno. "Who's she?"

Bruno lifted his tool, wiped his customer's reddened skin with a paper towel, then turned. "Oh, hey. Was that today? Shit, I lost track." He swatted the customer's butt. "Gotta take this, bro. Gimme five, awright?"

With a grunt, the customer rose and ambled toward the coffee station in the corner. Bruno patted the now-vacant chair. "Have a seat, sweetheart. Let's see whatcha got."

She sat and placed her glittery blue binder in his huge mitt.

He snorted. "Seriously? Looks like a high school kid's notebook."

Rosie flinched. She'd watched dozens of online videos about how to make your tattoo portfolio, and plenty used binders like this.

Bruno rolled his stool close enough to feel the heat rolling off his bulky body. He flipped through her drawings, stopping here and there to huff into his wiry beard. Finally, he closed the binder with a snap and laid his palm on her knee. Which would be fine if they were friends. But they weren't, and the gleam in his eye held a predatory edge. "You got potential, kid, but I don't see nothing in here that makes me wanna shout hallelujah, ya know? Skulls, roses, all the usual crap. Training a new artist is a pain in the ass, and I'm not seeing that individual spark." He slid his hand a little further north and kneaded her thigh like bread dough. "You want an apprenticeship? Convince me you're worth the trouble."

Heart thundering, she lifted his wrist and sucked in her cheeks. One more chance, just in case he was one of those touchy-feely types who didn't mean anything by it. "So, what exactly are you looking for? You know, to make you shout hallelujah?"

Bruno arched an eyebrow, his gaze raking her from head to boots. The artist at the next station snickered.

Rosie's scalp prickled as she realized the buzzing had stopped and all eyes were trained on her. She'd stepped right into the trap.

"Tell you what, darlin'." Bruno rubbed his shaved head. "You do a couple months on the front desk, get a feel for the clientele. If you do all right, we'll start workin' you in—supplies, clean-up, assist the artists."

"You're offering me a job, then?"

Bruno's hand fell on her knee again. "That ain't how it works, cupcake. You pay us to teach you. Five thou."

She'd been warned about this. Some old-school tattoo artists expected an apprentice to be their shop bitch, doing all the grunt work in exchange for on-the-job training. And some charged for the privilege too. Apprenticeships were hard to come by, and Tacoma's tattoo scene was especially competitive.

Last chance, horndog. She peeled his fingers off her leg. "What about the girl up front?"

"Candy? She can't draw worth shit. Just wants free tattoos."

I wonder if Candy knows that, or if she thinks she's their apprentice. She rose to her feet. "You know, I've got a job

I love. I'm not sure I could make this work."

Bruno shoved her folder into her stomach. "Suit yourself." He stood and crossed his beefy arms over his belly. "A little advice before you go. Clean up your act. That folder's a mess. Show something more original." He loomed closer and leered. "And loosen up a little. You're a pretty girl. Customers like that. Use what you got to get what you want."

She didn't trust herself to bite back a snarky retort, so she spun on her heel and forced herself to stroll out, putting a little extra kiss-my-ass sway in her step. As much as she'd like to roast Bruno's sexist ass, word would get around and maybe slam other doors in her face.

When she passed the front desk, she waggled her fingers at the receptionist. The girl cupped her mouth and whispered, "Buncha assholes, right?"

Rosie spluttered a laugh—because crying wouldn't do any damn good. She'd known from the start she was up against a system that rewarded macho bullshit. But times were changing. There were lots of female tattoo artists nowadays. She'd find her place. And Screaming Eagle damn sure wasn't it.

* * *

Hunched over the bar, Eddie scribbled in his notebook. "So, it's Chambord, vodka, and…"

"Seven-up or Sprite." River added a shot of soda to the deep purple cocktail. "Just a little squirt. Like you, buddy."

Ignoring the gibe, Eddie sipped. Rich berry notes and the

clean burn of vodka. "Garnish?"

"Fresh blackberries."

Whenever River's drink special featured vodka, Eddie jotted down the recipe for his future menu. River was an excellent bartender, creative, fast, and entertaining. Too bad he was planning to open his own place. Collaborating with him would be worth the ribbing.

"Bring on the thirsty mob." River laced his fingers and stretched. His knuckles popped like firecrackers.

"Cut it out, Riv." Kiara tossed a balled-up bar towel at his head. "That noise gives me the willies."

Surprising to see both bartenders working on such a slow night. Until the playoffs started, Thursday meant football at Bangers, along with Diego's Game Day Tots—served in a football-shaped dish, loaded with extra-sharp Tillamook cheddar, pepper bacon, thinly-sliced green onions, with sour cream laces. Only a few dozen customers had braved the January sleet for tonight's tots, topped with pulled pork and drizzled with fiery barbeque sauce. The tempting scents wafting from the kitchen made Eddie's stomach rumble, but breaktime was hours away.

"Rosie's night off?" River asked, polishing a glass. "Bet you miss her."

He did, fiercely, but they were sticking to their just-friends pact, even after last week, when he spent the night drooling into her lap. Sure enough, his mama had spotted Rosie's car outside—hence the muffin delivery—and ever since she'd been bugging him to ask Rosie over for dinner. Soon, he'd have to either spill the truth or hook her into trying Mama's Kulebyaka—a meat and cabbage pie heavy enough to hold down a hot-air balloon on a windy day.

Eddie sliced lemons for drink garnishes. "Rosie's checking out tattoo parlors tonight."

Kiara reached across him to grab the squirt bottle of simple syrup. "You gonna let her tattoo you?"

"No comment." If getting a flu shot made him queasy, no way he could sit still in one of those dentist chairs while she zapped him with a buzzing electric torture device. Then again, he'd get her focused attention for a few hours, something he'd been trying to do with little success ever since their last sexless sleepover.

"Yo, sweetheart." Gus called from his perch at the end of the bar. "Beer me."

"Ugh." Kiara gave a dramatic eye roll. "Eddie, pretty please."

"On it." With Dawn out tonight visiting her sister, Gus was technically their boss. Or so he said. Everyone knew River was in charge when Dawn was away. Eddie pulled a Rainier draft and set it in front of the grizzled grump.

Gus raised his drink and winked. "Stolichnaya, kiddo."

"I think you mean Nasdrovie." Not that Russian people actually said that when toasting, but try and convince Americans of that. If it's in the movies, it must be true, right?

"Eddie, get me a fresh Woodford, would ya?" River called.

"And more Kahlúa," Kiara added.

When Eddie returned from the supply room, he spotted Rosie's sapphire curls. Bracketed by Kiara and Lana, she slumped on the bar, cradling her blotchy face in her hands.

His stupid caveman heart leapt. *Must. Protect. Woman.* He hurried to her side. "What's up, Ro?"

Why did I call her that? Only Lana calls her that. I'm a mega-dork.

Rosie wiped her puffy eyes with the back of her hand.

"Another no."

"Oh, hon." Lana wrapped her arms around Rosie. "If they're too stupid to see your amazing talent, they don't deserve you."

Rosie fixed Eddie with a watery gaze that made him want to pulverize whoever upset her.

He clasped her hand. "Tell me."

"That guy you called Harley Dude? He said my portfolio was a joke." She laid a sparkly blue binder on the bar.

Eddie flipped through the pages. That guy was delusional—Rosie's artwork was sharp, vivid, original. He tapped a skull with a snake slithering through the eye socket. "Look how this one seems to move. And the color on those scales is all shimmery."

Lana leaned in. "This is really good, Ro. Don't let that asshat get you down. There are hundreds of tattoo parlors in Tacoma, right?"

"Yeah, and I've already visited half of 'em. That guy is right—I need to find my angle, something I'm really good at that'll make me stand out."

Eddie squeezed her hand. "What about the Russian eagle?"

She pulled the notebook he gave her from her purse. "That one's not finished yet."

"So finish it. You wanted something different? Bingo."

"Maybe…" Her eyes brightened. "You know what I'd really like to draw? That phoenix on your quilt. And those flowers on your mom's tablecloth. They've got clean lines, but they're different from the roses everyone does. They'd make a great tattoo."

Lana giggled. "Eddie has inspiring bed covers?"

He felt his cheeks heat. "It's a traditional Russian design. My grandma made it."

Kiara skewered cherries and orange slices onto a cocktail pick. "So, the Chinese-American artist does Russian tattoos?"

"Well, I could do Chinese designs—got plenty of those at home—but everyone and his brother does dragons."

Eddie arched an eyebrow. "Do they all look alike, though?"

Kiara smacked the bar with her palm. "My dad collects these masks from West Africa. They'd make great tattoos."

"And if you want flower ideas, my ma does Swedish embroidery," River added. "Their living room is drowning in pillows."

Lana bounced on her toes. "And my tía brought back this gorgeous tapestry from her trip to Machu Picchu."

Rosie sat up straighter and beamed. "You guys are the best!" She smooched Lana's cheek. "I'm feeling inspired. Bartender, gimme a—what's the special tonight, River?"

"It's called a Zipper." He shot Eddie a grin brimming with mischief. "Eddie'll make you one."

"Great!" She hopped off her stool and scooped up her notebooks. "I'm gonna camp out over there. Gotta strike while the iron is hot."

Eddie bit back his disappointment and got to work on the drink. How unfair—he started the ball rolling on the folk-art idea, but Lana got the kiss he craved. He was used to being overlooked, but coming from Rosie it stung.

Before delivering her drink, he swung by the kitchen where Shelby, Diego's assistant, was pulling a fresh batch of tots from the fryer. "Hey, Shel, I need an order of mushroom-Swiss tots."

"Sure thing, champ."

He told River he was taking his break, then carried the tots and cocktail to Rosie's table.

"Here you go." He slid the greasy goodies toward her, careful not to smear her sketchpad.

Glancing up, she surveyed his offering and rumpled her forehead. "For me?"

"It's your favorite, right?"

"Aww, Eddie. You don't have to feed me." She squeezed his hand. "But thanks."

His inner caveman grunted happily. Who needs to hunt mastodon when you've got tater tots?

She popped a tot into her mouth, carefully wiped her fingers on a paper napkin, and picked up her pencil.

He cleared his throat. "So, you want to sketch that phoenix on Babka's quilt?"

"Could I?"

"As it so happens, Mama's been hounding me to ask you over. She wants to feed you."

"And grill me?" Her gaze fell back to her swiftly moving pencil.

"Most likely. But you can inspect her tablecloth—" He nudged her foot under the table. "And help a friend out."

The slide of her leg against his sent a flash of pleasure zinging northward.

"Well, since you're my muse and all, I guess I owe you one." She sipped the cocktail, and her eyebrows shot up. "Excellent muse juice."

"I'm your muse?"

One corner of her mouth quirked up. "Thanks to you I'll have three unique designs for my portfolio—the eagle, the phoenix, and the Russian flowers. That's worth another night of pretending to be your girlfriend."

Eddie winced. Okay, he'd started the whole fake-dating scheme, but couldn't they move past that? He'd bared his soul to her last night, pouring it all out at her feet—his career dreams, the tangle of family duty and love holding him back, everything!

Pushing up from her seat, Rosie leaned across the table and pecked his forehead. "You're going to make some lucky girl a fabulous boyfriend." Her tone was breezy, but he caught the flicker of something darker shadowing her smile.

Watching her sketch, her blue curls shaking softly from her hand's jerky movements, he felt resolve crystalize in his chest, clear and sharp. He was going to be *her* fabulous boyfriend. He'd make her see how right they were for each other, even if it took a mountain of tots, an ocean of cocktails, a flood of ideas, a torrent of praise.

You're going to be mine.

Chapter Eight

Rosie paused at the Volkovs' front door and gave her outfit a final once-over. Her modest top let a few tattooed rose petals peek out, but everything else was covered by her long sleeves, skirt, and heavy tights. More toned-down than her usual look, but a reasonable compromise for dinner with Eddie's parents. Besides, it was too damn cold to show off her ink.

Whether she and Eddie succeeded at pulling off this charade until his cousin's wedding, she did care about remaining his friend. Almost scary, how much she cared. Three weeks since falling into his bed, two weeks since falling asleep on his couch, she still couldn't stop thinking about him—the ease and comfort of talking through the night, the sexy rumble of his voice, the gleam in his chestnut eyes. If only he weren't so strait-laced and serious. Plus, they worked together, and no way would she be responsible for Eddie losing his job, not to mention her own.

But if they didn't work together, she'd never have met

him—so there you go. Just friends.

When she raised her fist to knock, the door flew open to reveal Alina, arms wide, beaming. "Rosie, at last. Welcome, welcome."

Eddie stepped into the hallway holding a platter with an enormous log of pastry. He flashed an apologetic half-smile. "Hi. Just let me set this on the table." The rich scent of meaty, oniony goodness made her stomach rumble.

"There you go." Alina patted Rosie's tummy. "I like a woman with a healthy appetite."

Awkward! Rosie surrendered her coat and bag and followed Alina into the dining room. The TV was off this time, but Eddie's dad sat in the same spot on the floral couch, his nose in a newspaper.

"Vadim," Alina snapped. "Our company is here. Enough sports page." She inclined her head and stage-whispered, "He pretends to check the scores every evening, so he doesn't have to help."

"Bull dookie," the older man said as he pushed himself up. "I do the dishes. Don't make me sound like a sexist dinosaur." He clasped Rosie's hands and fixed her with an intense gaze eerily similar to Eddie's. "Welcome to our home, Miss Rosie." He lowered his voice. "Good luck."

"Sit, sit." Alina beckoned them all toward the table.

"Jeez, Mama, give us a minute." Eddie moved to her side. "Can I say hello to Rosie first?"

"Make it quick."

Eddie hooked her arm and pulled her into the hallway, out of his parents' line of sight. "Hey." He shoved his hands into his pockets and grinned down at his highly polished shoes. "Thanks for coming. I tried to talk Mama into making her salmon pie instead, but she insisted on the beef bomb. Hope you're hungry."

"I am." She kissed his cheek, enjoying the prickle of his short scruff against her lips. "You look nice."

"Yeah, well—" He rubbed the back of his neck. "I came down in jeans, and the boss sent me back up to change."

She fingered the collar of his crisp blue dress shirt. "This color looks great on you."

He gave her a shy smile and wound one of her curls around his finger. "Reminds me of you." His fingertip brushed her earlobe. "I like being reminded."

His touch triggered a smorgasbord of sensations—flutters and tingles and a flush of heat. Who knew ears could be such an erogenous zone?

"Are you done kissing?" Alina called. "Dinner's getting cold."

Eddie rolled his eyes and whispered, "Sorry."

Surrendering to a foolish impulse, Rosie slipped her finger inside his collar, tugged him forward, and pressed her lips to his. Just a quick, chaste peck. "There. Now we're done."

Eddie flushed and blinked, then grinned. "You're really good at this fake dating thing."

"Anything to help a friend." He looked so adorably flabbergasted that she kissed him again.

Alina popped her head through the door frame. "Enough, already. Let's eat."

They sat on opposite sides of the table—just as well, since that removed the temptation to nudge him whenever something struck her as funny, which was often.

Alina preened as she cut into the monstrous pastry. "Kulebyaka," she intoned. "My grandmother's recipe."

"So fancy," Rosie said. "Smells marvelous."

Alina plated a thick slice, using the spatula to point out the layers. "Pastry, beef and rice, pancakes, egg and rice, pancakes, mushrooms and onions, pancakes, pastry." She passed the plate, then watched as Rosie forked up a big bite.

"Mmmm. Delish." It really was, thank God. Sour cream and dill gave the carb-and-meat bomb a silkiness that belied its heft.

Eddie mouthed "thank you" and dug in.

While Vadim silently plowed through his meal, Alina peppered Rosie with questions about her family, her artwork, and whether Eddie was as quiet at Bangers as he was at home. "A shy little mouse, our Eduard." She leaned in and stage-whispered, "Between you and me, I was surprised to see him so taken with a colorful girl like you."

"Mama," Eddie groaned.

She batted away her son's objections. "What? That's not an insult. I like her."

Poor Eddie squirmed in his seat. She knew that feeling well from dinners with her extended family.

"Eddie's given me some great ideas for my art portfolio. Speaking of which—" She pulled her phone from her skirt pocket. "I'd love to take some photos of this tablecloth. The design would make a—it's very interesting." Better not to rub the tattoo business in their faces.

Alina dropped her fork onto her plate with a clatter. "No problem." She clapped her hands. "Fellas, clear the table, please. I'm going to give Miss Rosie a tour of the house."

Eddie's brow rumpled. "Mama, please don't—"

"My house, my rules." She patted her son's cheek. "You can show her your place later."

Vadim coughed into his fist. "She's already seen it."

Rosie bet her cheeks flamed just as bright as Eddie's.

Alina linked her arm through Rosie's and towed her toward the hallway. "First, my sewing room."

The little room's shelves were stuffed with neatly folded cloth in every color, an expensive-looking Pfaff sewing machine, and a dress form displaying a chiffon gown in deep aubergine. Alina fingered the half-finished jacket. "For my niece's wedding. The bride, she likes purple." She nudged Rosie with her hip. "As soon as this is finished, I'll start on a purple baby quilt." She pantomimed a pregnant bulge. "I hope you and Eddie are more careful."

Despite her distractibility, Rosie was scrupulously careful with birth control. Still, Alina's comment left her spluttering. "I, uh, we—"

"Of course you are." The older woman grabbed her arm. "Now, we go upstairs."

A loud clatter rang out from the kitchen.

"Eddie, get the dessert from the fridge, please. Come, Rosie."

The stairway wall was a patchwork of family photos: a much younger Alina and Vadim on a dance floor, gazing raptly into each other's eyes, stiff wedding photos, and shots of little Eddie, a solemn, skinny tot with huge brown eyes and unruly curls. Alina tapped a frame. "Always so serious, our Eddie. I expect great things from him." She shot Rosie a sharp glance that melted into a smile when they reached the top. "And this is Eddie's room."

He wasn't kidding—the room really was a shrine stuffed with trophies, framed certificates, photos, and ribbons. A twin bed with a faded Spider-Man comforter held well-loved cuddly toys, including a threadbare Incredible Hulk.

Footsteps pounded up the stairs. "Mama, wait."

Puffing, Eddie burst into the room. "Do we really have to do this tonight?"

Alina lifted her chin. "Son, if you care about this girl enough to bring her to our family table, you care enough to show her your trophies."

He slipped an arm around Rosie, buried his face in the crook of her neck, and murmured, "I'm sorry."

"Don't be," she whispered back and rubbed her cheek against his soft, soft hair. "Your mom's adorable."

"Which year was this, Eddie?" Alina pointed to a trophy depicting a snarling wrestler.

Eddie sighed. "Junior year."

"State champion in his weight class." Alina whacked his arm. "You didn't tell her? His coach called him Volkov the Vicious. Look here." She pulled a framed newspaper clipping from the kid-sized desk and pressed it into Rosie's hands.

"Wow. Very impressive." A teen Eddie growled at the camera, neck corded and biceps bulging. Skinny, yes, but muscly and fierce, and sexy as hell in a singlet that left nothing to the imagination. Even back then, he packed an impressive package. She read aloud, "Stadium High student brings home state championship again..." *A hundred thirty-two pounds?* Her stomach lurched. *God help me.*

Eddie pried the frame from her fingers and set it face-down on the desk. "Nothing like a photo of me looking like a plucked chicken to impress the ladies."

"Baloney." Alina waved off his objection with a flick of her fingers. "You were handsome then, and you're handsomer now. Right, Rosie?"

"Absolutely." She took his hand and wished she could drain away the embarrassment twisting his features.

"Okay, enough bragging. Let's have dessert. I made your favorite, Eddie." Alina left them alone to scrape their respective self-esteem off the floor.

Eddie raked his fingers into his hair and paced. She bit her lip, imagining him walking off a defeat in the wrestling ring, wearing that tight little leotard that cupped his butt like a second skin.

Finally, he flopped onto the bed. "Am I dead yet?"

She sat beside him. "It's not so bad. Your mom's proud of you." She kissed his forehead. "And you looked really hot in that singlet. Do you still have it?"

He stared at her open-mouthed, then burst into deep, belly-shaking laughter. She slid her arm around his shoulders, and he buried his face in her chest, shuddering with mirth. Heat flooded her core. Had he ever fucked a girl on this narrow bed? Would the padded headboard slam against the wall? Would the box spring squeak?

Just a friend, just a friend, just a friend.

Finally, he raised his damp, red face, wiped his eyes, and grinned. "You are truly the best. Thank you." He hauled her to her feet. "Let's go have some chocolate salami."

"Chocolate what?"

"Sounds gross, right? It's actually like fudge, with broken vanilla wafers and walnuts. When you slice it, it looks like salami." He squeezed her hands. "If you can choke down a slice or two, we can get out of here."

"Hey, I got no problem with your mom's cooking. Or your mom. She's a sweetheart." She pecked his cheek and tried to turn toward the door, but he held her hands and her gaze for a long, silent moment. What was cooking behind those long-lashed, dark eyes?

Finally, he huffed and dropped her hands. "You're right. She's a good mom. Let's go."

Chapter Nine

It took every last bit of Eddie's self-control to finish the fudgy treat his mom made to please him and his "new girlfriend" before fleeing to the safety of his own apartment. Guilt twisted his stomach as he accepted the plate of leftovers she pressed on him "In case you two get hungry later." God, she was probably planning their wedding by now.

Time to stomp the brakes.

In the hallway, he helped Rosie into her coat. "You want to come up and take a picture of the quilt?"

"Yes please."

Behind them, his mom tittered.

"Good night, Mr. and Mrs. Volkov," Rosie said with a wave. "Thanks for a wonderful meal."

He pulled her through the door and toward the stairs.

"What's the rush, Eddie? It's not like we have to work tonight."

Usually, he took Tuesday nights off. Dawn had made a sour

face when he asked to switch his night off to Wednesday, same as Rosie, but offered no comment beyond, "Remember, no relationship drama at work."

Eddie opened his apartment door and waved her through. "We need to talk."

"Ruh-roh. Sounds grim." She shrugged halfway out of her coat. "Or should I keep it on?"

"What? No." Did she think he was giving her the boot? Then again, why wouldn't she think that? He was using her to appease his family. By lying to them. *I'm a shitty son and a shitty excuse for a friend.*

"Please, let's sit. You want some tea?"

She shook her head, her gaze never wavering from his.

He took her hand. No words came.

She inclined her head. "Out with it, pretend boyfriend. What's eating you?"

"This." He pointed from his chest to hers. "I should never have asked you to pretend you like me."

Her eyebrows drew together. "I'm not pretending, Eddie. I do like you. A lot." She wove her fingers through his.

Damn, she was not making this easy. Well, this was his pile of shit to shovel. Time to dig in.

"Thanks, Rosie. You were fantastic tonight. An Oscar-worthy performance. But I've been using you, and I can't anymore."

"Oh." She released him and folded her hands in her lap. "Guess I misunderstood." She huffed a wry chuckle. "My specialty, jumping to conclusions."

He knuckled his eyes. If he could just find the right words to express how much he wished this phony relationship could be real, could be more. But talking about feelings was never his strength. No way to turn this emotional clusterfuck into a neat bullet-point list.

Rosie stood and headed for the door. He bolted after her, grabbed her elbow, and spun her around. "Please, Rosie. I'm absolute crap at this, but let me try."

Her shaky sigh stabbed him right in his messy, gooey middle. "Okay. Explain."

He shoved a hand into his hair and paced. "What I'm trying to say is I was wrong to ask you to pretend. I brought you up here on New Year's Eve, and I have no right to try and control the outcome. We got caught. That's on me. If all you wanted was a one-night stand, I have to accept that."

"Eddie, I never—"

"I know, you didn't mean to hurt me. None of this is your fault, and I was a wimpy weasel to try and lie my way out of it."

Tears sheened her eyes. "My feelings for you aren't a lie, Eddie."

He spun away again, wearing a groove in the floor with his nervous pacing. "I like you too—a lot. You're the most interesting, exciting person I know. But we can't keep up this stupid charade." He flung a hand toward the house below. "Mama's getting attached to you. I can't let her get even more attached between now and the wedding, then tell her we broke up. That's just cruel."

He couldn't let himself get more attached, either. If they were going to be friends, he needed the insulation of the bar. Surrounded by all those people, he could resist temptation. Here, he just wasn't strong enough.

He thumped his fist on the breakfast counter. "It's not your job to protect me from their old-fashioned notions."

"You'll go to the wedding alone?"

He shrugged. "So what if the relatives cluck their tongues? Situation normal. I can handle it."

"What about work? Everyone thinks—"

"Let them think what they think. Their assumptions don't control us." He closed the distance between them and took her hands. "Tonight made me realize what a fuckin' idiot I've been. I know you don't see me as boyfriend material, and I hope we can—"

"Shut up, Eddie." She closed her eyes and squeezed his hands vice-tight.

Heart hammering, he braced himself for the dressing down he so richly deserved.

"You're not the only one who figured something out tonight." She released him and gestured toward his bedroom. "What happened here was amazing, and I panicked. Because guys like you have never treated me as more than a temporary plaything. I'm not the girl they bring home to their nice family and show their high school trophies to." She pinched the bridge of her nose. "So when I woke up in your bed, I figured the smart thing to do was to shut it down before I got hurt." Her voice wobbled. "And then, you brought me home to your parents. And your mom made us fudge, and…" Her eyes screwed shut, and her words dissolved into a sob.

"Hey, hey now." He wrapped his arms around her quaking shoulders.

She fisted the front of his shirt and snuffled into the crook of his neck. "I just wanted it to be real, you know? To believe we could actually be more than horny work friends who accidentally fell into bed together. I wanted the sweet guy who humored his mom, and the Spider-man quilt, and the trophies, and the weird fudge, and—"

The tight knot in his chest burst open, and he stopped her torrent of words with a ravenous kiss. Her lips parted on a sharp inhale, and then she hiccupped, a sound so cute he had to kiss her again. And again.

"Rosie," he whispered against her lips, "I want that too. So much. Ever since that night, I can't stop thinking about how much I want you. Not just in bed. I mean all of it."

Her hands slid to his hips and tugged him tight against her. His cock hardened to the point of pain, grinding between his zipper and her soft, warm flesh.

"Thank God." She kneaded his ass through his jeans. "Do you know how hard it's been to keep my distance at work, when all I want is to—uhng." She rolled her hips, and the speech center of his brain short-circuited.

He duck-walked backward toward the bed, kissing her non-stop. Along the way, they bonked into the breakfast bar, crashed into the bookshelf, and knocked over a lamp. No matter, the gravity of the bed pulled them in, strong and true. The backs of his knees collided with the mattress, and he collapsed with her atop him.

She straddled him and clasped his jaw with both hands, her dark eyes glittering. "No getting carried away this time. Is this what you really want?" Her lush breasts pressed to his chest, and his hips ground up on autopilot, seeking her moist heat. Her breath was hot on his face. "I need to hear the words, Eddie."

"Yes," he hissed. "I want this. I want you."

"And afterward?"

"We'll figure it out together. Please, Rosie."

She answered with a kiss that singed his soul.

Planting his heels, he rolled her onto her back and slid his hands beneath her top. She helped him peel it over her head, then lay back while he stroked her silky skin from waist to throat. A lacy blue bra imprisoned her breasts. He tunneled his fingers beneath her, searching for the clasp.

"It fastens in the front."

He grappled in vain, afraid of ripping the delicate fabric. With a sexy chuckle, she flicked it open, and her glorious breasts spilled out, creamy golden skin, dark rosy nipples, heavy and warm and delicious. With a hungry moan, he trailed kisses over the vine tattoo that wound behind her ear and along her collarbone before twining among the red and pink roses across her chest. The closer he came to her pebbled nipples, the more she squirmed on the mattress.

He cupped the heaven-soft mounds and circled their tight peaks with his thumbs. "Impatient, aren't you?"

"Hell yeah." She raked her fingers into his hair and pressed his face to her chest. "I've been wanting this since New Year's."

"Me too," he growled, and sucked one firm bud into his mouth.

"Sweet Jesus." She threw her head back and bit her lip.

Watching her surrender to desire fired his blood to the boiling point. He rolled and sucked and pinched her nipples until she gasped, then pushed up and raked his gaze over every gorgeous, golden inch of her. "You're a goddess, you know that?"

Fire flashed in her eyes as she reached for his shirt. "Take this off. All of it. I want to feel your skin against mine."

He shucked his clothes, then tugged her skirt and tights off, leaving only her blue satin panties. He knew he wouldn't last long after weeks of imagining this moment, and he wanted to give her as much pleasure as possible before plunging inside her.

With a hungry, mewling sound she reached for him, but he slipped from her grasp and kissed his way down the soft curve of her belly, his fingertips teasing her thighs apart. He swirled the tip of his tongue over the lotus blossom framing her navel, then grasped the elastic of her panties in his teeth. Though they'd had no wine with dinner, he felt drunk with desire, dizzy and reckless as he tasted the succulent skin he'd dreamed of every damn night since she left his bed.

He skimmed her panties over her hips. She kicked them away and giggled when they landed atop the bedpost. "Hard to keep your place tidy when I'm here."

"Fuck tidy," he growled. "Let's get messy." He parted her soft pussy lips with his thumbs and dove in.

She sighed his name as he licked and nibbled her tender inner flesh, so pink and plush beneath his tongue. Her tangy wetness eased his way as he slid one finger, then another inside her tight channel, all the while circling her firm clit.

Her hips lifted off the bed, her moans growing breathy and ragged as he sped his motions, gliding in and out, flicking his tongue over the hot little bud that made her muscles tense and jerk. The scrape of her nails on his scalp sent a flash of joy straight to his cock, but he kept on pleasuring her until her whole body tensed, and her soft thighs clamped around his ears, muffling her cries.

When she finally relaxed her hold, he wiped his sopping beard on the sheet and scaled her boneless body, soft and lax as a gorgeous Persian cat. The pulse at her throat thrummed beneath his lips.

"Eddie," she whispered breathlessly as she wrapped her arms

and legs around him. "Give it to me. Please." She rolled her hips, and the tip of his cock slid inside.

He allowed himself that split-second of bliss, one shallow thrust, another, before jerking back. "Condom."

"Wait." Her hands wove into his hair, holding him in place. "After the last time, I got tested, just in case." Her heavy-lidded gaze promised untold pleasure. "Did you?"

"I, uh, yeah. I mean, we used protection, but—" How could he phrase this without spoiling the mood?

She feathered kisses over his face and undulated beneath him. "I'm healthy, Eddie, and I want to feel you bare inside me. Can we do that?"

The sensitive head of his cock slid between her slick folds, achingly close to the place he longed to be. "I'm healthy too, but what about—"

"Pill." She lifted her hips.

Inch by inch, he eased inside her liquid fire. Wide awake and stone sober this time, he relished her softness surrounding him, gripping his cock until he was seated to the root.

"So good." She raked her nails down his back, a delicious counterpoint to the pulsing grip of her pussy. "Just like I remembered."

Kissing her deeply, he dropped to his elbows, his chest pressed tight to hers. Magic and mayhem inside her mouth—silk and velvet stroking his tongue as her inner muscles gripped his cock. He knew he would come too damn quickly, but he had to move. Now.

Arching his back, he pulled out until the tip of his cock nearly slid free, then slowly drove in again. Sparks danced up his spine, filling his body with pleasure and his mind with stars. She nipped his lower lip. "Faster, Eddie."

Chapter Nine

His body screamed at him to drop the reins and race toward climax, but he held onto control—barely. "Can you come for me again, beauty? Tell me how to get you there."

With a wicked smile, she grasped his hand. "Here." She drew the pad of his thumb in a circle around her swollen bud. "Fuck me hard, Eddie. Please."

What could he do but obey? Rosie's wild abandon aroused the hungry animal in him. Grunting, he pummeled her with hard, deep thrusts while his thumb ground against her tender flesh. His balls drew up tight, release just seconds away.

Propping himself on his free hand, he gazed down into her face. Head thrown back, glowing hair spread across the rumpled sheets, flushed and gasping, she'd never looked more beautiful. He withdrew and rubbed his shaft between her swollen folds. "Let go, Rosie. Come with me."

Her eyes flew open, and she watched his straining purple cock grind over her clit, back and forth. "God, Eddie, now—"

He plunged into her. Her legs clamped tight around his waist as his final, frantic thrusts rattled the bed frame. She arched and dug her nails into his hips and screamed his name, her channel pulsing and fluttering around his cock. Lightning flashed through his body and blanked his mind. Nothing existed but her flesh, her breath, her jagged cries.

* * *

Long moments later, Rosie came back to herself to find Eddie lying half-atop her. The soft scratch of his beard on her neck tickled deliciously as he murmured her name over and over—until his breaths grew deep and even.

Her heart squeezed. *He fell asleep in my arms!* This time, there'd be no bolting out the door. She was spending the night in this rumpled, sticky bed, curled up with the man who shook the stars from the sky.

As she toyed with his soft curls, she giggled at the memory of his high school wrestling photo. He made the same face in the throes of passion—clenched jaw, glistening brow, fierce concentration. Never had a guy put so much effort into making her come. And they were just getting started. She could only imagine the heights they'd reach once they really got to know each other's bodies and developed their own mutual rhythm.

Eddie jerked and lifted onto his elbows. "What's funny? Did I snore?" God, he was adorable, his chocolate curls mussed, his lips kiss-swollen, his eyes heavy-lidded.

"No, baby. You're just so pretty. And powerful." She patted his bare ass. "I don't think I've ever come so hard in my life."

His aw-shucks grin twanged her heartstrings. "I'm glad. Me too." Withdrawing his softening cock, he gave her hip a playful smack, then trotted to the bathroom and returned with a fluffy towel. "Here, let me just—"

Kneeling over her, he dabbed her damp chest and belly. Even after two exhausting orgasms, she felt a stirring as he wiped the mess from between her thighs.

"You are a such a love." She pulled him down for another kiss, then took her own turn in the bathroom.

When she returned, he lay stretched out beneath the phoenix quilt, fingers interlaced behind his head. His smile stretched a mile wide, but there was wariness behind those sparkling eyes. "Will you stay the night?"

She dug her bare toes into the bedside rug, suddenly self-conscious. "I'd like to, if that's okay."

"It's more than okay, babe." He flipped back the covers and patted the mattress. "Is it all right if I call you babe? I hear some girls hate that."

The moniker was a little cheesy, but also endearing, coming from Eddie. "I don't mind—if you mean it."

"Oh, I mean it." He scooted aside to make room for her. "You're definitely a babe. Also a goddess, an angel, a full-blown rose, a sexy vixen, a hot, horny she-devil..."

Snuggling beside him, she dissolved into giggles. He'd found her sweet spot, all right. Starved for praise, she basked in his flattery and, for now, allowed herself to believe he meant every word.

"Handsome, good in bed, and a killer vocabulary. What else you got?"

"Let's see." He pushed back her hair and nibbled her ear. "You smell delicious, your voice is like a sexy alto sax, your eyes are full of mischief, your pussy is a cave of wonders, your skin is an art museum..." He sighed and drew her head onto his chest.

She felt his heart thudding beneath her cheek and thought she might die from loving him so much.

What? She fisted the sheet.

"Too much?" Eddie toyed with her hair, oblivious to the panic clogging her throat. "Okay, I'll back off. You're pretty cool, Rosie."

She unclenched and rubbed a slow circle over his chest. "You're pretty cool too, Eddie." *And you smell good, and you feel good, and you're so beautiful, and you scare the shit out of me.* But running off now would ruin their chance of seeing where this surprise connection could take them. Too late to safeguard her heart. She was already in so deep that leaving would hurt, no matter who ended it, or when. So she closed her eyes, stroked his warm skin, and let sleep claim her.

Chapter Ten

Eddie pulled to the curb in front of Rosie's house, a neat little one-story of dark clinker brick with juniper hedges and a soggy winter lawn. When he opened his car door, a cloud of pirozhki-scented steam billowed in the icy air.

Rosie had answered his text about her latest interview with a curt —*No luck. Story of my life*— so he zipped across town to the Russian deli on Center Street in search of edible comfort. When someone he loved was hurting, his first instinct was to drown their sorrow in calories. Must've learned that from his mother.

Last night's surprise had him floating ten inches above the ground all day, but it would be weird to declare his eternal devotion this early in the game, especially when Rosie was so skeptical about their chances. Better to corral his runaway feelings and stick to the plan he'd carefully sketched out in his notebook:

1. *Get to know her interests and history and quirks.*

2. *Set up some normal dates.* Wrangling time away from the dry-cleaning shop would be tough, but leapfrogging over the usual courtship stuff had rattled Rosie. Time to back up and prove his sincere interest in her as a person, not just a fuck buddy.

3. *Sexytimes.* Because damn! Their passionate connection was definitely chipping away at her "just friends" armor. As Dedka always said, you get the job done with the tools at hand.

Before pressing the doorbell, Eddie sucked in a steadying breath. The first impression he'd made on Rosie's mom was hardly ideal—panicked and bleeding all over the floor. He had to do better this time.

Ms. Callas opened the door, barefoot but otherwise still in her teacher clothes. Crisp, professional, no-nonsense. If it weren't for her dark curly hair, curvy figure, and olive complexion, he'd have a hard time believing this woman was Rosie's mother.

"Hello, Eddie. Nice to see you." She gave him a quick up-and-down glance with eyes just as sharp as her daughter's. Behind her, a travel show flickered on the TV and stacks of papers covered the coffee table. Tweed sofa and armchairs, family photos on the walls, brick fireplace crackling—all very middle-class bland. No clue that someone as extraordinary as Rosie shared this house.

"Hello, Ms. Callas. Rosie's expecting me."

"Diana, please." She gripped his hand and pursed her lips in cool appraisal.

Bet she intimidates the hell out of her students.

He held up the greasy paper sack. "I brought her pirozhki. There's extra in case you want one."

Finally, she cracked a smile. "No thanks, hon." She patted

her curvy hip. "I'm still working on my Christmas pounds. Better go knock on her door. Once she sinks into a drawing, she loses track of time." She inclined her head toward the hallway. "Third door on the left. You can't miss it."

Indeed he couldn't. While the other doors were unadorned dark wood, Rosie's was painted magenta with a swooping cursive R trailing flourishes and stars. Did she have a tattoo like that? He still hadn't conducted a complete inventory. He made a mental note to remedy that.

Woo-woo electronic music drifted through the door, along with a high-pitched buzz. He knocked and waited. No answer. At his second knock the buzzing stopped, and Rosie opened the door. Hair gathered in a messy topknot, leggings and baggy sweater skimming her curves, she looked—drained, he decided, her face pale, lips bare of their usual scarlet, eyes a little puffy. Fixing this was going to take more than greasy snacks.

She gave him a weak smile, wrapped her arms around his neck, and whispered, "Hi" against his lips.

"I brought pirozhki. Sure-fire cure for a shitty day."

"You're the best, Eddie." She released him. "I'll go get some plates."

While she went to the kitchen, he checked out her room. Drawings covered a wall of cork tiles. An antique-looking rug in deep reds and blues held a dragonish creature in the center. On her desk, ceramic cups and beer mugs overflowed with colored pencils and markers. More art supplies lay scattered on a small table beneath the window. Twinkle lights and strings of mirrored stars and moons dangled from the ceiling. Her bed was barely visible beneath a mountain of throw pillows in satin and velvet. Giant potted palm in the corner. Happy, colorful chaos—totally Rosie.

She returned with a tray and set it on the table. "Lemme just clear this off."

"Jesus!" Eddie nearly shat himself when she turned toward him holding a severed hand. He jolted backward, landing on her bed with a bounce.

At last, she cracked a smile. "Don't freak out. It's just silicone, for tattoo practice." She tossed him the rubbery appendage, which bounced off his lap and onto the floor. Gingerly, he picked it up by the pinky. A half-finished floral design, delicate and somehow familiar, was etched across its back, with vines and leaves trailing up the fingers.

"Recognize the flowers from your mom's tablecloth?" She cleared away tiny pots of ink, paper towels, squirt bottles, and a black device that looked like a nose hair trimmer.

"Is that a tattoo gun?"

"We prefer tattoo machine. And yeah, just a cheap model to practice. Mostly on sheets of synthetic skin, but I got a hand and foot last week. I'm saving up for a set of tits."

He didn't know whether to laugh or gag. Needles were creepy enough, but rubber body parts? Still, his mission was to show his support, not get all squicked out by her artwork.

Rosie set the little table and opened a second folding chair while he unwrapped the pirozhki. "We got beef and onion, potato and cheese, cabbage and mushroom."

"Can I try a little of each?"

"Good choice." He divvied them up, and they dug into the greasy pastries. Rosie chewed slowly, then leaned back in her chair and groaned—a sexy sound that made him want to toss her onto the bed and do dirty, dirty things to her.

Focus. "So, lousy interview, huh?"

"I mean, the woman was nice, but she'd already picked an apprentice by the time I got there. Said she'd pass my card to her tattoo artist friends." Her shoulders slumped as she poked at her food. "She told me not to get discouraged, but it's so fuckin' frustrating."

"Hey." He scooted his chair closer. "It's gonna happen for you. I can feel it in my bones." He squeezed her knee, then massaged his way up her thigh. "What can I do to make you feel better?"

She didn't take the bait, but she did snuggle his shoulder. Her soft curls tickled his neck. "You're the best—bringing me food and listening to me whine."

"It's natural to feel frustrated when you have to knock on a million doors before one finally opens."

"Exactly. And on top of that, my period started during the interview. So, rejection plus killer cramps. It's been a shitty day on all fronts."

"Except this morning?" He rubbed her lower back in slow circles.

"That seems like a million years ago." She chuckled, a low, gritty sound. "But yeah, last night was amazing."

"Any chance we could try again tonight?"

Her groan was answer enough.

"Okay, I'll wait as long as you need. Just know that I don't care about, you know, messy sex."

"Really?" She sniffled. "The guy who turns green when he sees a rubber hand isn't squeamish?"

"As long as no needles are involved, it's fine." He lifted her hand and feathered a kiss over her knuckles. "No pressure, though. I want you to want it too."

A crooked smile played over her lips. "So noted." She

smooched his cheek before forking up another mouthful. "Wow. Who knew cabbage could be this delicious?"

Watching her eat with such honest enjoyment only made his stupid dick stand up and beg for attention.

"Please don't take it as a rejection." She patted her lower belly. "It's just that right now everything down here hurts, and I don't want to poke the beast."

"Right. No beast poking." He wiped his hands and dug out his notebook. "Let's talk dates."

She blinked rapidly. "Dates for what?"

"For us to, you know, hang out. Get to know each other away from the bar."

"And out of your bed?" Her grin brimmed with mischief. There—at least he had her smiling again.

"Well, I'm hoping we'll land there as soon as you're willing. But in the meantime, are you free on Saturday afternoon?"

"Don't you work at your parents' shop then?"

"Normally, yes. But you made such a good impression they're giving me the afternoon off." It had taken some pleading on his part, but she didn't need to know that. "Tell me where you like to go, what you like to do."

"Mr. List Maker." She chuckled. "Tell you what—why don't you take me somewhere you like to go. That way I can get to know you better."

He chewed the inside of his cheek. This was not going according to plan. Besides, other than occasional trips to Seattle to visit his family, he didn't really go much of anywhere this time of year—just work, home, and Jojo's garage. He'd have to pick Lana's brain tonight at work. He snapped the notebook shut. "No clues, huh? You're making this hard on me, Chu."

116

She ran her stockinged foot up his calf. "Not my intention, Volkov. If my mom weren't home, I'd do my best to relieve your"—she snickered—"hardness."

His gaze slid to the door. Diana's TV show was still audible, though probably not loud enough—unless they were very, very quiet.

Rosie must've picked up on his thoughts because she wiped the grease from her lips before sashaying to the dresser and cranking up the volume on her little speaker. Cascades of tinkling notes, soft drumbeats, and wordless alto warbling filled the room. She lifted a fat satin pillow from her bed and dropped it at his feet.

"C'mere," she purred. "I want dessert."

"But I thought—" Her mixed signals were making him dizzy.

She feathered the back of her forefinger over his jawline. "You're so adorable when you're turned on. I want to touch you, Eddie. Can I do that?"

"You don't have to."

Her smile bloomed with wicked promises. "I know. But I want to."

He murmured a prayer of thanks as she knelt between his knees, hands firmly kneading his thighs. His poor cock throbbed, pressed so hard against his zipper it must've left permanent teeth marks by now.

Rosie's chuckle vibrated all the way to his bones. "You're so responsive." Holding his gaze, she unfastened his belt and slowly slid his zipper down. "I love the way you hold your breath when I touch you."

Because I'm fighting not to come in my pants like a teenager. He bit his lip while she tugged his jeans and boxers down.

"So pretty," she murmured as she stroked him firmly from

117

root to crown, the pleasure so sharp he nearly levitated off his seat.

"Can I touch you?" he whimpered.

"Here." Eyes sparkling, she took his hand and slid it beneath her sweater. Sweet baby Jesus, she wasn't wearing a bra. "Gentle. They're sore."

Keeping his touch light, he caressed her heavy breasts, circling her nipples with his thumbs.

"That's the way. So nice," she purred before bending forward and sucking him into the molten heat of her mouth.

He spread his legs wider, his head lolling back as she worked him with sure, firm strokes. Her velvet tongue did magical things to his crown. Pressure built, gathering low and radiating down his legs and up his spine. She released him and—with a low, smoky laugh—licked down his shaft to tongue his balls.

"Rosie—I—oh God—please—"

Her hand sped, pumping him mercilessly while sharp teeth nibbled the sensitive inside of his thighs. Helpless, mindless, he bucked into her grip until the world around him exploded—pure light, pure sensation, pure bliss.

When he came back to himself, she was laughing softly, her cheek against his bare thigh. He hooked his arms under hers and pulled her up for a fierce kiss. "Rosie, thank you. That was—I don't even have words."

"You don't need words." She tilted her head to nibble his ear. "You showed me how much you enjoyed it." Pulling back, she glanced down at his shirt, now smeared with streaks of cum.

Mortified, he groaned. "Sorry about the mess."

She pushed to her feet. "Doesn't bother me. It's proof you had a very good time. Here." She pulled a T-shirt from her dresser. "Mom won't notice you've changed."

He refastened his jeans and replaced his soiled shirt with Rosie's clean one, dark gray and emblazoned with the Tacoma octopus. "I'll wash this and get it back to you tomorrow."

"No rush." She hooked her fingertips into his belt and pulled him in for a kiss. "I know where to find you."

"You sure I can't?—" He squeezed her lush hips.

"Positive. I'll be fine in a day or two." She smacked his ass. "Now get outta here, Volkov. I need a shower before work."

She walked him to the front door. Diana waved from the sofa. "Oh, you've got one of those octopus shirts too." Her brow rumpled. "Weren't you wearing a flannel shirt?"

Rosie saved his ass. "We spilled grease on it." She pecked his cheek and shoved him out the door. "See you at work, Eddie."

He grinned all the way home.

Chapter Eleven

Saturday afternoon, Rosie vibrated with excitement as Eddie bundled her into his little Toyota. He'd refused to tell her where they were going, only cautioning her to dress warm and bring an appetite. Drumming on the steering wheel, he slid her a playful grin as they rolled down Sixth Avenue past weed dispensaries, bars, and record shops.

"C'mon, Eddie, give me a hint, at least."

The corners of his eyes crinkled. "We'll be outside, then inside, then outside, then inside—"

She huffed. "You're such a tease."

"Says the woman who wiggles her ass in my direction at work. You, madam, are queen of the tease."

As he turned onto Division, tiny snow pellets began to fall, bouncing off the windshield like bits of Styrofoam. "Look!" Rosie pointed to the graceful stone ladies at the entrance to Wright Park. "Someone knitted hats for the statues."

"First stop." He pulled into a free space near the park, then took her hand. "In case I forget to mention it later, thanks for coming, Rosie." He looked so earnest, she wanted to climb onto his lap and kiss him silly—impossible to do in his cramped car.

"Are you kidding? I wouldn't miss the chance to spend some daylight hours with you. Do you realize we share most of our time together in darkness? We're like a couple of bats." She flapped her fingers beside her face.

"That won't change anytime soon, sorry."

"Don't apologize." She wove her fingers through his. "It's just the phase of life we're in. You're working hard to achieve your dream. So am I." Parroting her mom's reassuring words should help more than it did.

"You're right." Sliding his hand to her nape, he pulled her in for a toe-curling kiss. "Someday soon, we'll both be in a better place. Fair warning, when that day comes, I plan to claim lots of your daylight hours."

Did he mean once he opened his own bar? That would take years. She bit her lip as he popped out of the car and jogged around to open her door. "Would my lady care to stroll through the park?"

"I love this park." She smooched his cheek and wound her arm through his. Despite the wind's wintery bite, they shared the path with several families whose kids chased pigeons and squirrels on the rolling hills. Towering overhead, the skeletal trees stood out in stark beauty against the pale gray sky. Rosie pointed. "I saw a tattoo like this once—just bare winter branches. Wonder why the guy chose that image."

"Do tattoos always mean something?"

"Usually. Mine do."

He slid his arm around her hip. "You know, I still haven't

seen all your tattoos. Once your clothes come off, we usually get right to business, then conk out."

She pulled him in tight, holding him as close as their puffy coats allowed. "We'll have to remedy that."

"As soon as you're feeling better."

Period sex had always been something she avoided. Between cramps and worries about her partner's potential disgust, she found it hard to relax and enjoy the moment. But Eddie had been straight with her so far—maybe he really didn't mind. Worth a try.

"I'm actually feeling okay. Still a little messy, but not too bad." She wiggled her hips, pressing against him. "Your parents' shop is closed on Sundays, right? Maybe after work tonight…" She kissed him, just a light, teasing touch. "Or this afternoon?"

She could see the wheels turning as his gaze darted from her face back toward his car. His lips compressed and his nostrils flared. Finally, he gave a little grunt. "Let's make it tonight. I planned this date, and I want to stick to the plan."

She rolled her eyes. "That's my Eddie, man with a plan. Did you write it in your notebook?"

"As a matter of fact, yes." He grasped her hand and started toward the pond.

"Can I see?"

"Nope." His grin held a devilish gleam. "Let's feed the ducks." He pulled a plastic bag of bread scraps from his jacket pocket and dangled it like a cat toy before a kitten.

She clapped her gloved hands. "How did you know?"

"Everyone likes feeding the ducks."

As soon as he opened the bag, the quacking flotilla paddled furiously to her and Eddie's feet. Rosie laughed aloud as the ducks battled for the best bits. "Cut it out, you greedy bastard," she shouted when a pushy drake snapped at a smaller female.

"I'll distract him." Eddie scooped up a rock and tossed it past the glutton. Sure enough, the drake went for it, giving Rosie the chance to feed the other ducks.

"My hero." She smooched his cheek. He rewarded her with an adorable grin.

When the bag was empty, she wrapped her arms around Eddie from behind and rested her chin on his shoulder. "When we were little, Mom would bring Amara and me here the day after Christmas to feed the ducks. We always saved a few dinner rolls for the duckies." She giggled at the memory. "Saltines too. Crackers for the quackers. Probably terrible for them."

He pecked her cheek. "Ducks are tough. Let's go warm up."

They climbed the hill to the Victorian conservatory. Inside, Rosie peeled off her hat and gloves and filled her lungs with warm, humid air. "Smells like a jungle in here."

"Right? Extra oxygen." He patted her butt. "Let's explore."

Ooo-ing and ahh-ing, they strolled through the verdant jewel box. Lacy palms stretched overhead, reaching for the glass dome. Big ceramic pots held ferns and orchids, while Spanish moss and bromeliads hung from walls and tree trunks.

Rosie bent to examine a particularly striking bloom and felt Eddie's hand snake under her open coat and brush the side of her breast. She chuckled. "Sure you don't want to scrap the date and head back to your place?"

"Nope." He nuzzled her neck. "I'm enjoying the anticipation."

So was she. Each teasing caress fired her impatience to peel off his winter clothes and stroke the satin skin beneath. But he'd planned out this day, and she was equally eager to see what surprise came next.

"You hungry, Ro?"

She liked Lana's nickname on his lips. Grinning, she smooched him again. "Famished."

Their next stop was a new Asian fusion restaurant she'd been wanting to try. "How did you know?"

Another shrug. "It just seemed interesting and colorful—like you."

No way. He'd been asking around. Who had she mentioned this place to—Charlie? Lana? This thoughtfulness tickled her. Not many guys from her past had put so much effort into planning a date. In fact, no one had.

The hostess seated them at a communal table with a gas fire in the center and presented them with an extensive list of daily specials. While waiting for their order, they sipped hot jasmine tea.

She leaned onto her elbows and laced her fingers under her chin. "So, tell me more about your bar. Will it be like this place, or more like Bangers?"

"Definitely like Bangers, but a little more polished. Less sports stuff."

"Will you have darts? Is that a Russian thing?"

"Absolutely. Shuffleboard table too. I'm aiming for Russian flair, something different to stand out from the other bars. But I still want that homey feel like we have at Bangers." He pulled his little notebook from his jacket pocket.

Rosie tapped the open pages with her chopstick. "Taking notes?"

"Yeah, I really like this fire table. I don't get out to bars as often as I'd like." He flashed a wry grin. "Pretty busy. When I do, I try to notice what makes each place special."

"To use in your future bar?"

"Maybe. There's a lot that goes into it—layout, traffic patterns, decoration, furnishings, entertainment options."

"Sounds like you're building a killer business plan."

"You know about business plans?"

Her cheeks heated. "I'm not all boobs and ink, you know. I took business classes at TCC."

He set his hand over hers. "I never doubted your smarts. But most people find this stuff pretty boring. They just want beer and food. They don't care how it gets on their table."

"Well, I do have a little insight there. You can bounce ideas off me anytime." Just then, the server set down a plate of shrimp and chive dumplings and little dishes of dipping sauce. She tasted one, clutched her chest, and moaned. Eddie's eyes bugged out. Really, she shouldn't torture the poor guy like this, but teasing him was so much fun.

"Sooo good!" She dipped another dumpling in the garlicky sauce and lifted it to his lips. "You gotta try these."

He took a bite, closed his eyes, and sighed—just like he did when she kissed him.

Next came crispy salt and pepper tofu cubes drizzled with spicy garlic-scallion oil. Rosie sampled one and sighed. When she opened her eyes, Eddie's gaze was lasered onto her mouth.

"What will you serve at your bar? I'm guessing it won't be tater tots."

"No, but lots of dumplings—steamed ones called pelmeni, and fried pirozhki. There's a Russian dumpling place in Seattle that does all kinds of fusion flavors—bacon cheeseburger dumplings, kielbasa and sauerkraut, stuff like that. Plus I'll serve fried brown bread fingers with cheese dip—the best beer snack ever. And all kinds of pickled veggies—delicious with beer or vodka."

"Yum." She sampled a fresh spring roll—tender wrapper surrounding crisp lettuce, bean sprouts, scallions, and prawns. "Will you use your mom's recipes?"

"Maybe." He set down his chopsticks and sighed. "If she's still speaking to me by the time I finally scrape together the capital."

She laid her hand atop his. "You really think this could break up your family?"

"Honestly, I don't know. Nearly all my relatives work in the laundry industry." He wove his fingers through hers. "I hope they'll see this as honoring our family roots in a different way."

He picked up his chopsticks again and tried to lift a sticky Korean-spiced chicken wing. She nudged him with her elbow and picked one up with her fingers.

"What about your family?" he asked. "Do they support your tattoo career?"

"Hell, no." She huffed a curl from her forehead. "But I came to terms with that long ago. My sister hasn't given up on getting me back in school, but Mom says it's my decision to make. Funny that the only teacher in the family is the one who gets it—school just isn't my thing." She dropped the chicken bones onto the plate and nabbed another wing. "My grandparents are dentists. They offered to pay for dental hygienist training, but—ugh. Spending all day inside people's mouths?" She rubbed her thigh against his. "Unless it's your mouth, of course."

"You're gonna give me a heart attack, you know that?"

"This topic is too grim for such a delicious meal." She pointed a chicken bone at him. "New topic: How did you get so good at date planning?"

He waggled a finger. "Not divulging my sources. But I'm glad you're having fun."

"I am." Their gazes met and held. In tandem, they sucked in a deep breath, held it, then released it in a laugh.

"So, what's up next, planner boy?"

His eyebrows arched. "You'll see when we get there."

He paid for lunch, refusing her offer to split the check. They drove downtown to Antique Row, two blocks lined with quirky second-hand and vintage shops.

She clapped her gloved hands. "I love this place. How did you know?"

"Just an educated guess. You're collecting ideas for your portfolio, right? Figured we might find inspiration here."

"And you might find something for your bar?"

"Just ideas at this point. Let's go."

They wound through Smith and Son, a three-story warren whose wares ranged from antique furniture to junk jewelry, old furs, artwork, plus mini boutiques offering everything from comics to lingerie. Rosie snapped photos of Art Deco brooches that would make great tattoo designs. Eddie blushed like a strawberry as she flipped through racks of silky little nothings she could never afford, holding them up for his approval. *Note to self—wear good lingerie tonight.*

On the ground floor, they paused in front of a huge, mahogany-framed mirror trimmed with intricate carved flora and fauna.

Eddie whistled. "Can't believe it's still here."

Rosie wound her arm around his waist and squeezed. "This would be perfect for your bar, right?"

"Is there a stronger word than perfect?" He gazed reverently at the gorgeous old piece. She watched his reflection as he traced every detail. And then his gaze shifted to her, his eyes shining with banked fire. "I guess there is. It's Rosie." Holding her reflected gaze, he wound his arms around her middle. "From now on, that's what your name means—better than perfect."

Suddenly tongue-tied, she sputtered a nervous laugh.

He buried his blushing face in the crook of her neck. "Sorry. I suck at romantic words."

Warmth filled her chest. "No, Eddie. You definitely do not suck."

For a long moment, they stood entwined before the giant mirror, a mismatched couple who shouldn't fit but somehow did. Perfectly.

Finally, he patted her hip. "Welp, if I haven't scared you off with my bad poetry, we've got one more stop."

The snow fell harder as they drove down Pacific Avenue and parked across from the brick arches of the Washington State History Museum. As soon as the wipers stopped, fat flakes patted the windshield, covering them in a fluffy white blanket that muffled the street noise beyond their little cocoon.

"Damn." Eddie thunked his fist on the steering column. "I was hoping for clear skies for this last part."

"We could just make out in your car." She leaned across the center console and fluttered her lashes.

With a groan, he raked his fingers into her hair and mashed her lips in a hungry kiss. "Gonna need a bigger car if we want to do more than this. You up for a walk across the Bridge of Glass?"

"Absolutely." She tugged her fuzzy beanie over her curls. "More room to kiss there."

They dashed across the tram tracks and onto the slender

pedestrian bridge decked with Dale Chihuly's blown-glass artwork. Eddie pulled her to a stop beneath one of the poles topped with chucks of translucent blue-green glass, like giant rock-candy swizzle sticks. "Gotta kiss here. It's good luck."

His kiss warmed her right to her toes. "Wow." She blinked against the stinging cold. "Never heard of that tradition before."

Eddie chuckled. "I just made it up. C'mon." He tugged her to the shelter of the glass roof holding hundreds of blown-glass sculptures shaped like undersea plants and creatures—a fantasy coral reef in dazzling colors. By now the sun was low in the sky, and snow atop the glass ceiling contrasted with the rainbow overhead.

Huddled close, they shuffled from spot to spot, necks craning as they drank it the visual feast.

"Did you ever look through a microscope at those little pond water creatures?" Rosie asked, her head on Eddie's shoulder. "Reminds me of the way they dance, a tiny hidden world."

He nibbled her earlobe, his touch deliciously distracting. "Show me your favorite."

"You mean pick just one? Impossible."

"Nah, it's very possible." He pointed. "That one's my favorite." Still holding her tight, he maneuvered them beneath a wide tan blossom flecked with gold. Wavy glass petals flared from a chestnut center, and a brilliant cobalt rim circled its scalloped edge.

"Why this one?"

"It's your colors. See? Amber like your skin, warm brown like your eyes, and the bright blue matches your hair."

Her eyes blurred with tears. Though he denied his skill, Eddie had a way of spinning a compliment that arrowed right to her heart.

I love you. The words throbbed in her chest, pushed at her throat, struggled to escape her tightly pressed lips. She swallowed them down. *Too soon. Too fast. Don't blurt and ruin this.*

Misunderstanding her tremors, Eddie squeezed her tighter. "You're shivering. Let's get you warmed up."

Rosie kept silent during the ride home, her hand on Eddie's thigh, gulping deep breaths against a rush of emotion that threatened to tumble her ass-over-teakettle.

They pulled up in front of her house a little before five. Turning to face her, Eddie's forehead rumpled as he rubbed her arm in slow strokes. "You okay, Rosie?"

"It was—" Her voice came out squeaky. She cleared her throat. "I had such a good time, Eddie. You're an amazing date planner."

His tense expression relaxed into a brilliant smile. "I'm glad. I was worried you'd be bored."

"No way. Every detail was absolutely perfect."

"You mean absolutely Rosie." He kissed her hand. "You're kind of intimidating, you know. It's not easy for a boring guy like me to impress someone like you."

Cupping his whiskered cheeks, she pressed her forehead to his. "You are the polar opposite of boring, Eddie. And tonight after work, I'm going to show you just how impressed I am."

Chapter Twelve

"Hot tots comin' through." Lana nearly mowed Eddie down as she headed from Bangers' kitchen to the bar floor. "Hey, Eddie. How they hangin'?"

"Um, great?" He shifted his ice bucket from one hand to the other. As far as he knew, he and Rosie were still officially "taking things slow," but Lana was Rosie's best friend. How much had Rosie shared about their rapidly shifting relationship status?

"Heard you and Ro had a fun afternoon." She nudged him with her sharp elbow. "You better treat her right, you hear?" Another poke, and she strode into the crowd, her long pigtails swaying.

After refilling the ice well, he glanced around for the next task. River was chatting up a pair of cute girls while Kiara pulled beers and Dawn shelved freshly washed glasses. At the end of the bar, Gus stuffed his fuzzy face with chili-cheese tots. Eyes wide, he grunted and pointed to the screen.

A roar engulfed the room as the TV announcer bellowed, "Touchdown, Huskies!"

Eddie stayed too busy to watch the screen—not that he gave a rat's hairy ass about college football. Now and then he caught the blue flash of Rosie's hair as she hurried from bar to tables and back, but that was it. No greeting, no sexy glances, just full-speed hustle to keep up with orders.

When a final cheer roared to the rafters, Gus rang the ship's bell behind the bar and wiggled his baggy butt. "Huskies win! Eat my shorts, Beavers!"

Eddie had to laugh. This was the most animated he'd ever seen the old guy.

By closing time, his poor feet throbbed. Falling into bed was going to feel so good tonight—especially with Rosie beneath him. Or astride him. Or spooned beside him. Who cares, as long as they were naked and together.

Rosie finally trudged to the bar with a tray of dirty glasses. He off-loaded them and flashed her a smile. "Hey, gorgeous. I missed you."

"Missed you too." She leaned onto the bar and trailed her finger up his arm, making every hair on his body stand at attention—other parts, too. "I had so much fun this afternoon." She tickled the sensitive crook of his elbow. "My overnight bag's in my locker. I've got a little surprise for you."

"What is it?" His mind raced—a new tattoo? Lingerie? A sex toy?

"As somebody told me this afternoon, you'll just have to wait." She boosted herself up on the foot rail, clutched the front of his shirt, and pulled him in for a kiss that made him forget his name—

Until a stinging smack on his arm brought him back to

earth. Indiana Jones and his bullwhip had nothing on Dawn O'Malley and her bar towel.

He rubbed the sore spot. "Sorry, boss. We got carried away. Won't happen again."

She huffed, but there was humor behind it. "Seems I've heard that phrase from you two before. Something about my bar makes you kids horny?"

Rosie ducked her head, but there was no hiding her radiant smile. "It's not the bar, it's him."

"It's us." He held her gaze.

Dawn tilted her chin toward the top of the carved back-bar. "Must be that cherub up there, shooting love arrows at my employees."

Gus rounded the corner pushing a wheeled mop bucket. "Maybe you're next, pretty lady."

"What the hell you still doing here, old man?"

He sniffed. "My job. I'm co-owner, ain't I?"

Eddie left the oldsters to their squabbling. He and Kiara restocked the bar for the next day while the servers wiped down tables and stacked chairs.

After tip count-out, Dawn called them all to the bar. "Listen up, y'all. I want to get started on plans for our Anti-Valentine's Day Party."

Kiara tilted her head. "Say what, now?"

"Tell 'em, Gus." Dawn nodded to her business partner, who puffed up his flannel-covered chest and clasped his hands behind his back.

"I figure we can't compete with all the restaurants puttin' on fancy Valentine's Day dinners, so why not do the opposite?"

Rosie bounced on her toes. "I heard about this. You throw a party for everyone who's not attached."

Dawn nodded. "Or folks who don't want to shell out a fortune on roses and champagne. River's coming up with drink specials. Diego's got some menu ideas. Lana's compiling a playlist. If anyone's got ideas for games and competitions, let me know." She exchanged a glance with River, who nodded and cleared his throat.

"I'm gonna be pretty busy helping Dawn with the planning, so I could use some help with the posters." River illustrated window signs for Bangers' events and weekly specials. His cartoon doodles were cute, but nowhere near as skilled as Rosie's drawings.

Bent over a booth, her lush hips jiggling as she scrubbed, Rosie evidently didn't notice everyone's eyes on her. Eddie cleared his throat. "What do you say, babe?"

She straightened and turned, her cleaning rag clutched to her chest. "You want me to draw like River?"

Dawn sauntered over. "No, doll. I want you to draw like you."

Rosie backed away, bonking into a table and tumbling the napkin dispenser to the floor. "It's just, River's cartoons are so cute, and—"

Dawn patted her shoulder. "He suggested I ask you. Didn't you, River?"

River's mouth was currently fastened to Charlie's, but he flashed a thumbs-up.

"Um, I guess—"

Their coworkers dispersed, pulling on coats and hats against the nasty sleet.

Eddie looped his arm through Rosie's. "Breathe, babe."

With a windy sigh, she sagged against his shoulder. "It's just—I don't want to step on River's toes. Everyone loves his posters. If mine are better, then I'm taking something away from him, you know?"

Eddie nuzzled her hair. "I doubt he'll see it that way."

"Funny, isn't it? All my life I've wanted to be an artist, and now when someone offers me the chance to put my artwork on display, I get spooked."

"Fear of success. I heard about that on Doctor Phil. Or was it Doctor Oz?"

Rosie squinted. "You watch those old-lady shows?"

"Babka does. Sometimes I keep her company." Suddenly self-conscious, he fumbled for a more comfortable topic. "You know, I have markers at my place. You could practice your cartoon skills."

Rosie's eyes widened. "How did you know?"

"Know what?"

"Never mind." Her expression relaxed into a sexy smirk as she tickled beneath his chin. "Let's go."

* * *

Rosie stopped nibbling Eddie's earlobe long enough to murmur, "Hurry." While he fumbled with the lock on his apartment door, she tunneled inside his coat, greedy to unwrap her prize. Finally, the knob turned, and they tumbled inside.

Ever the old-fashioned gentleman, he helped her out of her coat. "You want something? Tea? A snack?"

"I want you, Eddie." Sweet of him to offer preliminary gestures, but once they started kissing on the stairs, her libido stomped on the gas.

Flashing a Christmas-morning grin, he reached for her blouse buttons.

She batted his fingers away. "Bathroom first. I need to insert my surprise."

His kissable mouth opened and closed like a startled goldfish. Did he think she was packing a strap-on in her purse? Teasing him was fun, but fucking him was even more delicious, and she was eager to get on with it. She fished in her bag and pulled out a foil packet.

His head tilted. "Condom?"

"It's a menstrual disk. It holds back the flow so period sex isn't messy." She'd never tried one, but Lana swore by them. "Never had one leak," she promised.

"Umm…cool?" He blinked rapidly. "I mean, I'll try anything you want, Ro, but you don't need to—"

Pressing her hips to his, she unfastened the top buttons of his shirt and kissed the tender skin where his shoulder met his neck. "This is for me. The mess makes it hard for me to enjoy myself."

His head lolled back, inviting more kisses. "Your enjoyment is my number one priority." He rocked his hips into hers, and the firm ridge behind his zipper sent a cascade of shivers down her spine.

"Number one, eh? Do I get my own page in your notebook?"

"You get your own chapter." His fingertips danced over her back in mesmerizing spirals. "I need a new planner just for all the things I want to do with you." He grasped her ass, snugging her tight against him. "Now go put in your thingy before I explode."

Grabbing her overnight bag, Rosie repaired to the bathroom where she took care of business and freshened up. Clean, perfumed, and insured against leaks, she pulled on the itchy but sexy lace bra and thong she'd brought, then wrapped up in her red satin robe embroidered with Chinese dragons. Fluffing her hair, she purred at her reflection, "Let the games begin." She pulled her second surprise from her bag, opened the door, and strutted through.

Eddie sprawled on the couch, thighs spread wide, the light of a dozen candles reflected in his glittering gaze. Barefoot, he'd unbuttoned his shirt but left his jeans on, a delicious gift for her to unwrap. The corner of his mouth hitched upward as he gestured to the package in her hand. "What you got there?"

"Tattoo pens." She dropped them on the coffee table before climbing onto the couch and straddling him. "I figure this game of show and tell will be more fun if we both have ink. Now, which of my tattoos haven't you seen yet?" She untied her sash and let the robe fall open.

His hands skated over her flanks, his touch light and teasing. "I've become pretty well acquainted with this beauty." Leaning forward, he pressed a kiss over her heart. "What inspired your rose bouquet?"

She chuckled. "When you're built like me, people stare at your chest."

"How could they not? It's dazzling." He nuzzled the spill of flesh above her lace bra cups.

"So I put my name there. Figured it might help people remember."

"You're unforgettable, Rosie." His hands slid up her sides to knead her breasts. "Good thing you're name's not Ursula."

"Yeah, I'd have to tattoo bears on my tits. Hey—" She swiveled and snatched up the markers. "You need a Russian bear. Lie down."

Still gripping her hips, he stretched out on his back.

"Hold still." She uncapped a brown marker and, in quick strokes, sketched a snarling bear on his left pectoral.

"Rosie," he moaned, bucking his hips beneath her.

She settled her full weight onto him, pinning him in place. Despite the distracting press of his erection on her most sensitive spot, she finished the snarling beast. "Done." She grabbed her phone and snapped a photo. "See how pretty you look with a little ink?"

"You're prettier." His hands closed on her breasts again, rolling and pinching her nipples.

The answering throb between her legs tempted her to drop their tattoo game and peel off his clothing, but the longer she drew out the tease, the stronger their ultimate release.

"When choosing a tattoo design, you need to consider your essence." She rose, flicked the robe aside, and bent forward to show him the rainbow swirl at the top of her thigh. "Me, I'm colorful. Always in motion, like the wind."

Eddie's fingers traced the design. With a low grunt, he sank his teeth in her ass.

Fiercely aroused, she jumped and squeaked.

"What's my essence, Rosie?" He slid a fingertip inside her thong and stroked her slick folds.

"Fiery." She slid from his embrace, snatched up markers in red, orange and gold, and shoved him back onto the couch. Kneeling beside him on the floor, she unfastened his belt. "You keep it hidden, but you've got this intensity. It's hypnotic, Eddie, like crackling flames. You're so passionate."

His hands fisted and his eyes glinted with lust as he watched her open his jeans and slide them down just a few inches. Despite the chill, a bead of sweat trickled between her breasts, dampening her lacy bra. Her panties—well, they were already soaked.

He toyed with her hair while she sketched dancing flames low on his belly, blending orange into crimson. Goose bumps rose on his skin with every feathery touch. She capped the marker and blew on her design. His breath stuttered.

"Beautiful." She traced a finger along the line of dark, wiry hair below his navel. "See, you don't want to tattoo here unless you plan to shave on the regular." Lips followed finger, feathering kisses. "And that'd be a shame, because your happy trail is so hot."

Eddie growled and reached for her.

"Just be patient." She pressed a kiss to the insistent bulge struggling to escape its denim prison. "You promised I could decorate you, and I'm having so much fun." She tugged his jeans a little lower. "Now, let's see. What shall I draw on your ass?"

With a roar, he grasped her arms and pulled her up, sealing his mouth to hers. His tongue plundered and stroked while his clever fingers found her bra clasp and popped it open. "Rosie, I can't take it anymore. I need you." He slid beneath her and fastened his mouth over her nipple. Every ravenous draw echoed in her clit.

"Wait." Grasping his shoulders, she pushed him back onto the mattress. "I want to see how your tattoo looks without all this cloth in the way."

She kissed her way down his heaving chest, pausing to swirl her tongue around each nipple, then circled his navel. He curled up to watch, lifting his hips as she eased his jeans and boxers down. His thick, ruddy cock sprang free to rest atop the flames she'd drawn, a crystal tear on its fat, rosy head.

A zing of pleasure shot right to her core at the sight of all this satiny skin and firm muscle on display just for her. She had to taste him.

She grasped him by the root and stroked, slow and firm. "Here? You need me here?"

Groaning, he writhed on the cushions.

"Like this?" She swirled her tongue over his velvet crown, tasting his salty precum.

"God. Yes. Please." He bucked into her grip in short, jerky motions.

"Or like this?" She ghosted her lips down his shaft and brushed a kiss over his silky balls, which contracted at her touch.

"Yesss," he hissed. "Like that. All of it. Anything. You're so good…" Eyes shut tight, he trailed off on a hungry moan. His abs tensed and jerked beneath her palm.

She laughed aloud, giddy with power and drunk on pleasure. Even though her impatient pussy tingled, she'd gladly delay her own release for the joy of teasing him right to the edge and then pushing him over, a free-fall into bliss.

She licked up his length in firm, broad strokes, then sucked him in as deeply as she could take him, humming her pleasure.

His thigh muscles trembled as he arched higher off the couch. "Rosie, uhng, I'm gonna—"

She gripped his shaft and met his frantic gaze. Deep inside her, something feral growled. "That's the idea, love."

"But I want to—"

"Later. Give me this." Another swirling lick over his velvet crown. "I'm having too much fun to stop."

He sank back with a gasp. The rug rasped her knees as she shifted to afford a better angle before engulfing his shaft again.

Faster and faster she worked him, using both hands and her tongue to stroke and caress and tease until his whole body stiffened and his cock pulsed, filling her mouth with hot, salty cum.

She relaxed her hold on him, peppering his belly and thighs with kisses. His chest rose and fell beneath her palm, his heart thundering. Despite the ache in her neglected pussy, she glowed with raw, animal satisfaction.

Eddie's fingers wove into her hair, the gentle pressure delicious. "That was—God, Rosie, I don't have words."

She chuckled and flicked her tongue over one flat nipple. "You don't need words. You showed me how much you liked it."

"No, I didn't." His dark eyes sparkled with delicious promise as he tugged her onto the couch, then straddled her, kneeling as he ran his fingertips over her body from neck to knees. Trapped between his strong thighs, she had no choice but to relax into his feathery caress.

"You are stunning," he murmured, bending low to kiss her throat and shoulders. He cupped her breasts reverently while his lips and tongue teased her nipples to stiff, tingling peaks. "I want to taste every inch of you."

She arched her neck and rolled her head against the couch, helpless and drowning in pleasure.

His lips trailed down her belly while his palms stroked her sides and hips. "Every time I see you, my cock aches. You're so lush and ripe and sweet." He bit the tender skin inside her thigh, sending a shock of pleasure straight to her clit. "I'm starved for you, Rosie."

He slid her panties off, then his thumbs teased her open and traced her folds, his touch infuriatingly light. "You smell like sin." He nipped her again, and she cried out.

His tongue soothed the sting away just as his thumb slipped inside her, parting her inner walls and stroking her in maddening circles while his tongue flicked over her clit. He answered her every gasp and jolt with happy grunts and murmurs. "That's right, love. Let go. Give yourself to me."

Sweet pressure built, shortening her breath and tightening her muscles. His tongue circled and flicked and stroked—and withdrew.

Blinking and breathless, she rose onto her elbow and found him kneeling between her spread thighs, heavy lidded and flushed, fisting his erection. How could he be hard again so soon? What was left of her brain muttered something about gift horses.

"You make me wild, you know that?" He nudged her thighs wider and settled into the cradle of her hips, notching himself at her entrance. Inch by delicious inch, he thrust home.

"Faster." Greedy for more delicious fullness, she smacked his tight little ass.

Chuckling like a horny demon, he churned in and out with frustrating slowness. "Didn't somebody say something about patience?" He kissed her, his tongue sweeping inside to dance with hers.

A few more sweet, torturous thrusts, and her breath caught. Fast or slow, hard or tender, she was seconds away from erupting like a volcano. She clasped her legs around his hips and hung on.

Sensing her readiness, Eddie sped his thrusts, rattling her bones as he slammed into her again and again. The last thing she saw before tipping over the edge was his fiery gaze. And then she shattered into a million sparks, floating free on waves of magical pleasure. A million miles away and right there under her skin, Eddie followed, flooding her with the heat of his release.

Slowly the room rematerialized around their joined bodies. Sweat-slick and panting, they clung together. She slid her fingertips in spirals over Eddie's damp back. He nuzzled the crook of her neck and sighed. "That was one for the record books."

She laughed into his soft hair. "We won the gold medal for sure."

He pushed himself up on shaking arms. "So much for your tattoos." The designs on his chest and belly had dissolved into streaks of color and bled onto her skin. "Too bad—that was a very fine bear."

She patted the smudge on his chest. "Once I get a position, I'd love to ink that on you. Or even better, the two-headed eagle from your belt buckle. It's your perfect symbol—fierce and stern, looking forward to the future and back to your heritage."

His smile faded. "Not so fierce, actually." His bit his lip. "Arrgh—this is so embarrassing."

She cupped his jaw and waited until he met her gaze. "Don't be embarrassed. Just tell me."

His chest rose on a deep inhale, then dropped. "I'm terrified of needles."

Blinking rapid-fire, she struggled to suppress a grin. She lost the battle.

"Gah," He flopped onto the couch and covered his eyes with his forearm.

"No, listen." She threaded her fingers through his. "Lots of people hate needles. I promise you, I'm not one of those kinky

143

types who gets off on pain. But really, it's not that bad, and after the first few minutes, you get used the feeling and you kind of relax."

Eddie grimaced. "You'd have to drug me up real good."

"Well, it's a moot point anyway. The rate I'm going, I'll be a bar server forever." She snuggled against his side and pulled the fuzzy throw blanket over them both.

The slide of his fingers through her hair was hypnotic. "You'll be a tattoo artist long before I open my own bar."

"Nah. You're a champ Eddie." She yawned into a throw pillow. "You'll find a partner with big bucks—like Gus invested in Dawn's place."

"Partner?" He huffed. "No way. I'm not gonna break my parents' hearts just to compromise on my vision."

The intensity in his voice pierced her sleepy fog. "You really think your parents won't understand?"

"Lately, Dad's been harping on every picky detail at work. I've got a bad feeling." He yawned in her ear. "Stay with me tonight?"

"Of course." How could she refuse, with him looking like an adorable, sleepy-soft puppy?

Wrapped in their shared blanket cape, they shuffled to his bed. Eddie wound his arm around her middle and threw his leg over hers. In less than a minute, he drifted off to dreamland, long lashes fanned against his cheek, razor-sharp jaw relaxed, plush lips parted.

But she lay awake, staring at the frost blossoms on the attic window above their heads, unable to sleep while the wheels in her head whirled. She wiggled her butt, seeking a more comfortable position. Eddie muttered in his sleep and tightened his grip.

"Clingy," she grumbled through a grin.

"Mmmrf." He head-butted her breast like an affectionate cat.

Threading her fingers through his hair, she stroked the silky strands. She'd nearly pushed him away because she thought they'd never fit together. Giddy emotion fluttered her belly and sheened her eyes with happy tears. "Aw, Eddie," she whispered. "Look at us. Has there ever been a more mismatched couple?"

His only answer—a soft snore.

If not for Bangers, they'd never have met. Their paths weren't parallel—hell, they weren't even in the same county. Tangled in someone else's family drama is the last place she wanted to be—and Eddie was headed for a major blowout when he finally told his parents of his plans. If his faith in her was well-founded, she'd soon be juggling two jobs—Bangers and a tattoo apprenticeship—leaving her even less time to spend with him. But in this cozy little apartment, none of that mattered. If only...

With a contented sigh, she stroked his arm and let her imagination wander. She could set up her laptop and drawing supplies over there, in the empty corner by the door. Eddie would scribble in his notebook while she sketched. She'd try out new design ideas on his virgin skin, smoothing ink over muscle and bone. Endless repeats of tonight, laughter and supernova sex and easy, honest talk.

A glowing warmth suffused her chest. The words bubbled up, fizzy as champagne froth and just as impossible to contain. "Oh Eddie, I'm so in love with you."

His eyes fluttered open. A dreamy smile danced on his lips. "You are?"

She tensed in his arms, her heart karate-kicking her ribs.

His sleep-scratchy voice held so much vulnerability. She couldn't lie to him now, couldn't deny the truest thing she knew.

She pressed her forehead to his. "Yeah, I am."

Eyes wide, he clasped her arms, his jaw working silently.

Nausea gripped her as she whirled down a vortex of self-doubt. Should she have denied it? Pretended to be asleep? Had she just screwed up everything by blurting her stupid, impulsive feelings?

Her words tumbled out. "It's too soon, right? You don't have to say it back. I just—I care about you, and I love that you care about me, and I love the way you're always on my side, and the way you touch me, and your huge, mushy heart." She lay her palm over his chest. "I wasn't looking for a boyfriend or anything, but I think about you all the time and whenever something good happens I want to call you, even though I know you're busy, and last night I dreamed you were holding me and I woke up and you weren't there and I was so sad and—well, here we are." She grimaced. "Does that make sense?"

The corners of his eyes crinkled. "Perfect sense." He brushed his lips over hers. "You're a fuckin' poet, Rosie. I love you too."

"Yeah?" Warmth bloomed beneath her sternum, spreading up and down and out until she was sure she must be glowing like neon.

"Absolutely." Grinning, he kissed her. "And it's not too soon. I've been crushing on you since the day we met."

Giggling, she wrapped her leg around his hips and pulled him tight against her. He sank into her embrace, and a moment later sank into her. Slow and sweet and so, so good, they rode this new feeling, soaring high and then floating down to earth together, each the other's shelter, safe and warm.

Chapter Thirteen

"Welcome to Daisy Fresh Dry Cleaning," Eddie intoned for the umpteenth time that morning.

"Patel. Three suits." The harried-looking customer didn't even look up from her phone.

"Right away, ma'am." He verified her receipt and handed over her freshly cleaned suits. The woman addressed his mother, who hovered at his shoulder. "Such a lovely young man, Mrs. Volkov. You've raised him well."

I'm twenty-eight, not twelve, for fuck's sake. He pressed his lips in a tight smile before returning to the back room, glancing in the mirror as he passed. His beard hadn't fallen off. His Adam's apple still protruded. Yup, still a grown-ass man. Hard to feel that way, though, working under his parents' close supervision. They'd been extra fussy lately, reminding him of procedures he knew by heart, peering over his shoulder as he worked the register or the steam and press machines, patting him like a goddamn puppy. "Good job, son. Good boy."

They could afford to hire someone else to help at the front desk, but they'd found fault with every clerk they hired over the past few years. Not that he had any right to complain—they paid him a fair wage and didn't charge him rent for the apartment, a potential income that could hasten the retirement Dad joked about on the regular. He'd never retire, though, just collapse into the sorting bin at the age of one hundred and float up to heaven, a freshly starched angel.

Eddie snatched his jacket from the hook by the back door. "Pops, I'm taking off now. Be back by two."

"You put those shirts in the machine?"

"Yes, Dad."

"And changed the tape in the register?"

"Yes, Dad." He yanked his wool beanie over his ears.

Mama brushed imaginary lint from his jacket. "Tell Miss Rosie hello from us, right Papa?"

His father grunted.

"And ask if she got a dress for the wedding. If not, we have something on the unclaimed rack that might work."

"Ma." He grasped her shoulders. "Rosie is not going to wear someone's leftover prom dress to Irina's wedding."

"Let the boy go, Alina," Dad grumbled. "Someday all this will be his, and there will be no more time for long lunches with cute girlfriends."

Though the temperature in the back room was near sauna-level, an icy finger slid down Eddie's spine. He pecked his mother's cheek and slipped out the door.

A wide grin bloomed as he cranked his engine and started for Rosie's house. No high in his life matched the feeling of waking up to her warm, curvy body in his bed. In fact, since she spent every night there, she might as well move in, right?

How long should he wait before asking her?

Cool your jets, idiot.

Rosie's mom greeted him at the door, her hair in a messy topknot, wearing sweatpants and a fuzzy fleece top—odd attire for a high school teacher on a Thursday.

"Hi, Diana. No school today?"

"Caught strep from a student." She gave him a sharp-eyed smile that raised the hairs on his nape. "Listen, Eddie, you and Rosie are both adults, so this isn't really my business. But I can't help noticing the change in her schedule. She used to come back from work around two or three in the morning. Now she comes back at seven or eight."

His throat constricted.

What do you say to your new girlfriend's mom? *Gosh, ma'am, I sure love boinking your daughter? Any chance you'd like to turn her room into a guest room?*

He shuffled his feet on the carpet. "I, uh, really like spending time with Rosie. With my day job and her job search, we don't get much time together." He risked a glance at Diana and found her smiling, just a little. "I wish we could have more, but for now I'll take what I can get."

She patted his shoulder. "Relax, hon. Rosie seems happy lately. I'm glad you two found each other. Nice to see her with someone who isn't covered in ink. So, you two going to Doyle's?"

"Yes ma'am." Of course, he'd take careful notes of their menu, décor, seating, serving arrangement, special events, foot traffic… But this outing was mainly about spending time with Rosie. So far, they'd only been on one proper date, and that bugged him. Love wasn't supposed to come this easy, with no effort at courtship.

"Well, have fun." Diana returned to the living room and wrapped herself in a crocheted afghan. "Assuming you can pry her out of her tattoo lair."

Eddie knocked on the hot pink door, which flew open to reveal Rosie just as rumpled as her mom. But on Rosie, rumpled looked sexy—probably because of his delicious memories of rumpling her.

She clapped a hand to her mouth and tugged him inside. "Shit, is it noon already? Lemme get dressed." She kissed him hard and deep, tugged a fuzzy sweater over her T-shirt and a short skirt over her leggings. While she unsnarled her hair, he sat on her bed.

"Whatcha working on today?"

She pointed with her brush to the window table, where a half-tattooed foot sat.

Suppressing a shiver, he examined it. An elaborate Celtic knot design on the instep unraveled into vines climbing the ankle, complete with green leaves and thorns dripping blood. "You show these to your prospective bosses?"

Her eyes grew round. "No way." She fastened a jeweled clip into her riot of curls. "It's considered bad form to start on this stuff before you get an apprenticeship. Makes you look like an amateur."

"This doesn't look amateur to me."

"I don't make the rules." She dabbed on scarlet lipstick, doing that sexy pucker-kiss thing.

Closing his arms around her middle, he watched her oral gyrations. "I'm just gonna kiss it off, you know."

She wiggled her ass against him. "I like to look pretty for you, babes." She'd taken to calling him that lately, and it tickled him to no end. So did the pressure of her hips against his.

He nuzzled her curls. "Maybe we should skip lunch?"

She smacked his rear. "I was promised a fahn-cy lunch, and I'm holding you to it."

Mid-day traffic wasn't too bad, and soon he parked across from King's Books. The Irish pub next door was nearly full, but he found a table in back. A gum-popping server brought them leather-bound menus and pointed out the specials.

Rosie glanced around. "Great ambiance, right? Love all the dark wood."

He nodded. "No dartboards, though. Weird, in an Irish pub."

Rosie flipped through her menu. "Did you know Bangers was originally an English-style Pub? My parents used to go there back in the day. Speaking of bangers, I'm going to try them. Never had a real one." She winked. "You know how fond I am of a spicy sausage."

His cheeks heated.

Of course, Rosie noticed. She slipped off her shoe and stroked her foot up his calf. "Succulent and firm and juicy."

His face burst into flame.

The server interrupted, thank God, before Rosie's teasing reduced him to a pile of horny ash.

After he ordered shepherd's pie and Rosie ordered the bangers and mash, Eddie pulled his notebook from his jacket pocket and scribbled a few observations about the floor plan.

Rosie tapped the open pages with her fork. "Taking notes again?"

He pointed to the mic stands in the back corner. "This place has live music. Good choice. Brings in new customers."

The server delivered their plates. Rosie forked up a mouthful of mashed potatoes, clutched her chest, and moaned. His stupid dick perked up, pressing painfully against his zipper.

"Sooo good!" She lifted a forkful to his lips. "You gotta try these."

He had to agree, they were fuckin' superb, creamy and rich with hints of garlic.

While they traded bites and double entendres, the couple at the next table vacated their spot, and someone sat beside him in a flurry of unfurling coats and scarves. He kept his focus on Rosie. Who knew mashed potatoes and sausages could be so sexy? Then a hand clamped onto his arm.

"Oh my God, Eddie?"

Mashed potatoes everywhere—that's what happens when your ex-girlfriend you haven't seen in years plops down next to you, just as you take a bite.

Rosie grabbed her napkin and wiped gobs of his lunch from her face and chest.

He leapt from his seat, yanking his arm free from Courtney's grip. "Oh God, Ro, I'm so sorry."

Rosie made a choking sound, her expression froze somewhere between horror and laughter.

Courtney clapped a hand over her mouth and tittered. She'd changed. Her formerly wild hair was slicked into a smooth twist, her glasses were gone, and she'd lost weight. But she still had that irritating high-pitched giggle. Her lunch companion grabbed napkins from the next table and handed them over. "Everyone okay?"

Rosie stood and scraped a blob of mashed potato and gravy from her skirt.

"Eddie can get that out, right Eds?" Courtney assured her.

By now, the ruckus had attracted their server's attention. She hustled over, cleared away their plates, and wiped the table while Courtney chirped apologies.

Her date handed the server his credit card. "I'll get your lunch. She's bringing fresh plates." He tucked his wallet into his expensive-looking tweed jacket.

"Oh, Eric, you didn't need to do that," Courtney simpered. "That was totally my fault."

Eddie found his voice at last. "Rosie, this is Courtney Jurich."

"We used to date," she added.

It had been six years since their graduation from Tacoma Community College. Headed for UW's business program, Courtney promised they'd keep their romance alive despite the distance. Two weeks into the fall semester, she broke it off. He'd braced himself for that message but found it didn't really hurt all that much. They were on different paths, and their two-year affair had run its course.

Courtney's date cleared his throat.

"Oh, this is my fiancé, Eric Feinberg."

Rosie shook both their hands as if it were the most normal thing in the world to meet your boyfriend's ex in a shower of carbs.

Eddie clasped Rosie's hand under the table. She squeezed back and pulled their joined hands onto the table in clear view of his giggly ex.

No one spoke, just lots of awkward seat wiggling and darting glances. Finally, Rosie turned to Eric. "Are you from Tacoma?"

He flashed a wide smile that brought out a dimple in his Superman chin. "Kent, actually. Court and I came down for a conference."

Courtney nodded vigorously. "Twenty-first Century Business Leadership." She beamed at her tall, buff boyfriend.

"You finished your MBA, then?"

"Two years ago. Didn't I tell you? How about you?"

No reason to feel defensive, yet his spine still stiffened. "Still working on my Bachelor's."

"Oh." Courtney's brow furrowed as if he'd just confessed to cutting a fart.

The server arrived with their new plates and leaned in to whisper to Eric, who nodded and pushed back his chair. "Court, that window table you wanted just opened up. Let's let these two enjoy their lunch in peace."

"Oh, okay." She gathered her coat and bag. "It was great seeing you again, Eds. Tell your folks I said hi." She followed her fiancé with a lingering, over-the-shoulder glance.

With a groan, Eddie dropped his head into his hands.

Rosie had every right to be pissed, but she just chuckled and rubbed his back. "Don't worry. You're dating the queen of clumsy. I've spilled on more people that I can count. Though I've never spewed mashed potatoes before." She dropped a kiss on his jaw. "Besides, I know a good dry-cleaner."

"Ungh." He kissed her palm, then tackled his lunch, courtesy of his ex's boyfriend.

"So, tell me about giggle girl over there." Rosie dug in. Gotta give her credit—she didn't let little obstacles shake her.

"We met in a business class at TCC. Haven't seen her in years."

"Miss her much?"

Okay, maybe Rosie wasn't as unbothered as she appeared. "Honestly, I haven't thought about her in ages. One of those deals where you hook up because you find yourselves in the same place at the same time." *Sounds like I'm talking about us. Fix. Now.* "I mean, we didn't have much in common, really." *Shit, I'm making it worse.* "We were on different paths, you know?"

Rosie slurped her iced tea and raised an eyebrow. "Sure."

Mayday! Change the subject. "Am I gonna bump into any of your exes around town?"

"Nah." While she chewed another bite of sausage, her gaze flicked toward the front window where Courtney chattered with her new guy. "The only one who meant anything moved away."

His common sense told him to drop it, but the topic was like an itchy scab he couldn't stop picking at. "What was he like?"

"Who?"

"Your ex. The one who meant something."

"Tattoo artist. Picture Jojo, but with lots of ink."

"Were you in love with him?" Really, he must have a death wish today.

She shrugged. "I thought so once, but I'm over him." She inclined her head toward the window. "Were you in love with giggle girl?"

He shrugged. "I mean, I liked her, but when she left I got over it pretty fast. So I guess not."

"Love." She stabbed her second banger. "Funny word. It can mean so many things." Her gaze flicked up to his, then skittered away.

He closed his hand over hers and stilled the sawing motion of her knife. "What does it mean to you?" His heart hammered as if that knife hovered over it, ready to slice.

"Well—" She inhaled deeply. "It means that when we break up, it's really going to hurt."

"When?"

She set down her knife and squeezed his hand. "If. I meant if. It's just—meeting your teeny tiny little ex has me kinda shook."

Like knowing she'd been in love with a huge, Jojo-sized bruiser. But she was with him now, not her ex.

"Your turn." Rosie pointed her fork at him. "Define love."

The food in his stomach turned to cement. But he'd led her into this minefield, so she had every right to ask. "I guess, love means knowing someone's on your side, no matter what."

Rosie's guarded expression relaxed. "I'm on your side, Eddie." She rubbed her leg against his. "But I'm not gonna call you Eds. I hope that's not a deal-breaker."

"Please don't. I never liked that." Relief flooded him. Whatever insecurities Courtney's intrusion might've poked, Rosie shook them off like raindrops on a duck. She was such a strong, gorgeous, funny woman, and he was lucky beyond belief. "I'm on your side too, you know."

"Good." She unleashed a devilish grin. "You know, there are many sides of me." She took his hand and stroked his fingertips up her thigh. "There's the front side." She slid it behind her knee. "The backside."

His jeans were suddenly too damn tight. "I'm really fond of your backside."

"I noticed." Horny mischief twinkled in her eyes. "Then there's the inside."

He shivered. "That's my favorite side of all."

She dropped her silverware with a clatter. "You know, I'm just not hungry anymore."

"Let's go." He pulled her to her feet.

"I have an appointment at three, though."

"I can be quick."

Chuckling, she slid her hand into his hip pocket. "A nooner with my sweetie. How delicious."

He checked with the server to make sure their bill was covered, then slung his arm around Rosie and headed for the door. But she pulled him to Courtney's table.

"Thanks for lunch, guys. So nice to meet you both," she chirped in a tone just like Courtney's before planting a noisy smooch on Eddie's cheek. "We have to dash. Just enough time for a quickie before we go back to work. You know how it is—busy, busy."

Chortling, she towed him out the door.

"Claiming your territory?" He nuzzled her as they waited for the crosswalk signal.

"Damn straight." She kissed him again, a hot, lingering press of lips with just a taste of her velvet tongue. "Light's green. Let's go."

* * *

An hour later, sated and grinning, Rosie prepped for her next interview.

"Girl, what happened to your hair?" Lana dug a brush from her bag and tackled the snarled curls at the back of Rosie's head.

Rosie giggled. "Eddie happened."

Lana smacked her butt with the brush. "No way, a nooner? You're a naughty, naughty girl."

"Our third this week. I'm a lucky, lucky girl." She leaned into the mirror and reapplied the eyeliner that smeared during her romp with Eddie. True to his word, he'd made her come hard in just a few minutes, thanks to his talented tongue and fingers, then blew her mind a second time when he bent her over the breakfast counter and rode her like a buckaroo. Her well-used pussy still tingled. Every woman should feel this gloriously satisfied. Speaking of... "You talked to Jojo yet?"

Her friend's button nose crinkled. "What for?"

"Hello. He's besotted with you. But he'll never make the first move. You gotta give him a nudge."

Lana's eye roll smacked of over-acting. "Girl, I don't have time for that love nonsense." She moved to the closet and rifled through possible interview outfits. "I'm glad about you and Eddie, though. Never in a million years would I have put you two together, but you actually make a cute couple. And you seem more confident lately."

Rosie snapped her fingers. "I'm always confident."

"At the bar, yeah. But after all that talk about becoming a tattoo artist, you're finally going for it. Plus, those window posters you drew for work are mega-cute. Shoulda volunteered for that ages ago."

Lana had a point. Despite her worries about stepping on River's toes, everyone at work praised her illustrations for their weekly window posters—River loudest of all.

Lana held up a sparkly sweater, scrunched her lips to the side, then hung it back in the closet. "And Eddie's talking in full sentences instead of just grunting. I never noticed before how sweet his smile is. You two are good for each other." Lana handed her a pair of stretchy dark jeans. "These make your ass look like a peach."

"I'm interviewing with a woman, you know."

"So? Maybe she digs girl butts. You never know." Lana resumed her rummaging.

Rose shed her yoga pants and wiggled into her wardrobe

mistress's choice. "Something weird happened at lunch, though. We were at Doyle's."

"By the bookstore? I love that place. Their Reuben sandwich makes me wanna strip naked and rub it all over my body."

"Kinky. Anyway, this woman sits down next to us. Turns out to be Eddie's ex."

"Really!" Lana spun, clutching an armload of tops. "Eddie has an ex?" At Rosie's frown, she added, "I mean, of course he does. Just none of your caliber. What was she like?"

"Petite. Blonde. Giggly." She flashed a wry grin to cover her itchy discomfort. She should be stronger than this, but knowing Eddie once fell for someone so conventionally cute flipped her insecurity switch to Red Alert.

Lana dumped the tops onto the bed, grasped Rosie's shoulders, and fixed her with a stern look. "Ah-ah, none of that. You're a gorgeous, sexy woman, and Eddie's with you now."

She sighed. "The operative word is now."

"Bullshit. He looks at you like he won the lottery. Don't go chasing down that comparison rabbit hole. Nothing good lives down there."

"You're right." She blew out a breath and peeled off her T-shirt. "Which top?"

Lana tapped her pursed lips. "This tattoo lady is how old?"

"Don't know, but word is she's been around for a long time. One of the oldest studios in Tacoma."

"I'd keep things understated then. Older ladies appreciate class, not flash." She handed her a wrap-waist black sweater, then rummaged through Rosie's jewelry box.

"Uh huh. And you know all about older ladies."

Lana's playful grin melted away. "Considering I have to keep my tías happy if me and my brothers wanna stay together, yeah.

I've had to learn about the psychology of the over-fifty woman. Not to mention social workers."

Rosie wrapped her arms around her friend's shoulders and nuzzled her sleek black hair. "Hey, I'm sorry." Since her parents' death in a car crash, Lana had put her own career plans on hold to keep her two younger brothers together in the home they grew up in. She relied on her Bangers job and the good will of her family to keep the boys from being split up among the older relatives, all of whom had firm ideas about how to whip teen boys into shape.

Lana waved her off. "I'm fine. We're together. Rent is paid. Pedro's keeping his grades up, and Leo made the wrestling team."

"Must be nice, being able to make your own choices without constantly hearing how you're getting your own life wrong."

Lana snorted. "Don't gimme that shit. Everybody's family has opinions. Means they love you, even if they're a hundred percent wrong about what you need. My little brothers have endless opinions about my life—like they know shit about adulting."

"Sounds like my sister. Do you listen to them?"

"Sometimes. Doesn't hurt to keep an open mind. Also, appearing to consider their advice gets them off my back faster. Now, role play." She wriggled out of Rosie's embrace, plopped onto the bed, and poked her plush Cthulhu doll with her fingernail. "Buzz, buzz, buzz. I'm giving this guy a tattoo. Grab your portfolio and impress me."

Chapter Fourteen

Rosie closed her eyes and whispered a prayer to the tattoo gods before pushing open the door of Inky Dreams Tattoo Studio. She stepped into a narrow hallway with exposed brick on one side. On the other, a huge, curved arrow in iris blue pointed to a spiral iron staircase. Tucked behind it, an old-fashioned elevator with a folding metal grate instead of a door.

Clutching her new and improved portfolio, she sucked in a breath, smoothed her jacket, and started to climb. She'd topped Lana's chosen ensemble with a vintage blazer in dark purple velveteen—serious, but still cool. Small but attention-grabbing iridescent jewels sparkled from her ears. Similar jewels glittered from the eyes of the silver skull pendant nestled between her breasts. "Sophisticated lady," Lana had pronounced, "with just a whiff of bad-ass bitch."

Her steps echoed on the metal stairs. The small upstairs foyer held an empty desk, coat hooks, and rows of wooden cubbies. Rosie inspected the flash sheets covering the walls. All the classic designs were on display: cartoons, anchors, skulls, hearts, "Mom," pin-up girls, snakes, eagles—plus snarling Samurai warriors, lifelike portraits of people and dogs, and variations of the Tacoma octopus. A velvet curtain obscured her view of the studio beyond and dampened familiar sounds—the rhythmic buzz of tattoo needles, soft conversation, and mellow electronic music. Atop the desk, an old-fashioned hotel bell sat beside a hand-lettered "Ring me" sign.

When Rosie dinged, a husky female voice called, "Shoes off, please. Put 'em in a cubby."

Well, shit. So much for bad-ass. She'd worn her lucky fuzzy socks, candy-striped in pastel colors. She followed orders before peeking around the screen.

Black and white tiled floor, slate-gray walls covered with neatly framed drawings. A band of glass bricks high on the rear wall let in light, supplemented by frosted glass fixtures that reminded her of an old-time saloon. Bronze velvet curtains separated the large room into work areas for each tattoo artist.

"C'mon back, don't be shy," a woman called from behind a curtain on the right.

Rosie followed the sound. The tiny artist inside glanced over her shoulder before returning to her client, a large person with short salt-and-pepper hair whose broad back she was inking with a very detailed tarantula. "How you holdin' up, hon?" she asked the customer.

"Gotta piss," Spider-person said and lifted off the chair, holding a towel to their chest.

"I got a meeting with this youngster," the artist said. "Gimme ten minutes. There's coffee in the break room."

"Roger that." The customer eyed Rosie up and down on

their way out. "Good luck, kid."

That sealed it. This petite woman had to be Magda Wosniak, the only female studio owner she'd met so far. A Bangers customer tipped Rosie that Magda's apprentice had been arrested, leaving her in need of a new one. "Watch out," the guy warned her. "Magda don't take no shit off no one. Tried patting her ass once. She 'bout broke my arm."

With her thick silver mane and delicate build, Magda looked like an aging beauty queen—that is, if beauty queens came with full-sleeve tattoos and a neck design of bloody barbed wire. She raised one perfect eyebrow. "Well?"

Afraid her voice might wobble, Rosie cleared her throat. "Good afternoon. Thanks for seeing me, Ms. Wosniak." She extended her hand.

The older woman took it and squeezed. Hard. "It's Magda. Never Maggie. Got that?"

"Yes, ma'am."

The boss inclined her head toward the recently vacated tattoo chair. "Have a seat."

Rosie sat and clasped her portfolio across her lap, feeling like a second grader called to the principal's office.

Magda pivoted her wheeled stool and fiddled with the ink caps on her tray. "How old are you, kid?"

"Twenty-five, ma'am."

She clucked her tongue. "Enough with the ma'am shit. This ain't the army."

"Um, of course."

Magda peeled off her black nitrile gloves and held out her hand. "Let's see what you got."

Heart hammering, Rosie passed her the portfolio. Magda flipped through far too fast, her face stony. "Adequate. Show me the one you like best."

Worry snaked through Rosie's belly. This was like those job interviews where they asked you to name your biggest flaw. So much riding on this. Rather than let her mental wheels spin out, she decided to trust her gut. "These two. This one's a Chinese phoenix. My grandmother's design."

One perfect eyebrow rose. "Your granny's an artist?"

"A dentist. She works in embroidery floss instead of ink, but yeah, she's very artistic." She tapped the other page. "This one's a Russian phoenix, from a quilt my boyfriend's grandmother made."

"Huh." Magda tapped her lips with one fingertip, then flipped through the binder again, more slowly this time.

"I have more stuff on my website." She fished one of her new business cards from her jacket pocket. Charlie's idea, the glossy cardstock displayed one of her Chinese dragons. The flip side held her contact info and the URL of her new online portfolio.

"Huh." Hard to tell if that soft grunt meant approval or disdain. Magda slid the card into the pocket of her low-slung jeans. "You like kids?"

"Uh—sure?" *Kids in a tattoo studio?*

"Victoria, my right-hand girl, sometimes has to bring her baby in. Cute little bug. We keep him in the break room. He likes company." Another elevator glance. "I like the hair. Let me see your ink."

"Oh, I, uh—" She shed her jacket, untied her sweater at the waist, then glanced around.

"Just your arms, hon'. You ain't shy about skin, are you? Not a good look on a tattoo artist. You'll be up close and personal with tits, asses, all kinds of body parts."

Rosie peeled off her sweater, leaving her in just a flimsy satin camisole. Magda circled her, peering closely. "This Bernie Smith's work?" She tapped the chubby cherub on Rosie's right shoulder.

"Yeah. It's the angel from the bar where I work."

"Angel bar?"

"It's called Bangers. There's this carved back bar, huge antique mahogany piece from a saloon in Alaska."

"Ohhh." Warmth threaded into Magda's whiskey voice. "Dawn's place. I inked her dad's face on her calf."

Rosie blinked in surprise. Dawn had never let on that she had any ink under the hoodies, jeans, and Seahawks jerseys she wore to work.

Magda moved around her back. "You any good at portraits, kid?"

No use lying. "Depends on the face. I'm working on that."

"How about lettering?"

"Pretty good. Lots of samples on my website."

Magda chuckled. "Nowadays, everyone wants big ol' chunks of text on their skin. I don't get it, but since when did fashion make sense, right?"

"Sure."

Magda poked Rosie's elbow. "What's this clusterfuck supposed to be?"

"Amethyst geode. Gift from my Dad when I was little. The artist's sketch looked great, but—"

"Color's wrong. Looks like a squashed flower. Who did it?"

"Guy in Bremerton. Willie something."

Magda snorted. "Total hack." Finished with her inspection, she sat on her stool, crossed her ankle over her knee, and massaged her stockinged foot. Rainbow polka dots, Rosie noted.

"Okay, kid. Here's what I'm looking for." She ticked off on her fingers. "Front desk, over there. Paperwork and phone skills. You gotta deal with assholes who want what they want right now. I'm booked up for months. You can't let anyone bully you."

"Got it. What else?"

"Clean-up, fetch supplies for the artists, watch and shut up and learn. Tattoo oranges. When you prove your skills there, I might let you try some simple line work. I'll pay you for manning the desk from noon to six Monday through Friday."

"What about weekends?"

Magda grinned. "Don't work weekends anymore—privilege of my position. Sometimes Vicki and Tina do, though. Up to them." She stood and hollered toward the back corner where a tattoo machine buzzed over the sound of giggling. "Yo, Tina!" The buzzing stopped. "Come meet the new girl."

Hope fluttered in her chest like a freakin' butterfly convention. "You mean I got the job?"

Magda wagged her finger. "Don't get ahead of yourself. You got a two-week trial. You start tomorrow. Bring a sack of oranges, and don't be late."

* * *

Grinning like a loon, Rosie bounced into Bangers, then stopped short when she found the entire crew gathered at the bar sharing a pre-shift platter of tater tots. Gus sat on his usual stool—no surprise there. But how odd to see Diego and

Shelby outside their kitchen when they were usually warming up the grills and prepping ingredients. Eddie beckoned. Why did he look so flushed? Was Lana teasing him again?

Dawn glanced up. "There she is. You're late, kiddo."

"Late?" Rosie checked the Seahawks clock above the entrance. "I'm ten minutes early."

"Didn't you get my text asking you to come in twenty minutes early?"

She tapped her phone screen. Sure enough, there was the alert she hadn't noticed. "Sorry."

"Well, you're here now. Grab a seat."

She slid onto the empty stool beside Eddie, who rubbed her knee and flashed a nervous-looking grin. Were they in trouble? They'd both kept their hands to themselves at work—well, mostly.

Dawn clapped River's back. "River's done a fine job as my assistant manager, but I promised him time off for his fishing trips."

Jojo snorted. "You're going fishing? In January?"

River grinned. "Commercial fishing on my granddad's boat. My cousin is captain now, and he needs a spare hand on a squid run down the Oregon coast. Mama Dawn says I can go." He reached across the bar and clasped Charlie's hand. "My other boss gave permission too. Must want a break from my snoring."

Charlie flushed and clucked her tongue. "It's just a few weeks. You've always wanted to do this, so go do it."

Such a sweet, funny couple. Before Charlie arrived in December, River's flirty smiles were all for show. Anyone with half a heart could see that his was dried up as a prune. Now, he beamed happy energy, especially when Charlie slipped behind

168

the bar to squeeze his butt—which she did often.

Dawn stuffed a tot into her mouth before continuing. "That fall off the ladder before Christmas made me realize I was pushing myself too hard. I like having a right-hand person who knows the routines and can step in if I need a break."

Gus cleared his throat and puffed out his chest.

Dawn slid him a fond smile. "Not you, old man. You're my ideas guy, but I'm not gonna ask you to deal with broken plumbing or missing orders." She surveyed her employees. "While River's away, I need someone who knows the business from top to bottom."

Rosie's eyebrows inched upward. So that's why Eddie was flushed. He squeezed her leg and pinched his lips together, his knee bouncing a mile a minute.

Dawn rapped her knuckles on the counter. "And that's why I'm turning the position over to Eddie while River is gone."

The servers and bartenders exchanged confused glances—except for River, who thumped Eddie on the back.

Kiara raised her hand. "What about bartending?"

"Eddie does that already. I'll step in when I'm needed. In a pinch, Gus can take over on beer taps." She nodded toward the servers. "So can any of you girls. Questions?"

Shrugs and nods all around as the team dispersed. Rosie threw her arm around Eddie's shoulder and kissed his cheek. "That's great, love. You get to try out your management skills."

He flashed a sheepish grin. "I still can't believe she asked me."

"Of course she picked you. And hey," She hopped down from her stool. "I have news too." Bouncing on her toes, she leaned in closer and whispered, "I got an apprenticeship!"

He blinked open-mouthed for a moment, as if her news

did not quite compute, then a wide grin bloomed across his face. "That's great, babe." He gave her a quick, dry, suitable-for-work peck. "Um, your new job won't interfere with your hours here, will it?"

Her heart skidded to a stop. *That's it? Where's my hug? My squee? Okay, I guess guys don't squee, but give me something!*

She crossed her arms. "Your enthusiasm is overwhelming. I start tomorrow, in case you care." Jaw set, she grabbed her things and stalked to the locker room. How could he be so blasé about the best news she'd had in forever? He knew damn well how much this meant to her.

Eddie trotted behind her. "Rosie, wait. I'm sorry." He followed her in. "That's fantastic news. I'm really happy for you—just surprised."

She huffed through her nose. "Told you I had an interview today."

"You did?" He raked a hand through his hair, mussing the soft brown curls. "Oh, right. At lunch. It's just, with everything that happened, I guess I forgot." He rumpled his brow and made sad-puppy eyes.

She blew out a breath and fought back a wave of snark. Biting his head off was just the kind of workplace drama Dawn warned them against, the kind that could get them both fired. No matter how pissed, she'd never do that to him.

"I'd just like you to be as happy about my news as I am about yours. This is a big deal for me."

He shuffled closer and slid his hands into her hip pockets. "I am happy for you, Ro. And proud of you."

"That's better." *A little.* She leaned into his embrace. Maybe his reaction was just a careless slip of the tongue. God knows she made those all the time.

170

He cleared his throat. "About your work hours, though, will that be a problem?"

She planted both hands on his chest and shoved. "For fuck's sake, Eddie. Way to spoil the moment."

"What?" His brow rumpled. "Dawn's putting me in charge of scheduling while River's away. I've gotta make sure the Superbowl party is covered, and the Anti-Valentine's thing." He stretched his hands out wide. "This is my first chance to prove I can run a bar. I can't screw it up."

As she knotted her apron, she spit out her words like broken teeth. "Don't worry, boss. I'll show up for my shifts." She slammed her locker door. "It's not like you don't have a day job too."

Eddie trailed her to the bar floor, stammering apologies.

She spun and glared. "Let's just drop it."

"I don't want to fight with you, Rosie." He looked positively nauseated.

"We're fine." She bit that last word extra hard.

"Clearly, we're not. Can we talk about this after work?"

Her better angel whispered to cut him some slack. He couldn't read her mind, couldn't know the kind of enthusiastic reaction she'd craved.

She smacked that little pest like a mosquito. "Think I'll head straight home. I have a headache."

"Ro, I swear I didn't mean to shit on your good news. Please don't be mad."

"Well, I am. I can't snap my fingers and make my feelings stop."

She just needed to get over this sour mood—and nothing did the trick like a blast of external validation. If Eddie wouldn't give it to her, her customers would. She picked up her tray, checked her cashbox, then strutted to her first table.

"Hi, boys. What'll you have?"

"Yo, tattoo mama." Her customer grinned. "Give us a platter of onion Swiss tots with extra bacon, and a pitcher of Rainier."

His friend added, "Love your rose tattoo. My girlfriend wants one like that."

"Yeah?" She shot a glance over her shoulder. Behind the bar, Eddie stared, bug-eyed. "I just started working at Inky Dreams Tattoo, down by the Tacoma Dome. All female artists. She should check it out."

She circled her section, collecting orders and flirting with customers. Okay, maybe she was laying it on a little thick tonight, but damn it, the more she replayed Eddie's comments, the more they stung. A guy who really loved her would've been over the moon to hear her dream was finally coming true. What a painful wake-up call.

Maybe she'd got it wrong. Maybe all she and Eddie shared was a hot sexual connection and their love for Bangers. How stupid to blurt out the L word before thinking it through. She should've kept things casual. All the sex, none of the messy feelings.

At shift's end, she counted out her tips, a good haul tonight. Must be all the phony smiling. Avoiding Eddie's gaze, she stuffed his share into his tip mug. Her emotions still churned in a vortex of anger and self-blame. Better cool off before talking to him. She needed time to figure this out on her own.

As she turned toward the locker room, a soft hand fell on her shoulder. "Hang on there, kiddo."

Shit, shit, shit. She molded her face into what she hoped passed for a relaxed expression. "What's up, boss?"

"Eddie tells me you have news." Dawn raised an eyebrow.

For a woman who never had kids of her own, she had that omniscient Mom stare down pat.

"Yeah, actually. I got a tattoo apprenticeship. I start tomorrow."

Dawn beamed and threw her arms around Rosie, squishing her against her chest. "That's awesome! Hey, guys, meet Tacoma's newest tattoo artist." She clasped Rosie's hand and raised it high.

Lana sprinted over to join the group hug, followed by Charlie, Kiara, and all the others, chanting her name and bouncing up and down in a big, squealing love scrum.

"Get in here, Eddie." Dawn drew him into the center. "Aren't you proud of your girl?"

"I couldn't be prouder." He cupped her cheeks and pressed his forehead to hers. "Truly."

Really, Eddie? No way to know, since Dawn put him on the spot. Tears blurred her vision. Let them think they were tears of happiness.

"Sign me up," Jojo said with a pat on her back. "Been thinking about getting a vampire on my arm. Get it? Phlebotomist? Vampire?"

River groaned. "We get it, weirdo."

Rosie swiped her leaky eyes and wiggled out of Eddie's grip. "It'll be a while before I'm allowed to tattoo people."

Jojo shrugged. "I can wait. I'll save you this spot right here." He flexed his massive biceps.

With some careful sidestepping, she avoided Eddie's attempts to pull her aside, slipping out the back while his attention was diverted. A cowardly move, but she was too emotionally wrung out to face him.

As she pulled into her driveway, her phone lit up with a text from Eddie.

—*I'm so sorry, Ro. I love you*—

She powered her phone off and thunked her head against the steering wheel.

A guy who loved her would've smooched her silly and shouted her good news for all to hear. Sure, he told the others later, but only after she blasted him with her disappointment. Too little, too late.

Chapter Fifteen

"That's time, gentlemen." Jojo set his kettlebell at his feet. "Hit your mat."

Thank God. Eddie dropped his much smaller kettlebell and collapsed to the floor. Despite the frigid temperature in Jojo's garage, sweat streamed down his face and stung his eyes. Lifting a noodle arm, he wiped his face on his sleeve and awaited their next round of torture.

"Next up, in Eddie's honor, Russian twists. Feet up. Two minutes. Go."

Balanced on his rear, Eddie lifted his feet, clasped his hands over his chest, and twisted from side to side until his whole torso burned. Normally, the pain was a welcome distraction from his everyday worries, but today, it wasn't working. Rosie was still avoiding him. Did anyone else notice how phony and brittle her smile turned whenever he approached? And who could blame her? Distracted by his new work responsibilities, he'd really stepped in a big, steaming pile of verbal doo-doo.

Rosie went home alone again on Friday night, claiming a headache. Saturday night, she was expecting a phone call from her cousin in Hong Kong. Each time, she shrugged off his apologies with "We're fine." He might not be an ace with women, but he knew enough about the feminine mind to recognize "fine" for the landmine it was.

Huffing and grunting, he powered through until Jojo blew his goddamn whistle. "Gimme an up-dog. Stretch out those sexy abs."

River muttered a string of curses.

"Why are you even here, Riv?" Eddie asked. "Shouldn't you be packing?"

River huffed a dry chuckle. "And miss this torture? Besides, I wanna talk to you."

"Down dog," Jojo called. Five asses lifted in the air. Along with Jojo's brother Kai, Diego had joined their morning workouts.

"Child's pose."

With a grateful moan, Eddie folded up and pressed his forehead to the mat.

River poked his shoulder. "No need to stress, man. Dawn wouldn't ask you to step in if she didn't think you could handle it."

Eddie's sigh emptied his lungs. "It's not the job."

"Aha," Diego murmured from the mat next door. "Lady troubles."

Jojo's sharp ears didn't miss that. "What up, little man? You and Rosie squabbling?"

Eddie rolled onto his back and hugged his knees to his chest like a dead bug. "To do that, we'd have to be on speaking terms."

"Holy shit, Volkov. What did you do?"

"More like what I didn't do. Or say." He winced at the shrill whine of Kai's blender. "When she told me she finally got a tattoo apprenticeship, I was all in my head about my new job responsibilities. Shoulda made a big fuss about her win, the way she made a big fuss about mine."

River furrowed his brow. "What did you say, man?"

Eddie swiped a palm down his sweaty face. "Asked her if her new job would interfere with her shifts at Bangers."

"Oh, shit." River winced and clapped Eddie's shoulder. "You got some groveling to do, my friend."

The other guys nodded.

A moment later, a foot nudged his ribs. "Up, Eddie. Drink your spirulina shake and face your problems like a man."

He let Kai haul him to his feet and accepted a tall glass of green sludge. Sucking down a gulp, he added brain freeze to his list of complaints. Because why should anything go right today?

Jojo perched on a weight bench. "What happened to taking things slow?"

Eddie shrugged. "Things got fast. Now she's pissed at me, and I don't know what to do."

"Take some advice from the master," River said, draping his arm over Eddie's shoulders.

Kai snorted. "And so humble, too."

"Master of fuck-ups, I mean. Back in December, I nearly lost Charlie because I was a stupid, selfish ass. It took a lot more than pretty words to make things right. It took hard proof."

"What kind of proof?"

"Well, in our case I had to compromise with my Dad. The

landlord for Bangers was gonna sell the place to a developer, and Dawn couldn't afford to match his price. Dad offered the money she needed to buy the building, but I knew he'd turn it into one of those soulless hipster brewpubs." River scritched his blond beard. "I mean, I was right, but so was Charlie—save the bar first, then fight Dad's proposed changes. Anyway, Charlie was furious. Cut me off cold."

Jojo's brow rumpled. "Your dad's a partner?"

River shook his head. "Funny—I had this big, painful confrontation with Dad about how he's always trying to control my life. Lots of drama, but he finally agreed not to remake the bar—and then Gus stepped in with his insurance money, so Dawn didn't even need Dad's help. Charlie forgave me once she saw I was willing to swallow my pride. And now, I'm the luckiest bastard in Tacoma. I got a beautiful, smart lady who calls me on my shit and lets me go fishing."

Diego blotted his damp hair with a towel. "Ima give you a run for your money on that luckiest bastard title."

River clapped the cook's shoulder. "I feel better about leaving with you looking out for Anna and Charlie while I'm gone."

Diego grinned. "Like you say, man, hard proof. Anna still doesn't quite believe I'll stick around after the baby comes, so I'll just have to wait her out."

Eddie shook his head. Weird that Diego set his sights on a pregnant woman in the throes of a contentious divorce, but the chef knew what he wanted.

And so did Eddie. How to convince Rosie, though? Presents? Love letters? Abject begging? If only she needed something from him, he could give it to her. But all she wanted from him now was distance.

Chapter Fifteen

* * *

"Have another cookie." Lana shoved the tray toward Rosie. She'd lured her out for breakfast before her shift at the tattoo parlor. Turns out that "breakfast" meant a mountain of pastries, an ocean of caffeine, and the wisdom of their girl posse, including Charlie and her sister Anna. While some singer-songwriter murmured breathy, ironic lyrics and the coffee machine hissed, the three of them tried to jolly Rosie out of her lovesick funk.

Rosie slumped forward, head in her hands. "Cookies don't help."

"The hell you say." Anna chomped an oatmeal raisin bar.

Lana rubbed soothing circles on Rosie's back. "It's been nearly a week now. You should talk to him."

"And tell him what?"

Charlie scooted her chair closer. "Just be honest. Tell him how you feel."

"That's the problem—I don't know how I feel!" A headache poked the back of her eyeballs. Since last Thursday night, she must've shed a gallon of pointless tears, and for what? She deserved a boyfriend who cheered her victories, not a manager who put his job first—his temporary job, for Chrissakes—and put her feelings second. Eddie wasn't the guy she thought he was. Too bad she hadn't noticed that red flag before opening her heart like a damn barn door.

"Look," Anna said, "He definitely should've reacted better to your good news, but maybe you should cut him some slack. Not all guys are good with words. Just last week, Diego called me gordita."

Lana's jaw dropped.

"What did you do?" Rosie asked.

"Clobbered him with a pillow, called him a clueless mother-fucker, cried a little, then calmly explained that certain words are off-limits and why." Her eyes twinkled. "He groveled real nice."

Charlie wrinkled her nose. "I swear, you two are going to break that bed."

"The point is," Lana said, "you're miserable, Eddie's miserable, and you could fix this if you'd just talk to him."

"He's no good at talking about feelings. Neither am I."

"And how do we get better?" Lana sing-songed. "Say it with me, boys and girls. We praaaactice."

Charlie crossed her arms. "I'm with Rosie. Words don't mean shit. Actions do. Eddie needs to prove he supports you—your job, your feelings, everything."

Rosie's lip trembled. "What if it's my fault, though? What if I blurted three stupid words way too soon?"

"Hey." Lana squeezed her shoulder. "Number one, who's to say you guys gotta follow a timetable? Number two, if you really mean it, saying 'I love you' isn't stupid, it's brave."

Charlie took Rosie's hand. "If he's the right guy, he'll do what it takes to hang onto you. If he doesn't, then you can move on with a clear conscience. But you gotta give him a chance first."

Rosie shook her head. "I don't know. I keep coming back to how different we are. How could a strait-laced guy like Eddie and a wild child like me ever find our balance? Maybe the kindest thing to do is cut this off before we get hurt even more."

"Hmmph." Lana folded her arms. "Never thought my best

friend would turn out to be such a chicken."

Rosie threw up her hands. "Okay, okay! I'll talk to him tonight after work. Now pass me a fuckin' cookie."

"That's our girl." Charlie slid the tray across the table. "Now, tell us about your new boss. Is she scary?"

Rosie crunched into a frosted chocolate sugar cookie with rainbow sprinkles. "She's a total tattoo goddess. And the other two artists are women too. You know, I'd like to open a place like that someday. Just women artists. Customers won't have to wade through macho bullshit."

"Sign me up," Anna chirped. "I want my baby's name on my ankle. Or on my back?"

"Ankle hurts more." Rosie's glum mood lifted as her friends peppered her with questions about tattoos. There, at least, she knew what the hell she was doing. Maybe if she could keep her mind on work, this cloud of emotion would lift and let her see clearly again.

* * *

Under the pretense of checking supplies, Eddie ducked into Bangers' storage room and pulled out his notebook again. Since his Sunday pep talk from the guys, he'd been adding to his list of Rosie's fine qualities. Still stumped for hard evidence of his abject contrition, at least he had a list of things he found amazing about her.

His first draft was mostly filled with sensual details—the scent of her hair, the brush of her breath on his bare skin, the silky heft of her breasts, the hungry little moans she made when he kissed the inside of her thigh. But Rosie already knew she was a sex goddess. Any guy in the bar could tell her that. So he'd crossed those out and thought harder. Why was he so drawn to Rosie, so miserable without her? The more he pondered, the faster the ideas flowed: how she stood up to her family's narrow expectations and blazed her own path, her amazing artistic talent, her loyalty to friends, her confidence, her persistence, her dazzling smile, her kindness to his pushy mom...

He'd memorized them all like lines in a play. All the same, he tucked his notebook in his pocket, just in case her presence left him tongue-tied. Tonight, after work, he'd plead his case.

Trouble was, Rosie was nearly half an hour late. With River gone, monitoring timecards was his responsibility. His texts had gone unanswered—no surprise there. Dawn hadn't yet emerged from her office, but each minute that ticked by made it more likely she'd notice Rosie's absence. He could clock her in and make excuses, but that would be a betrayal of Dawn's trust. If he didn't, he was betraying Rosie.

Stomach churning, he returned to the bar. Trivia Night wouldn't start for another hour, but already the tables were filling up with thirsty customers. Laughter and conversation swelled over the bluesy wails from the speakers. Kiara was busy shaking up tonight's drink special, the Bangers Brawl—a lemony twist on a mint julep made with rye from a local distiller. Lana and Charlie hustled trays of burgers and tots. Gus filled beer glasses, sloshing foam everywhere. Still no Rosie.

Eddie nudged the old guy's shoulder. "Thanks, I'll take over."

Gus wiped his bulbous nose on his flannel sleeve. "Where's yer girlfriend, kiddo?"

Damned if I know. Or if she's even still my girlfriend.

Several minutes later, Rosie appeared at the server station, hair damp and disheveled, lips clamped in a thin line.

Eddie hurried to her. "Hey." He kept his voice low. "What happened? You okay?"

"I'm fine." Avoiding his gaze, she snatched a stack of cocktail napkins for her tray.

"You're late, though."

"Not my fault. I got here as fast as I could." Glowering, she adjusted the waist tie on her apron.

He peered closer. Her hands were shaking—with fury? At him?

"Come on, Rosie. I'm just trying to do my job here."

If looks could kill, he'd be a pile of smoldering ash. Through clenched jaws, she snapped, "I said. It wasn't. My fault."

"Whoa now." Dawn stepped up behind Rosie, her voice low and lethal. "What did I tell you two about relationship drama at work?"

Rosie sucked in a shaky breath and faced the boss. "I was just explaining to Eddie why I was late."

He spread his hands. "You didn't explain anything. You just—"

Jojo interrupted. "Someone to see you, Rosie." He pointed to the front door where a uniformed cop waited.

Rosie shot Eddie another glare over her shoulder as he trailed her through the crowd.

The cop held up her phone, its screen spiderwebbed with cracks. "Found it under that bozo's front tire."

Dawn joined them. "Problem, officer?"

The cop tipped his cap. "No problem, ma'am. Just returning Miss Rosie's phone."

"How'd it get broken?" Dawn asked.

"Nasty fender bender up by Taco Bell. Guy ran a red light."

Eddie's throat constricted. Here he was, jumping to conclusions like some paranoid jackrabbit, when the woman he loved was still shaking from a car crash. He clasped her shoulders. "Are you okay?"

She squeezed her eyes closed and nodded. "But my car's not."

"Fortunately, the guy who hit her has insurance." The cop pulled a card from his pocket and scribbled something on the back. "My cousin's body shop, down on South Tacoma Way. Tell him I sent you. He'll fix you up good."

"Thanks," Rosie whispered. A tear meandered down her cheek.

Eddie wrapped his arms around her and pulled her to his chest. It was like hugging a block of wood.

Dawn enclosed them both in a motherly hug. "Take her home, Eddie."

Rosie protested, "No, I'm fine, really. They checked me out at the collision site."

"You're shaking like a leaf. Go home." Dawn nudged them toward the back door.

"But Eddie—"

"Will come right back as soon as you're safely home. Won't you, Eddie?" It wasn't a question.

"Of course." His arm around Rosie, he navigated through the crowd. "Where's your car now?"

"They towed it to the Honda place." At her locker she wrapped up in her puffy coat, which did nothing to stop her shivering.

"You sure you don't want to see a doctor?"

184

"I'm not hurt. Just shook up." She trudged to the back door.

When they reached his car, he opened his passenger door, but she ignored his extended hand, dropped into her seat, and crossed her arms. "I can't believe you scolded me for being late."

He flapped his hands helplessly. "I didn't know. You didn't call."

"Hard to do when your phone is smashed." She swiped at her damp cheek.

"I was worried, okay? You haven't been answering my calls or texts. I didn't know what to think."

She whirled on him, jaw tight and eyes blazing. "A real friend wouldn't assume I was being irresponsible."

He pounded the steering wheel. The horn gave an anemic bleat. "I never said you were irresponsible, Ro, and I'm more than just your friend. I'm—"

Her gaze dropped to her hands, clasped tightly in her lap. "Please, just drive."

They rolled in silence through the sleet-slicked streets. When they got to her house, she sat staring dully through the windshield. "Thank you, Eddie."

Barely controlling the urge to scream or weep or kiss her—all at once, maybe—he reached for her hand. "I love you, Rosie. Please don't shut me out."

She pinched the bridge of her nose. "I can't have this conversation now. I'm too shook up."

"Okay." Now his voice was shaking too. "Whenever you're ready."

No response.

"Are you still coming to the wedding?" *Idiot! Haven't you shoved your foot far enough down your throat tonight?*

She leveled him with a dead-eyed stare. "If the boss gives me time off."

He flinched as if she'd slapped him.

Her breath whooshed out. "Hey, I'm sorry. Of course I'll come to the wedding." Her mouth twitched in a pale shadow of a smile. "It'll be fun, right?"

Somehow, he doubted that very much.

Chapter Sixteen

Eddie pulled into the parking lot outside the Seattle hotel where his cousin's wedding reception would start in—he checked the dashboard clock—fifteen minutes. Fifteen awkward, silent, prickly minutes. Rosie had maintained near-silence on the ride up and during the ceremony, thawing only to greet his parents and grandparents.

He reached for her hand. Might as well be holding a dead fish.

"I really appreciate your coming today, Ro."

"I said I'd come, and I keep my promises." Her gaze flicked to his, then darted away.

"So do I." He laced his fingers through hers. "Please, babe, help me understand what I did wrong so I can make it right. I love you."

With a groan, Rosie closed her eyes and let her head thunk back against the headrest. "That's the problem, right there."

He twisted in his seat, grunting in frustration as the seatbelt locked him in. "Fucker." He punched the button, and it thwacked against the door frame. "*What* is the problem? Explain it to me like the idiot I clearly am."

She rolled her head toward him and opened her misty, weary eyes. "Love. The word that caused this mess."

His stomach dropped like a runaway elevator. "You changed your mind?"

"No, I—it just slipped out. That's my problem, blurting out my thoughts. It was way too soon to tell you that." A tear trickled down her cheek.

"You didn't mean it?"

She swiped her damp cheek with the back of her hand. "I care about you, Eddie, and I think you're a great person, but maybe we're confusing sex with love. I mean, the sex is beyond amazing, and I like spending time with you, but we hardly know each other." She raised her teary gaze to his. "Saying the big L word sets up expectations, you know? I expected you to know what I needed. But you didn't, and that really hurt." She shrugged and spread her hands. "My head knows this clusterfuck is my own fault, but my gut is still tied up in knots."

Damn it, why did they have to tackle this conversation now, in a rapidly-filling parking lot? A trio of bridesmaids in fluttering pastel dresses shrieked with laughter as they passed.

"Ro, I'd do anything to turn back the clock and say the right thing. It's just—" He scraped a palm down his face. "Dawn trusting me to take over for River is a huge deal. I'm terrified of screwing it up. I was obsessing about that when I should've been listening to you."

"You'll do great, Eddie." She dabbed her eyes with a crumpled tissue. "You're smart and organized and logical.

You have everything you need."

He clasped her hand and pressed it to his heart. "Rosie, I don't want to break up with you. We were just getting started. Everything was so good between us."

"But you wouldn't have said I love you after just a few weeks. You'd have waited, like a person who has sense."

"Maybe, but only because I was scared. I would've dithered for God knows how long. Should I tell her? Does she want me to say it first? Are we still just friends? I was a coward, but you were brave and honest and real. Don't ever regret that." He kissed her clenched knuckles. He couldn't lose her. Not over a few clumsy words. Life couldn't possibly be that unfair.

"We don't fit, Eddie." She gazed out through the sleet pattering his windshield. "I knew that from the beginning, but I ignored it. You're a planner, a step-by-step guy. An ant."

"I'm a what?"

"You know that fable about the ant and the grasshopper? You're gonna be a success, I know it. But me, I'm a—" She made a sound somewhere between a giggle and a hiccup. "A fuckin' bumble bee, fat and clumsy."

How could she think he was hung up on her size, after the way he'd worshiped her lush body? No one with eyeballs and half a brain could deny her allure. "Rosie, you're the most gorgeous woman who ever breathed. There isn't a minute we're together when I don't want to undress you and taste every glorious inch of your skin."

She squeezed his hand. "Thank you, Eddie, but I'm talking about my personality, not my body. I'm such a bumbler, you know? Sometimes I land somewhere soft and sweet, like your bed. Sometimes I bonk into things—or people—and inflict pain." She shook her head so hard a sparkly hair pin dropped

189

into her satin-covered lap.

"Rosie, you're wrong." He cupped her cheek until she met his gaze with tear-bright eyes. "You fit me perfectly. With you at my side I feel brave and smart and sure. Every couple hits speed bumps like this, and I know we can work through it if we just—"

A rap on the window made them both jump. His parents stood there, Dad scowling at his oversize gold watch, Mama beaming, oblivious to the drama. "Come on, you two lovebirds. Don't want to miss the open bar."

He cracked the window. "We'll be there in just a moment."

"Come on, Alina," Dad grumbled. "They're kissing. Let them be."

Mama's giggle trailed behind her. "Remember when you used to kiss me like that?"

The irony curdled his stomach. Here they were at a wedding, a celebration of lasting love. Watching his cousin and her fiancé exchange vows, he imagined himself and Rosie at the altar, her in a frothy white gown that hugged her curves, him in a snazzy tux. And now she was pulling away.

He pulled his key from the ignition, then paused. "Should I just take you home?"

"No." With her soggy tissue, she blotted the smudges beneath her eyes. "I said I'd stick with you through the wedding, and I will." She squeezed his hand. "Let's try to have fun."

"And afterward?"

She didn't answer—just popped out of her seat, squared her shoulders, and waited for him. Arm in arm, they slogged through the slush toward the twinkling ballroom.

Ballroom, gloom, doom. He couldn't even get drunk to ease

the pain, since he was Rosie's ride home. This was going to be a nightmare.

His hand on the small of Rosie's back, Eddie paused in the ballroom doorway. Cousin Irina and her proud parents had pulled out all the stops. A bazillion twinkle lights fluttered overhead and from bundles of gold-painted twigs in tall white urns.

As they passed, Rosie bopped a cluster of pale pink heart-shaped balloons and muttered, "Looks like the sparkly love child of Winter Wonderland and Valentine's Day."

His aunt beckoned them toward a seating chart on an easel. "Eduard, sweetheart, how big and handsome you've grown!" She clutched his shoulders and pecked his cheeks. "Introduce me to your lady love."

A grimace flicked over Rosie's face. She extended her hand. "Hi, I'm Rosie Chu, Eddie's friend from work."

Might as well stab me with an icicle.

The woman winked. "Just a work friend? That's not what Alina tells me." She enveloped Rosie in a tight hug. "I'm Auntie Anna. Welcome to the family, darling."

Anna pointed them toward a round table tightly packed with gold-rimmed place settings and scattered with heart-shaped confetti. There was no way he and Rosie could continue their discussion, or even eat without getting jabbed by relatives' elbows.

As they wove through the crowd, Eddie whispered, "So we're back to fake dating again?"

She looped her purse handle over her assigned chair. "We'll talk later, okay? We're here to put on a show and keep your family off your back."

He grabbed her hand. "Rosie, there's nothing fake about my

feelings for you. Don't shut me out."

The smile she flashed him was wide and phony and just this side of feral. "We'll. Talk. Later."

"Okay, okay." Time for a tactical retreat, but there was no way he would surrender this battle. "You want a drink?"

"Several."

While they waited at the bar, Rosie fielded introductions with the same playful warmth she showed customers at Bangers. Damn, she was a good actor, looping her arm through Eddie's and gracefully dancing around nosy questions.

"How long have you two been together?"

"We've known each other about a year."

True, and I've wanted you every single day of that year.

"How did you meet?"

"At work. Eddie's the new assistant manager." She pecked his cheek.

Yeah, for two weeks. If she kept this up, he'd have even more embarrassing questions to answer when he reverted to plain old barback.

His cousin Eva, always good for a few laughs, nudged him with her hip and pointed her chin toward the bar. "Could they be any slower? You should step in there and crank out some drinks before we all die of thirst."

"Right?" Rosie wound her arm around Eddie's waist. "We should've brought a flask."

Eva grinned. "I like this one, Eddie. Glad to see your taste in women is improving." She stuck out her hand. "Eva Petrov, black sheep of the family."

Eva's fishnet stockings and sparkly high-heeled sneakers were nothing compared to Rosie's abundant ink and sapphire hair. Even in a simple satin dress, she outshone every woman in the room.

She chuckled. "Rosie Chu. I'm Eddie's—" She turned to him, and her smile faltered. "You know, special friend."

"Gotcha." Eva clapped her shoulder. "Stop by our table later. I stuffed my purse with mini bottles."

At last, it was their turn at the bar, where they picked up tumblers of the bride's "signature cocktail," a bright pink, too-sweet mixture with lots of vodka and a spear of booze-soaked Rainier cherries.

Rosie took a sip and grimaced. "Wow. Maybe don't add this one to your menu." She nibbled a cherry, and his poor, clueless dick throbbed. "These are killer, though."

He gulped his drink, relishing the burn of alcohol. Maybe with enough vodka, he could get through this. Or maybe he'd melt into a puddle of tears at Rosie's feet. Either possibility sounded better than this prickly standoff.

Of course, on a day when Lady Luck decided to shit on him, he and Rosie were seated at the same table as his parents. Thank God, Uncle Pete was there too. At least they'd have someone fun to talk to.

"Hey, kiddo, good to see ya." Pete rose from his seat and thumped Eddie on the back. His favorite uncle had the same wiry physique that made most Volkov men look like plucked chickens, but on him it looked suave and elegant. Must be the expensive pinstriped suit. "And who is this ravishing creature?"

She giggled. "Hi. I'm Rosie."

Pete grasped her hand and gave her knuckles an air kiss. "Piotr Volkov at your service, dear lady. Meet my husband Bruno."

Looking GQ sharp in a sleek black suit, Bruno murmured greetings in his thick Italian accent.

Rosie fanned her cleavage. "My stars, Eddie, you didn't tell me there were so many gorgeous men in your family. I thought it was just you."

Was that twinkle in her eye just for show? Nothing he could do about it now, so he might as well play along. "Let's sit here." He switched the place cards so he and Rosie sat next to Pete and Bruno. Aunt Lada and Uncle Ivan could fend for themselves.

Pete rapped his knuckles on the table. "Tell me, young one, what is new with you?" He twinkled at Rosie. "Besides this bit of extraordinary good fortune."

Rosie took another healthy swig from her pink drink. "Eddie got a promotion. He's going to be the most excellent bar manager, don't you think?"

"Is that so? Tell me, Eddie."

She wobbled a little as she leaned across him. Should've taken her home when he had the chance. Better to beg off with some lame excuse about his date being sick than to have her spill his plans. The way the family grapevine worked, his parents would know in seconds. He threw a panicked glance around the ballroom, but they were nowhere in sight.

"It's just a temporary thing," he told his uncle. "I'm filling in for someone."

Just then, Cousin Eva trotted over with her girlfriend in tow. "Eddie, the DJ's taking requests for later. Come help us."

Zelda wheeled, "Pleeease. Otherwise, it's gonna be nothing but Sinatra and the Electric Slide." She patted Eva's rump. "Hey, did you know that song's about a vibrator?"

Eva clapped her hand over her mouth. "That's Babka's

favorite song! Do you think—"

Pete spoke up. "Now now, Eddie just sat down. Give us a minute to catch up."

"I'll go." Rosie popped out of her chair, smooched the top of Eddie's head, and trotted after the other two girls.

Bruno cocked an eyebrow. "She seems fun. Another drink, love?"

"Please." Pete nodded his head toward Eddie.

"Vodka rocks." If he didn't have to drive home later, he'd ask for the whole damn bottle.

Bruno patted his shoulder and left him alone with Pete. The youngest of his dad's brothers, he was yet another black sheep, having gone into family law instead of something more useful to the dry cleaning business.

Pete regarded Eddie over tented fingers. "You look like you're about to explode. What ails you, son?"

"What doesn't?" He dropped his head into his hands.

"Love troubles?"

"Big time." He huffed a sigh. "And work stuff too."

"Are they connected?"

Uncle Pete always saw right to the heart of the matter. "Yeah." He glanced around—still no sign of his parents. "If I tell you something, will you swear to keep it to yourself?"

"Sure." His broad hand dropped over Eddie's. "You in trouble?"

"I will be." He scooted his chair closer and, in a voice too low to be heard beyond their table, spilled it all—the vision board, the notebook, the dream of running his own bar.

"Well now," Pete stroked his thick mustache. "Sounds like a solid plan."

"Only two problems. No money, and my parents. They

expect me to take over their shop."

"Now?"

"Eventually. There's no way I can do both. I mean, I'm young and single, and already I'm exhausted at the end of the day. How am I going to handle two businesses and a family of my own? It's impossible."

"Not to mention soul-sucking." Pete chuckled. "I should know. After a couple years dealing with the family's business contracts—not my specialty at all—I finally told Pops I was through. And you know what? He got over it."

"Really? I thought you were kind of, you know—"

"An outcast? That didn't last long. Some of the oldsters still look at me funny, but that's more about Bruno than leaving the family business." He adopted a thick Russian accent. "How could he marry an Italian?" He chuckled. "This clan is big on tradition, but they're not heartless. Besides—a Russian themed bar with vodka and dumplings? That's brilliant."

"If I can ever get enough start-up capital."

Pete tapped his lips. "Can I tell Bruno about this? He might have some ideas."

Eddie nodded.

"When you're ready to tell your parents, give me a call. Vadim can be stubborn, but he has a soft spot for his baby brother."

He grinned. "I will. Thanks." Why hadn't he asked Pete's advice before? Caught up in worry about disappointing his parents, he forgot that Pete had already done the same thing and survived. All it took was helping a niece through her nasty divorce, and suddenly the fam saw the benefit of his specialty. Maybe they'd see his bar the same way.

Where the hell was Rosie? She'd left with Eva twenty

minutes ago. He stood to peer into the crowd and found her arm in arm with Babka, heading his way. Babka patted her hand and said something that pulled a hair-tossing, boob-shaking laugh from Rosie. Longing stabbed him right in the gut.

This couldn't be the end of the road for them. What's the point of all his plans if his nose-to-the-grindstone blinders cost him that laugh, that smile, that warm, soft body? This past week apart left him jittery, sleep-deprived, and so lonely he ached.

Just like one of his mom's chick flics—the lead couple breaks up at a wedding. How does the hero win her back? Serenade her? God no, she'd cover her ears and run for the exit. He was a crappy dancer too, but he'd spin her on the dance floor all night if that'd bring back her smile. Maybe he should grab the mic and declare his undying love. Nope, stupid idea. Already so nervous about love that she called it "the big L word," a public declaration would freak her out for sure.

With Rosie in tow, Babka reached their table and smacked Eddie's hand. "Eduard, stop chewing your paw like a mangy mutt."

He noticed the blood welling from his thumb. Great, now he was regressing to nervous habits from his childhood.

Without the tiniest flinch, Rosie grabbed the napkin from his place setting and wrapped it around the bloody digit. Her hair brushed his cheek as she whispered, "Pretty sure they're feeding us tonight. No need to resort to cannibalism."

He groaned, cheeks roasting. "I'd apologize, but it doesn't seem to make any difference."

"So dramatic." She clucked her tongue. "I'm still on your side, Eddie."

His mom bustled over, her lace jacket flapping. "The bride and groom are here. Let's go."

Rosie slid her arm through his, and they followed his parents and grandparents to the reception line. After greeting the newlyweds, along with their parents, stepparents, and more bridesmaids and groomsmen that he could possibly remember, they returned to their now-full table for frou-frou salads, chicken Kiev, and roasted potatoes. Rosie chatted amiably with his aunt and uncle to her left, gamely explaining the significance of her visible tattoos. The thought of the ones hidden under her clothing made him want to bite through his plate.

"Eddie, what is wrong with you?" Mama squinted. "This is good food. You got a stomachache?"

"Let the boy alone," Dad admonished, his dark brows rumpled. "He's grown. He knows if he's hungry or not."

Rosie bumped his knee under the table. "Must be all those canapes we had during cocktail hour."

Liar. They hadn't been near the hors d'oeuvre table. If she was still pissed at him, why was she running interference?

He nodded. "Yeah, those shrimp toasts were delicious."

"Shrimp toasts?" His uncle Leo scowled. "I didn't see no shrimp toasts."

Aunt Anna poked him. "Dorogóy, shrimp gives you hives."

Leo puffed out his chest. "Still, I would like to have the choice. Always so cheap at these things—one platter of the good appetizers, then it's cheese and crackers. I tell you, these young people today…"

While the older ones squabbled, Eddie lowered his voice. "You don't have to cover for me, Ro."

"Don't I?" She smiled sweetly. "I thought that was the whole point."

Pressure built behind his forehead, the first throb of what promised to be a killer headache. "A month ago, yeah. Now, everything's changed. I told you—"

Mom clapped her hands. "Hush, everyone. Time for speeches."

Who needs a wedding planner when you have General Alina Volkov?

At the head table, the bride's father tapped his glass with his spoon, and the room stilled for a string of maudlin speeches. By the time the best man finished his tribute, the whole crowd was sniffling. Beneath the table, Rosie clasped Eddie's hand.

He grinned in relief. Maybe all this lovey-dovey mush had softened her up enough that she'd listen to his pleas with an open heart.

His mom stood, raised her wine glass, and shouted, "Gorka!" Everyone joined in, except Rosie, who shot him a quizzical frown.

"It means the wine is bitter," he explained. "They have to make it sweet by kissing."

"Awww." She leaned against his shoulder.

Warmth spread through his chest. The wedding had worked its magic. It was all going to be okay.

The first dance came next, and Cousin Irina was a good sport when her tipsy groom's attempt at a romantic dip nearly dropped her on her ass. After the father-daughter, mother-son dance, guests flooded the dance floor.

Rosie nudged his shoulder. "We gonna do this?"

"Absolutely." Faking confidence he didn't feel, he led her into the throng. Thank God the floor was too packed to do more than sway in a circle. Rosie held herself stiffly at first, but as Sinatra gave way to John Legend, she sighed and relaxed into his hold, her soft breasts pressed to his chest, her fingers toying with the hair at his nape. Fortunately, his jacket was long enough to hide his erection from his grandparents, who danced just inches away. Babka reached out and patted his shoulder, her eyes misty. "You two look perfect together. I hope I am still alive to dance at your wedding."

Dedka chuckled. "She means don't wait too long."

"Is it so wrong for me to want great-grandchildren? My sister already has three."

Rosie thunked her forehead against his and whispered, "Damn, Eddie. At least my family isn't pressuring me to have kids." She gave a dry chuckle. "They probably don't think I could handle them."

"Nah, you'd be a great mom."

When her eyes bugged, he added, "I mean, someday. In the future. If you want to." He scraped a palm down his clammy face. "Sorry. Just stupid wedding talk."

"Yeah, all this happily-ever-after bullshit can fry your brain."

So much for softening her up. He stroked his forefinger down her bare arm. "Hey, any chance we could find a quiet corner and talk?"

Before she could answer, the DJ bellowed into the mic, "Game time!"

Babka grabbed Rosie's arm. "You come with me, sweetheart. This will be fun."

"But I—"

"Go play." Dedka flapped his hand toward the growing line of women along one side of the dance floor. "Eduard and I need to talk. Vadim, where are you hiding?"

Chapter Sixteen

* * *

Eddie's grandmother tugged Rosie to the side of the dance floor where his mom beckoned, bouncing on her toes like a giddy tween. "Oh, this is perfect. What part of Rosie should we give him?"

Her eyebrows shot sky-high. "I beg your pardon?"

"It's just a game," Alina assured her. "They blindfold the groom, then he has to identify his bride by touch. It's hilarious."

"So, a grope-athon."

"Don't be silly." Babka patted her hand. "You don't have to give him your boobs. Besides, that would be a dead giveaway. The bride is flat as a pancake."

"Mama Volkov!" Alina burst into giggles. "It's okay, Rosie. You just take his hand and put it wherever you like. But it would be hilarious if—"

Rosie rolled her eyes. *The things I do for you, Eddie.* But really, she was having a good time. Eddie's extended family were jolly and welcoming. So far, no one had openly ogled her tattoos.

"Here he comes!" The best man led the wobbly, blindfolded groom to the first woman in line, a sixty-something lady with a bosom like the prow of a ship, who took his extended hand and slapped it right onto her boob.

The groom gave her a squeeze, then recoiled in mock horror. "Madam! I'm a married man."

The room echoed with laughter.

"See?" Babka elbowed her. "It's fun!"

While she waited for her turn, she searched the ballroom for

Eddie. There he was, back at their table seated between his dad and granddad. Both older men leaned in close, gesticulating and talking rapidly. Eddie looked pale, answering in staccato nods. Probably grilling him about some picky detail of the dry-cleaning business. Was he ever going to tell them his plans? The longer he waited, the harder they'd take it.

Eddie glanced up and gave her a sickly half-smile. She mouthed, "Tell them." He gave his head a sharp shake. Didn't he realize this was the perfect chance? His parents would never flip out in front of all their relatives.

She gave herself a mental smack. *It's not like his future will impact me. We're on totally different paths.*

When the groom stepped in front of her, Rosie placed his hand on her waist. It slid down to her hip. "Mmm, nice," he purred.

A bridesmaid clucked her tongue. "Boy, you are in trouble."

The groom leaned in and took a big sniff. "Nope, wrong perfume. Sorry, miss." He threw his head back and wailed, "Rina, where are you? They've kidnapped my bride."

Once the bride had been identified and claimed with a dramatic movie kiss, Alina pulled Rosie aside. "Let's get a drink, dear."

"Actually, I think I'll have a water."

"Nonsense. It's a wedding." Alina towed her to the bar and ordered two champagne cocktails. She plopped into a seat at an empty table. "I want your advice. About Eddie."

Rosie sat beside her. "I'll help if I can, but I don't know him all that well."

When Alina raised an eyebrow, she added, "I mean, we've only been dating for…" She counted on her fingers.

"Five weeks." Alina nodded. "Plenty of time if you're in love.

So tell me, what is up with my son?"

Her pulse skipped, then sped. "Er—what do you mean?"

"Lately, at work, he seems distant, glum, bored. Has he told you why?"

Rosie's mouth went Sahara-dry. "Why would he tell me?"

Alina patted her hand. "It's okay, Rosie. When he was younger, my Eddie would tell me everything." She tapped her temple. "I could always tell when he was lying, so he didn't try to fool me. Now—" She shrugged. "He is grown. It's normal for a young man to share secrets with his sweetheart instead of his mama. But I can't help worrying. The business will be his soon, and he doesn't seem to care."

"Soon?"

Alina beckoned Rosie close enough to smell her Shalimar perfume and boozy breath. "We haven't told Eddie yet because we don't want to worry him, but we can't put it off much longer. So I need your help."

Her throat tightened, turning her voice to a squeak. "Why me?"

"When Eddie's with you, he lights up like Christmas. You two are like those—oh, what do they call the little parrots that cuddle all the time?"

"Lovebirds?"

"Exactly." Alina grinned. "Just now, on the dance floor—" Her gaze grew misty. "Vadim and I used to dance like that. Every Friday night, he would take me—" She sighed and gulped her drink. "No matter. These days, my husband is in too much pain to dance. Or to work."

"Oh no, is he ill?" That would explain Mr. Volkov's serious, frowny demeanor.

"His back. All those years of lifting heavy clothes." She

pantomimed hooking hangers onto an overhead rack. "And his blood pressure is very high. The doctor can't find the right medicine. She says it's time for him to retire. If he doesn't—" Her voice wobbled. "It's time for Eduard to step into his father's shoes."

Rosie's chest ached. All Eddie's plans, all the work and hope he'd put into his dream bar, flushed away. He'd never stand up for himself now—how could he, as devoted as he was to his family? His parents were dooming him to a lifetime of frustration and regret. He'd end up a bitter, withered old man with a bad back and probably cancer from the dry-cleaning chemicals.

She swallowed a spiky lump. "What if—now, don't freak out—what if he has other plans?"

Alina's eyes narrowed. "What do you mean, other plans? He's been training his whole life to take over the family business."

"Have you ever asked him, though?"

"Pffsht." Alina waved away the suggestion. "Why ask when the answer is obvious?"

"Here's the thing." *Don't fuck this up don't fuck this up don't...* "In my family, it's just assumed that everyone will go to college and become a professional. You know, like my grandparents are dentists and my mom's a teacher and my cousins are MBAs and CPAs." *You're blathering. Rein it in.* "I didn't want to let them down, but I hated college."

"And?" Alina folded her arms across her chest.

"Telling my mom I was dropping out was really hard. She was disappointed, but she understood, and I'm so grateful."

Alina's lips pursed. "Are you telling me my boy wants to make tattoos now?"

"No! It's just—" She raked her fingers into her hair, dislodging her stiffly sprayed updo. "You want him to be happy, right?"

"Of course we want that." Lips clamped tight, Alina rose. "What could make him happier than his own business? He'll have security and respect and..." She started across the dance floor, marching between dancing couples like a pissed-off, tipsy little general.

Hobbled by her tight skirt, Rosie hustled after her. "Alina, wait."

As they closed on their table, Eddie glanced up, his face bloodless, his lips pinched tight. Her heart plummeted. His dad must've just dropped the bomb. If she'd been at his side holding his hand like the friend she should be, he might've found the strength to tell his parents the truth.

Alina's sharp voice drew stares from the other tables. "Eduard Stanislav Volkov, what is this nonsense? You want to make tattoos now?"

Eddie's brow rumpled as he glanced from his wobbly mother to Rosie and back. "What? Ro, did you—"

She raised both palms. "I swear, I didn't—"

"Don't change the subject." Alina finger-stabbed her son's chest. "You've been scheming, the two of you." She whirled on her red-faced husband. "Don't be so judgmental, you tell me. Just because she has tattoos everywhere doesn't mean she's not right for our Eddie. Now look what happens. She's poisoned his mind against us."

Eddie grasped his mother's shoulders, urging her into a chair. "Ma, take it easy. What's got you so upset?"

More finger stabbing. "She tells me you don't want to take over for Dad and me. Now Dad will work himself into his grave and I'll die old and alone…" Her words trailed off into a wail.

Eddie's brows snapped together. "You told her?"

"I didn't! I just said she should ask you what you want, and—"

"Holy shit, Rosie!" He turned his back and gnarled his fingers into his hair as if snatching himself bald would help make sense of this.

"Tell me what?" Alina insisted. "What didn't she tell me?"

A new voice joined the chorus. "Hey now, let's just all simmer down." Arms spread wide, Uncle Pete stepped up, gathered Rosie and Eddie to his chest, and murmured through clenched jaws, "What in holy hell is this about?"

Eddie snarled, "Rosie told Ma about my bar."

"I didn't," she hissed back.

"Then why is she freaking out?" He could crack a walnut between those eyebrows.

"Let's take this outside." Pete shepherded them toward the lobby, calling over his shoulder to Bruno, "Get Alina some tea, would you, darling?"

In the quiet hallway, Pete deposited them both in plush armchairs. "Now, you want me to stay and referee?"

Eddie shook his head before dropping it into his hands. "Could you check on my parents?"

"Of course." He withdrew, leaving them with just a potted fake palm between them—hardly enough protection from Eddie's simmering rage.

Finally, he raised his red-rimmed eyes to hers. "What did you say?" His voice rasped like a rusty saw.

"Now, just calm down. Your mom—"

He shot to his feet. "Calm down? Are you serious?"

206

She clutched the arms of her chair. "Your mom's worried about you. Said you've been moping at work and you don't seem to care about the shop."

"That's what Dad said. And Dedka. So what?"

"Damn it, Eddie, you waited too long. You should've told your parents."

"I was going to tell them when the time was right. I've been building my plan, gathering all the details I need to convince them." He sank into his chair again, his eyes dull. Defeated. "You stole that chance from me."

She had to force the words past an ache in her throat. "I didn't tell her about the bar, Eddie. I just told her she should talk to you before deciding your future. Your dad—"

"Enough." He pushed to his feet with the heaviness of a much older man. "I have to go clean up the wreckage." He trudged toward the ballroom, then turned in the doorway. "Don't try to help, Rosie."

A sob doubled her over. Clutching her knees, she rocked back and forth. Ruined. All of it—thanks to her big, fat, blurty mouth and Eddie's stupid secret keeping. She'd been right from the start. They didn't fit. They never would.

She didn't know how much time passed before two pair of shiny loafers appeared before her. She glanced up to find Uncle Pete and Bruno holding her coat and purse.

"Did he tell them?"

"He's working on it." Pete knelt and patted her shoulder. "We got the DJ to turn up the music and drown out the yelling."

Still wracked by sobs, she choked out, "I swear, I was only trying to help."

"I'm sure you were, hon." Pete's dark eyes, so like his nephew's, shone with sympathy. "Sometimes a person has to hit the wall before they change course."

Bruno chuckled and smacked a fist into his palm. "Bam."

"Poor Eddie. Now he has no one on his side." She shook her head. "He's trapped."

"He'll figure it out. Do you want us to take you home?"

"No." She'd caused enough damage—Eddie was right about that. "My sister lives in Seattle. I'll call her."

"We'll wait here until you're sure."

Amara was not pleased—of course she and David had plans on a Saturday night. But she told Rosie where to find a spare key. Ten minutes later, her Uber driver pulled up. She thanked Pete and Bruno, wrapped up in her coat, and stumbled out into the icy night.

Chapter Seventeen

It was past midnight when the front door of David and Amara's apartment clicked open, throwing a beam of light from the hall right into Rosie's bleary, swollen eyes. For hours she lay shivering on her sister's leather couch, aching and wrung out. Sleep eluded her as, over and over, the memory of Eddie's devastated expression triggered fresh waves of tears.

She tugged the throw blanket over her head and groaned. "Why is that so bright?"

Amara clucked her tongue. "Hung over again?"

"No." This headache was the product of heartbreak, not booze.

She heard the thunk of Amara's shoes hitting the floor, then the soft pad of her sister's feet on the carpet. The couch cushions sagged.

"Hey." Amara lifted the blanket and peered beneath. "You okay?"

Rosie shook her head. Except for their dad's death, she'd

never been further from okay. Echoes of that shock buzzed in her bones. The same feeling of "How could this be true?" Just a few hours ago, they were on the road to reconciliation—Eddie's arms around her, his soft hair tickling her cheek as they danced.

But that wasn't really true, was it? Nothing had been right since the night Eddie under-reacted to her good news and she over-reacted to her disappointment. Like a runaway snowball, hurt feelings layered upon hurt feelings until the final icy crash.

She clutched the blanket to her cheek. "Eddie broke up with me."

"At a wedding?" Amara's eyes flashed. "What an asshole."

"He had his reasons." She sniffled hard. "I blew it, Am." She spluttered into another round of ugly, snotty sobs. She ought to be wrung dry by now, but the tears kept coming.

"Hey now." Amara pulled Rosie's head onto her lap and stroked her hair.

David's voice came from the kitchen. "I'll make you some tea." In this big, open-plan apartment with its wall of windows overlooking Lake Washington, he was bound to hear their every comment. Rosie was beyond caring. Might as well walk the streets of Seattle wearing a sandwich board sign: *I had a good thing, and I fucked it up.*

A moment later, David set down a tray holding a white ceramic teapot painted with blue peonies, along with cups and a plate of shortbread cookies. "Sorry you're hurting, Rosie."

"Thanks, David. You're a peach."

He rubbed the back of his neck, just like Eddie would've done. "Yeah, well, I'll go make up the guest bed." He dropped a kiss on Amara's head and left.

"He's a keeper." Rosie pushed upright and reached for the tea.

Amara gently swatted her hand. "I'll pour. You're too shaky."

"Pretty tea set. From Maa Maa Chu?"

"Of course." Her sister handed her a cup of lemon-scented tea. "When you move out, she'll give you the whole kit too—tea stuff, noodle bowls, and those soup spoons we liked when we were little, tablecloth, mah-jongg set..."

"You know how to play mah-jongg?"

"Nope. Don't tell Maa Maa." She put two cookies on a plate and set it on Rosie's lap. "You look really pretty, by the way. Except for the smeared makeup and the mashed hair."

"And the ugly-cry face." She chuckled through her tears. "I'm a zombie in a party dress."

Amara nudged a box of tissues toward her. "So, spill."

Fortified with tea and sugar, Rosie launched into the whole, pathetic tale.

When she finished, Amara pinched the bridge of her nose. "What a clusterfuck. What'll you do now?"

Rosie shrugged. "Nothing I can do except leave him alone." She clutched a throw pillow to her stomach. "And now he's my boss."

"What?" Amara's eyebrows flew up.

"Just for a few weeks, until River gets back from his fishing trip."

"You lead a complicated life, sis." Amara patted her knee. "Fishermen and tattooed oranges and vindictive Russian dry cleaners. Sure you don't want to come work for David's dad?"

"Thanks, but no. I worked too hard to get this apprenticeship, and I really like Magda. I'll just have to suck it up and make nice at the bar until this blows over." A sickening thought struck her—would Eddie have to give up his job at Bangers? Running the dry cleaners full-time would take up all his energy. Better that way for her, but he relied on their work family too. He'd be bereft without them.

David stepped out from the hallway and cleared his throat. "Babe, I can't find the pillowcases."

"Probably in the laundry room. I'll get them."

David sat down in her place. "You feeling better?"

"Nope." She leaned her head onto his shoulder. "Thanks for letting me stay. I hope you didn't cut your evening short."

"Nah, the party was dull anyway." He gave her a brotherly side-hug. "And you're always welcome. So, you need me to beat this guy up?"

The idea of pale, lanky David taking on Eddie coaxed a smile to her lips. He might be taller, but Eddie would have his pasty ass on the ground in no time.

"That's okay." She leaned onto his shoulder. "We didn't really fit anyway. I guess I knew that from the start."

"Hey." He squeezed her shoulder. "If he doesn't appreciate you, fuck him."

She groaned. "I don't think he wants to anymore."

"Oh, honey. You're a sexy she-beast." He threw a glance over his shoulder. "Don't tell your sister I said so, but seriously, if that guy—what's his name?"

"Eddie."

"Hmph. If Eddie doesn't see your beauty, he's an idiot."

"My looks aren't the problem. It's more like a difference in philosophy." She drew her knees to her chest. "Like, what's the right thing to do—pursue your own dreams, or sacrifice for your family?"

David put his feet up on the coffee table. "That opposites

attract stuff doesn't always work out in real life. It helps if you're on the same page most of the time."

"And we're not even in the same book."

"For what it's worth, I used to feel that way about Amara. It's hard to partner up with someone so bright and quick. Feels like I'm always lagging behind. Sometimes I still wonder what she sees in me."

She snuffled into a tissue. "Yeah, that's how I feel about Eddie."

David nudged her with his shoulder "Maybe that's how he feels about you. You're a live wire, Rosie. You know what you want and what you're worth. I feel sorry for anyone who tries to stop you."

"Room's all ready, Rosie." Amara stepped up holding a balding plush Basset hound. "You can sleep with Floppy tonight."

"You still have Floppy?" Rosie jumped up and hugged the one-eyed, well-loved toy to her chest. "I haven't thought about him in years." Back in their grade school days, she and Amara would argue over whose doggy he was, sneaking into each other's rooms to pilfer him during the night.

"Yeah, well, some things you hang onto. I'm sure he misses you."

Feeling very much like a tear-drunk eight-year-old, she cuddled her old friend and let her little sister tuck her into bed.

Amara patted her hair. "We'll go out for chicken and waffles in the morning. Good for hangovers and breakups."

Rosie grabbed her hand and kissed it. "You're the best, Am. Thank you."

"Yeah, well, you were there for me when Justin Kovic broke

my heart in seventh grade. I owe you." She turned out the light, then paused in the doorway. "Maybe I'll even let you give me a tattoo."

* * *

Kiara's voice cut through the rowdy crowd's din. "Eddie, we need more Pirate Punch."

Jittery under the press of impatient, thirsty patrons, Eddie glanced again at River's laminated recipe card. "Four ounces white rum, four ounces spiced rum..." He hollered across the bar, "Jojo, we're outta rum."

"Can't." Jojo hollered back from his stool at the entrance. "Checkin' IDs."

"On it." Gus wiped his beer-sticky hands and shuffled toward the storage room—at a snail's pace.

Eddie covered his sweaty face with his bar towel and let out a muffled scream. He figured there'd be less interest in Bangers' Superbowl Party after the Seahawks got knocked out of the playoffs, but fans packed in so tightly Dawn had to count heads and make sure they didn't exceed the fire marshal's limit. He'd been here since nine that morning, stringing up twinkle lights and balloons in team colors—the perfect excuse to delay a much-needed truth session with his parents. Last night his mom was simply too drunk and hysterical to listen to reason. They were still asleep when he slipped out, and though he half-expected his mother to storm in during the game, he'd heard nothing from them so far.

He and Kiara had scrounged River's file of cocktail recipes

for tonight's offerings, a fruity rum punch for the Tampa Bay Buccaneers and a cider and rye concoction called the Buffalo Bill. They hadn't counted on how thirsty the crowd would be.

Might as well double up. He dumped cranberry juice, pineapple juice, and orange juice into twin pitchers, measured in Amaretto, then made sure the garnish trays were loaded with cherries, oranges, and pineapple chunks. Passing with a basket of prizes for the Pick 'Em game, Dawn slapped the bar with her palm. "What's the hold-up, kiddo?"

"Gus is getting more rum."

She rolled her eyes. "He's probably back there sampling the bottles. I swear—" She poked his chest. "When you open your bar, think twice before taking on a partner." She elbowed her way toward the storage room.

"Right. Like that's ever going to happen," he muttered. Flattened by last night's bad news bomb, the only way to force himself out of bed was to focus on the demands of today. After this party ended, he had no fucking idea what his future held. But every time he saw Rosie's blue curls bobbing past, the hollow ache in his stomach reminded him what his future wouldn't hold.

How could she smile like that, flirting with customers, laughing at their stupid jokes, toting tater tots to people who, at the end of the day, didn't give a shit about her? Yet there she went, wiggling her lush ass and tossing her hair. To look at her, you'd think last night never happened. Clearly, she was over it—over him.

It had taken hours to talk his mom off the ledge. Every time he thought she'd yelled herself out, she started in again, wailing about his ingratitude and Dad's impending doom. She even hollered at him for denying her grandchildren. By the time they got her bundled up and into Dad's car, the whole family network knew something awful was up with the Tacoma Volkovs. God only knew what stories were burning up the family text string this morning.

"Be here now," he muttered. Tomorrow was soon enough to sit down with his parents and try to explain. Hopefully by then the yelling would've stopped.

Rosie stepped up to the bar and caught his eye for a microsecond before dropping her focus to her cash box, where she meticulously arranged singles and fives. "I need five pirate punches and two Seahawks-tinis."

Just at that moment, Dawn bustled up and deposited two half-gallon jugs of rum. She clapped Eddie's shoulder. "Would you believe he was rearranging the shelves?" She patted Rosie's hand. "How's my girl? You're both looking a little peaked tonight. No better party than a wedding, right?"

Again, Rosie's gaze flicked to his, revealing dark circles beneath puffy eyes. A dull heaviness clogged his chest, making it hard to draw a full breath. He reached for her hand. She drew it back with a sharp shake of her head.

Dawn chuckled. "When I said no relationship drama at work, I didn't mean you couldn't hold hands." She turned away to fill beer glasses at the taps.

Eddie twisted the caps off the bottles the way he'd like to wring someone's neck. But whose? Now that he knew about his dad's illness, Rosie's interference seemed less like sabotage and more like a clumsy attempt to help. And he'd jumped down her throat for it. With cleats on.

While he poured her drinks, she grabbed a cocktail pick and speared fruit from the garnish tray. Their hands collided, sloshing rum punch onto the bar.

"Sorry," they chorused.

He picked up a bar towel. "I got this."

"Just trying to help," she grumbled. "I should know better." She hefted the tray and spun away.

Kiara nudged him with her sharp elbow. "What's your deal, Eddie? Servers always help with the garnishes when orders back up."

His stomach dropped to his knees. *Could I be more of a dick?* He should run to her and apologize, but the flood of customers kept him pinned behind the bar, just like his parents' expectations kept him pinned to a life that didn't fit him. Or clipped his wings. Too many bug metaphors. He wrestled his focus back to the task in front of him, taking out his frustration by muddling oranges and limes. It felt good to smash something.

Hours later, the post-game crowd filtered out, leaving the bar nearly empty when Diego and Shelby emerged from the kitchen, flushed and sweaty. Diego waved to Eddie and bee-lined to the booth where Anna, Charlie's younger sister, greeted him with a hug. Shelby groaned and leaned on the bar, head on her crossed arms. Kiara clucked and massaged her shoulders. "Poor baby."

"I never wanna see another tater tot as long as I live," Shelby groaned.

"Go sit." Kiara patted her butt. "I'll make you a hot toddy."

Phone to her ear, Charlie smiled broadly. "Okay, I'll tell 'em. Yeah, promise. Love you." She smooched the screen, then held it to her chest and sighed. "River says hi, everyone. He caught a bazillion squid."

Shelby called, "What say we switch out tots for calamari?"

"You hush." Dawn mussed Shelby's short, spiky hair before

moving to the bar and ringing the ship's bell. "Closing early tonight, folks. Last call."

Eddie surveyed his work family. Everyone was pairing up—Charlie and River, Diego and Anna, Jojo mooning over Lana, and he was pretty sure Kiara and Shelby had something cooking. It was almost like that mahogany cherub atop the back bar was shooting invisible arrows. Its magic didn't last, though, at least not with him and Rosie.

God, he was going to miss this crew. He had to find a way to make things right with his parents, and with Rosie. His poor battered heart couldn't take leaving this place, these people behind.

Once the last customers trailed out, Dawn summoned everyone to the bar. "Gus has an announcement."

The grizzled old fart wiggled off his bar stool and pulled up his sagging jeans. "Yes, well, ahem." He shuffled his stained work boots.

"Get on with it, darlin'." Dawn's cheeks bunched in a fond smile.

Dawn and Gus? The boss was 50-something, he figured. Gus must be…hard to tell, actually. With that brown-gray beard and baggy face, he could be just a little older than Dawn, or twenty years older. Were they a couple too?

Gus cleared his throat and clasped his hands atop his belly. "So, my friend works at the women's shelter on Broadway. We got to talkin', and they need all kindsa stuff, bed linens and blankets, kids' clothes, toys, pots 'n' pans…"

Dawn cut in. "Seems every bar and restaurant in town is running something for Valentine's Day. All we got so far is our Anti-Valentine's Party. I've been wracking my brain for something to make it special when—bingo! Gus told me about the shelter. Here's what I'm thinking. You've all seen those posters in the bathrooms?"

Kiara nodded. "Love doesn't have to hurt."

Dawn smacked her palm on the bar. "That's our angle. We're gonna hold a fundraiser for the shelter. I found a printer who'll give us T-shirts at cost if we pay for labor. But we need a design fast. Like, yesterday." She beckoned. "Ideas. Hit me."

Eddie pointed to the troublemaker atop the bar. "How about him?"

"That little angel?" Kiara squinted. "He kinda looks like cupid. We could give him a bow and arrows."

Dawn clapped him on the back. "Great idea, Eddie. Now all we need is a design for the T-shirts." With a huge, shit-eating grin, she turned to Rosie. So did everyone else.

Rosie blinked for a moment. "Yeah, okay. I can draw our cupid, I guess."

"That's my girl." Dawn pointed. "Lana and Charlie, can you do a social media blitz like you did for our Christmas party?"

"On it, boss." Lana saluted.

Dawn wrapped her arm around Eddie's shoulder. That leaves you and me to finalize plans."

Eddie huffed a laugh. She was sweet to include him, but everyone knew he was just there to backstop the boss. Besides, his poor brain was so fried, not to mention his deflated heart, he doubted he could contribute any ideas worth shit tonight. "Okay if I think on it overnight?"

"Yeah, you look pretty rough." She tousled his hair. "We'll talk tomorrow."

While he and Kiara cleaned up the bar, Dawn and Gus conferred over mugs of coffee, and Rosie sketched, head down, her pencil moving in quick flicks. Once everything was set to rights, he stuffed his hands in his pockets and strolled toward her table, aiming for relaxed, casual—probably looking like a shambling idiot.

Her gaze flicked up toward the carved angel—and collided with him. She startled, clutching the pencil in a white-knuckled grip.

Eddie nodded toward her sketch. "Can I see?" He slid into the seat opposite her.

His heart squeezed when he saw she was still using the peacock-blue notebook he'd given her at New Year's. Seemed like a lifetime ago now. The angel was perfect—at once recognizable as the Bangers' mascot, but with a saucy grin, a heart-tipped arrow notched in its bow, and heart-spangled wings.

"You're amazing, Rosie."

"Hmmf." She bent over the page, adding bits of shadow here and there. "How's your dad?"

"Healthy enough to chew me out all the way home."

Keeping her eyes on her work, she hooked a stray curl behind her ear. "You told them?"

"Not yet."

Finally, her gaze met his. Never had her dark eyes looked so dull and vacant. "Will you ever?"

When he didn't answer immediately, she sighed and looked away. "Not my business, anyway." Scratch, scratch went her pen. "Funny how your mom told me before she told you."

"Maybe she wanted to practice."

"Maybe she was drunk."

Unable to resist her gravity one second more, his hand closed over her wrist. "She trusted you."

She snorted. "Right. For about thirty seconds. Then I

became the evil Jezebel luring you away from family duty. Anyway, what does it matter now? You're gonna do the right thing." She pulled out of his grip. "For them, not for you."

Eddie's heart thudded dully against his ribs. "I don't know what I'm going to do, Rosie. But you're right. I should have told them long ago. Now it's going to be harder than ever."

Closing her eyes, she scraped her hair back from her forehead. "It never woulda worked out, Eddie. We're on different paths. Besides, guys like you don't stick with girls like me. Guess I always knew that."

Her comment sliced him right to his core. She'd said the same thing at the beginning. Unwilling to let her go, he'd coaxed her back into his bed, pried open her guarded heart, even told her he loved her—then abandoned her after everything she'd done for him. The face-saving pretense, the nights of bone-melting passion, the warmth and support—he'd crumpled it up and tossed it away. She must hate him.

He dropped his head into his hands. "I'm so sorry, Rosie."

"Too late for that. But I hope you don't surrender your dreams. There's got to be a way you could do both—help your parents and open your bar."

Damned if I can see how. He laid his hand on the table, palm up. "You were right about one thing—it's time for me to man up and face this."

"Guess you don't have a choice anymore." Her lips twisted in a wry smile. "Funny what we can do when our back's against the wall." She slid her palm into his and squeezed. "You're a good guy, Eddie. You deserve a partner who'll help build your bar. I'm sure she's out there." She withdrew her hand, and instantly he felt the loss of her warmth. "I deserve that

221

too. Maybe someday I'll meet a guy more like me—someone who blurts and bumbles through life. There's someone for everyone, right?" She sniffled and swiped at her nose. "Now get outta here before I cry and smear this drawing."

He'd wounded her deeply, and still she was being a good sport, saving face by pretending in front of their friends. What could he do but leave her in peace?

Shoulders bowed under the weight of his defeat, he trudged to the locker room, pulled on his coat, and rested his spinning head against the cool metal of his open locker door. Rosie was right—she deserved someone who'd stand up for her, the way she'd stood up for him. She deserved someone as brave and strong as she was, and he had a damned long way to go before he qualified. Alone and aching, he slunk into the icy darkness outside.

* * *

"Okay, Uncle Pete. I will. And thanks." Eddie disconnected the call and tucked his phone into his pocket, then gathered his armor. He was as prepared for this battle as he could possibly be. Pete would set up a meeting with a law school friend who specialized in small businesses. He had a lunch date Saturday with Uncle Leo and Cousin Nadia. Hopefully, his parents would come. If not, Eddie would present his plan alone.

He slid his tablet into his briefcase, then pulled his vision board from its hiding place behind the TV. Before going downstairs, he paused for a lingering look around his cozy little apartment. Eight years ago, he helped his father and grandfather build this place from the studs up. He hated to leave it behind, but it was time.

The sky was still dark, and the icy wind nearly ripped the poster board from beneath his arm as he descended. A sign from above? *Fuck no.* He gripped harder, crossed the driveway, and opened the kitchen door.

Mama looked up from the pot she was stirring, her gaze flat, her lips tight. "Well, well. Look who's here, Papa. Our long-lost son deigns to join us at our humble breakfast table."

Dad looked up from his newspaper. "Enough with the drama, Alina. You knew he was coming. Why else would you make kasha porridge?"

She raised her nose and sniffed. "I happen to like kasha porridge. So warming on a chilly morning. And it reminds me of family." She pulled a ladle from a drawer, then banged it shut. "Family is so important, don't you think?"

Dad rolled his eyes and folded his newspaper. "Sit, son. Your mother is still in a snit, but I am ready to listen."

Mama slopped porridge into earthenware bowls. "Who says I'm not listening?" She banged a bowl down in front of Dad, then filled another for Eddie.

Dad passed the sliced strawberries before drizzling his dish with honey.

Mama clucked her tongue. "Not too much, Dorogóy. Think of your health."

"I'm not diabetic, for God's sake." Dad rolled his eyes. "Your mother, the dietician."

"Well, forgive me for wanting to keep you around a little longer."

Eddie blew on his steaming porridge. He knew better than to interrupt Mama when she was venting, but Dad had no such compunction. "Sit, woman. We need to be at work soon."

Grumbling like a disgruntled hen, she joined them at the table.

"So, what is this about?" Dad crossed his arms over his still-trim middle. Except for bags under his eyes and softness at his jawline, he looked as fit and vital as ever. Eddie kicked himself for not noticing his father's signs of pain. Hell, he'd probably seen little grunts and winces and written them off as Dad being his usual grumpy self.

Eddie straightened and faced his parents. "First of all, I apologize. We should have had this conversation long ago. I knew you'd be disappointed, and I wanted to be as prepared as possible. I had no idea you wanted to hand over the shop so soon."

"We didn't, until the doctor…" Mama dumped sugar in her coffee and stirred, clinking her spoon loudly. "Besides, you're a grown man, Eduard. You have a good head on your shoulders, a nice way with the customers, and if you'd just put forth an effort—"

"Let the boy talk, Alina." Dad pointed with his chin. "What's all this stuff you brought?"

Using the spare kitchen chair as an easel, Eddie set up his vision board. A magazine cut-out of vodka bottles fluttered to the floor. He slapped it back in place and cleared his throat. "As you know, I've been working at Bangers for a little over a year now."

Mama sniffed. "Carrying beers and mopping floors."

"Actually, I'm acting assistant manager. I'm learning everything I can about the bar business because someday I want to open my own place." He swept his hand over the board. "Here it is."

Dad rose from his chair and squinted. "Looks like a kid's school project."

Mama's eyebrows rose. "It's a vision board. Like on Oprah."

"Exactly. My Business Leadership professor says we should visualize our plans." He patted the board tenderly. "This is Dacha. Our specialty is Russian bar food and a hundred kinds of vodka."

"Dacha?" Dad cracked the tiniest smile. "Like a Russian country house?"

"Exactly." He tapped his tablet to life. "Here's the menu."

Dad scrolled through, nodding slowly.

"There are really a hundred kinds of vodka?" Mama asked.

"Thousands. We'll have beer and cocktails too, of course, plus Washington wines and Eastern European ones." He pulled a spiral-bound booklet from his briefcase and set it on the table between them. "My business plan."

His parents flipped through, exchanging pointed glances. Lots of eyebrow action, grunts, and pursed lips.

Dad finally pushed the papers away. "Where?"

"Depends where I can get a lease. I'm hoping for the Lincoln District. Lots of up-and-coming new bars in that area, plus there's an international flavor to that neighborhood, but no Russian places yet. In fact," he scrolled to a map. "there's no Russian bar in the Tacoma area, though there are a few in Seattle."

"Where will you get the money?" Dad asked.

Mama inhaled sharply. "You don't expect us to sell the shop?"

"Of course not, Mama. I'm working with Uncle Pete on possible sources of start-up capital."

Dad's expression remained stoic, but his gruff voice betrayed his emotion. "What about our business? We put our whole lives into that place. We were counting on you to keep it going."

"I wish you'd—" He sucked in a breath. *No shifting blame. Take responsibility.* "I should have discussed this with you sooner." He reached across the table and took his mother's hand. "And, to be honest, I dreaded disappointing you. I know how much the shop means to you."

"Not just us," Dad added. "My parents, their parents, the cousins, your Uncle Leo and Aunt Lada…"

"I understand. But don't you think I deserve the chance to build a business like you did? One I can be proud of?"

Dad's shoulders slumped. "Son, there is so much you don't know about running a business. I was going to teach you."

Eddie bit his lip to the point of pain. As much as he yearned for a business that was wholly his own creation, maintaining a strong connection with his parents was worth a compromise. "So teach me, Dad. But with the bar, not the dry cleaners. I'm sorry, but I just can't face a future chained to a business I don't love."

Mama's chest rose and fell on a shaky breath. "We just want to make it easy for you."

He squeezed her hand. "I don't want easy, Ma. I want this."

The corners of Dad's mustache drooped. "I guess we could sell the shop." But his crumpled expression said it all—that place was his pride and joy. Passing it on to a stranger would break his heart.

Eddie raised his forefinger. "Or you could consider keeping it in the family." He quickly explained the plan he'd brainstormed with Uncle Pete and Bruno—combine forces with other relatives running dry-cleaning and laundry businesses in the Seattle area to create one big company. Between their grandparents' mother ship in Seattle, plus Uncle Leo's shop in Bellevue and their cousins' shops in Kirkland, they had enough expertise to maintain high quality and even expand. "And you could keep working if you want to, Dad, but as management, not a floor worker. Stop by the shop for a few hours, make sure things are running to your satisfaction, then relax at home." He clasped his father's calloused hand. "You could turn my old room into a home office."

Mama's eyes brightened, and not from tears this time. "We could even travel, maybe? We haven't been to the beach in so long, Vadim."

Dad nodded slowly. "It's worth a discussion. Saturday, eh? Let's meet at that tea shop on Capitol Hill, the one with the good sharlotka. Maybe you can get their recipe, son."

Would his parents really acquiesce this easily? No doubt, they had months of negotiations ahead of them as the relatives carved out their own roles—if they even went for the idea at all. And he still had one more bomb to drop. He took his parents' hands, hoping he could get through this without tearing up. "Mama, Dad, I appreciate everything you've done to make my life easier and more comfortable. But it's time I move out."

"Out?" Dad's brows scrunched together. "What are you talking about? You moved out years ago."

"Living over your garage doesn't count. It's time I got a place of my own. My boss at Bangers has an apartment I can rent."

"You can afford that on a bartender's salary?"

"Assistant manager, Dad," Mama corrected him.

"I can manage." *Barely.*

Mama sniffed. "Our baby is a man now, Papa. He's leaving us."

227

Eddie's eyes stung. "Don't be so dramatic, Ma. I'll be ten blocks away. Besides, the rent from that garage apartment will pay for a lot of beach trips."

Dad massaged his chin. "This is a lot to consider, son. And you know I do not like change. But we will talk about it." He slapped his thighs and rose. "And now, let's go to work."

Head spinning, body light with relief, Eddie packed up his presentation. Rosie was right. They did understand—or at least they showed signs they might ultimately accept his decision.

His good mood fizzled as the truth weighted him like a lead blanket. If he'd told them before, he'd still have Rosie at his side today. It would take more than posterboard and a business plan to win back her trust. Time for drastic measures.

Chapter Eighteen

Rosie looked up from her sketchbook at the sound of footsteps climbing the stairs toward Inky Dreams Studio. Since cupids and hearts were classic tattoo motifs, she'd been riffing on the Bangers cupid, adding a devilish wink here, a floppy curl on the forehead there. Trouble was, the more she played with the image, the more the arrow-shooting pest resembled Eddie.

Magda stepped onto the landing, her silver mane sparkling with snowflakes. "Got a present for you." She set a slim rectangular package on Rosie's desk before toeing off her boots. "Go on, open it."

Rosie pulled out an envelope with a familiar label. Inside, sheets of synthetic skin for tattoo practice. "Um, thanks?"

The buzzing from Victoria's station stopped. She poked her shaved head through the velvet privacy curtain and waggled her multi-pierced eyebrows. "Hoo boy—fake skin now. Rosie's moving up in the world."

Magda pointed to the stencil machine on a side counter.

"Pick one of your more complicated designs."

Rosie bit her lip. To tell, or not to tell? After watching hundreds of tutorials and reading thousands of online articles, she knew the usual progression by heart. You start with fruit, then move to sheets of synthetic skin, maybe pig's ears, then to your own skin. Finally, an apprentice is allowed to tattoo another person, but only the simplest designs at first.

Never the patient type, she'd jumped the line, buying her own rotary tattoo machine last fall and filling sheet after sheet of synthetic skin with tattoos. Her first attempts were splotchy messes, but she was improving fast. Since last Saturday's wedding disaster, she'd filled her sleepless late-night hours with tattoo practice, drowning out memories of Eddie with the angry-hornet buzz of needles.

Rosie flipped through her sketchbook. Its peacock-blue cover was yet another painful reminder of Eddie, but her practical nature balked at wasting so many blank pages. Better to think of it as exposure therapy. Gradually, she'd come to tolerate reminders of him until sharing a workspace didn't hurt anymore. Because now, even the slightest glimpse of his dark curls behind the bar was like a gut punch. Every damn time.

She sighed and flipped the page. Which design to practice on today?

Magda's cool hand fell on her shoulder. "Go back a page."

Damn, she's sneaky. Must've been a spy before becoming a tattoo artist.

Magda tapped the page. "That eagle thingy. What is that?"

A dull, pulsing ache bloomed behind Rosie's forehead. "It's from a friend's belt buckle."

"German?"

"Russian Imperial Army."

Joining them, Victoria whistled. "Fancy. You should do that one."

Magda clapped her shoulder. "Make us a Russian eagle, grasshopper."

Rosie gulped down the huge, spiky lump blocking her throat. "I'd really rather not."

Magda's perfect eyebrow arched. "And who is the teacher here?"

She hung her head. "Okay, okay, one eagle, coming up." Couldn't let her personal feelings get in the way of her dream job. Maybe she could get through this task without bawling if she visualized the fake skin as one cheek of Eddie's smooth, taut, needle-phobic ass. She chuckled grimly as she headed for the stencil machine. But this flat, rubbery stuff had no shape, no sweet little curve she used to trace with her fingertips and tongue…

With a groan, she fed her photocopied design into the thermal printer. This would be easier if the shop were busier today—more noise to distract her, more chatter between artists and customers. Easier to quit replaying those bitter-sweet memories and just let the surrounding sounds flow through her. But Magda had cleared the afternoon to catch up on bookkeeping, and Tina was out for a medical appointment, leaving just Victoria and her stoic, silent client. The place was so quiet she could hear the tick of the antique clock behind her desk.

"Mind if I put on some music?" When no one objected, she switched on a soothing electronic playlist, very woo-woo and not at all sexy, and carried the stencil to an empty workstation. Mindful of Magda's sharp eyes on her, she gloved up and sterilized the fake skin with alcohol before smearing it with Stencil Stuff lotion. No need to shave it, at least.

"You skipped a step."

Shit. "It's not hairy," she protested.

"Nevertheless, you're building good habits. You want every step to become automatic."

"My bad." Grumbling inwardly, she wiped the sheet clean, squirted it with green soap, pantomimed shaving it, then finally applied the stencil. Before beginning, she sheathed her equipment in disposable plastic sleeves, set up her ink caps, and dabbed A & D ointment on the back of her hand.

Buzz, glide, wipe. Over and over, the steady rhythm claimed her focus and loosened the tension gripping her. Bit by bit, the Imperial eagle took shape, proud and scornful.

As symbols go, this two-headed bird was a pretty poor symbol for her lost love. It wasn't pride that kept Eddie from following his dreams, just a sense of duty and obligation to a family who loved him. Was that so bad? And she could hardly call him two-faced—he'd been straight with her about, well, everything. Which made letting go of him all the more difficult. His memory was inked on her heart.

She set down the tattoo machine and shook the stiffness from her hand. *God, I'm such a sap. Good thing I'm an artist and not a writer.*

Two hours later, she switched needles to ink the fine lines of the eagle's feathers. Her shoulders and back ached from hunching over her workstation, but Eddie's eagle was nearly complete. She'd snap a picture and show it to him tonight at work—

Heaviness seeped into her chest. That thought belonged to the before times—when Eddie was her sweetheart, her ally, her friend. The image before her blurred. A tear splashed onto the eagle, then another and another. A choked sound escaped her tight, scratchy throat.

Passing on her way to the break room, Victoria paused at Rosie's workstation. "Hey now, don't be upset." She placed a hand on her shoulder and leaned in to inspect Rosie's work. "This is really good. Why are you crying?"

Their exchange caught Magda's attention. Victoria's customer too. All three women huddled around Rosie, witnesses to her humiliating breakdown. The more they patted and cooed, the harder Rosie rocked with sobs.

Magda nudged Victoria. "Get her a cup of tea, will you?"

"And cookies," the customer added, holding her half-tattooed arm away from her body. Pretty design, a pair of joined hearts wrapped in a banner inscribed with dates, the whole image surrounded by a wreath of thorny roses. *Fuckin' lovey-dovey shit everywhere I look.* Her muscles tensed with the urge to bolt.

Magda's strong, wiry arm closed around her shoulders, pinning her in place. "Deep breaths, darlin'." She nudged the box of tissues closer. "I've seen artists cry over a failed design, but never over a successful one. What's this about?"

"A guy, most likely." Victoria placed a steaming mug beside Rosie. "Or a girl? I shouldn't assume."

Rosie bit her lip hard as she fought for control. "This guy." She tapped the tattoo.

"Ah." Magda nodded. "So that's why you didn't want to work on this design. Ex-boyfriend?"

Did she even have the right to call him that, after such a short time? "I'm sorry. This is so unprofessional." She clutched a handful of tissues to her soggy face.

233

"Don't apologize." Magda rubbed soothing circles on her back. "Tattooing is an emotional business. People get inked to commemorate lost loves, family members who've passed, places they loved and had to leave."

"Like me." The customer thrust out her ointment-smeared arm. "Lost my Johnnie to cancer last year." By now Rosie's vision had cleared enough to recognize the numbers on her arm as dates. Below the design, inked in looping script, "Always in my heart until we meet again."

A fresh wave of tears shook her, churning her stomach. Was she really going to cry until she puked? Way to make a good impression on her boss.

Magda gently shooed the other two women away, then pulled up a rolling stool and crossed her arms over the chest support. "Still raw, huh?"

"Just last Saturday."

"Well, you can't expect to heal in a week. Not if you really loved him."

"I guess I did." Rosie scrubbed her eyes with the heels of her hands. "But he was all wrong for me."

"Why?"

"Oh God, Magda, I don't wanna talk about it."

"You'll feel better if you do."

Rosie snorted. "I tried talking it out with my sister, my best friend, even my mom. Just makes it worse."

"What does make you feel better, then?"

She lifted the tattoo machine and pressed the power switch to make it buzz. "This. I can't sleep, but I can practice. I used up a dozen sheets—" She clapped a hand over her mouth.

Magda's scarlet lips curled in a smirk without venom. "Figured you didn't get this good just practicing on fruit."

"You're not mad?"

Her mentor shrugged. "Shows you're motivated, passionate about the art. That's not a bad thing, hon." She pointed. "Line's a little thick here. Otherwise, this is excellent. I think you're ready for some real skin."

"Whose?"

"Yours, of course." She smacked her own thigh. "Here's a good spot. Something small and simple will give you a feel for needle depth and…" She chuckled. "Don't tell me you've already done that too."

Rosie huffed a watery sigh. "I know it's supposed to be unprofessional, but I couldn't resist trying. Just a tiny shooting star."

"Well, let's see it." She pulled the velvet privacy curtain.

Rosie unfastened her jeans and slid them down. Magda set tiger-striped reading glasses on her nose and leaned in close. "A bit fuzzy in this corner."

"Yeah, went too deep."

She sat back with a chuckle. "Well, now you know. Tell you what—next time someone asks for simple line work, I'll let you try."

Rosie's jaw dropped.

"Just a line or two. I'll be right there. Now—" She tapped the eagle. "Let's see you add some gray wash shading here and here."

An electronic beep sounded. Someone coming up the stairs. Rosie yanked her jeans up and quick-stepped to the reception desk. She skidded to a halt when she saw the customer standing there, twisting a snow-dusted beanie in his hands.

"Eddie?"

Eddie clutched his beanie tighter, hoping it would stop his hands from shaking. "Hi." His voice came out strangled and squeaky. He cleared his throat and tried again. "I, uh, want to make an appointment. For a tattoo."

He and Rosie blinked at each other for a long, awkward moment. God, she looked beautiful. Her sapphire curls glowed extra bright in the pale winter light streaming through the high windows. Her cheeks were flushed, her eyes bright, if a little puffy, and her nose—

Shit. She's been crying. He took a step back. "Is this a bad time? I could come back later."

A petite woman with abundant silver hair and neck tattoos stepped through the curtain. "Problem, Rosie?"

Rosie gave her shoulders a little shake. Or was that a shiver? "No. He wants an appointment."

A bead of sweat trickled down the back of his neck. Just being this close to all those needles had his stomach rolling and his knees jiggling like Jell-o. But after a week of Rosie avoiding him at work and refusing to answer his texts, he had to try. Hopefully, he wouldn't spoil the moment by puking. Or fainting. Or—*What was I thinking? Run!*

He strangled his inner chicken and pointed to his belt buckle. "I'd like this design. On my shoulder, I guess. Or maybe on my chest?" He hadn't given much consideration to where, since thinking too long about the whole proposition made him nauseated.

The older woman dropped into a squat and peered at this belt buckle—as if this weren't already awkward enough. She raised an eyebrow and glanced up at Rosie. "This the guy?"

"Yeah." Rosie clutched her middle with clawed fingers.

"Holy shiitakes." The woman rose. "That's the mother of all coincidences."

She's been talking about me. That's good, right? His greatest fear hadn't yet come to pass. Rosie hadn't put it all behind her.

Glamour Grandma looked him up and down like a buyer appraising a horse. Or a pony, in his case. "I got time now."

He gulped. "Could Rosie do it?"

The woman's blood-red lips scrunched to the side. "Rosie's an apprentice. A good one, but she's not ready to do something this elaborate."

Damn it, that's the whole point. He had to show Rosie he was taking an interest in her work, facing his fears, trusting her. Too late to back down now. "I don't mind. It's my skin, right?"

"But it's my shop and my reputation." While Rosie's gaze darted between them, the artist stalked a circle around them both, tapping her pursed lips with her finger. "Tell you what. Rosie can assist, maybe add a few lines."

Rosie grasped her boss's arm and gave a strangled croak.

"Give us a minute, would you, hon?" The woman gestured toward a wall of cubbies. "Shoes and coat here. Coffee and cookies in the lounge." She pointed, then pulled Rosie through the curtains. He couldn't quite make out their flurry of whispers, but he was pretty sure he caught the word "Revenge." His balls tightened, and not in a fun way.

He followed the scent of coffee to the break room, where one of those single-serve machines sat beside a rack of pods. Caffeine was the last thing he needed, so he chose a chamomile tea and waited while the machine sputtered and hissed. The tray of iced cookies looked tempting, but his roiling stomach reminded him to abstain. Instead, he scanned the photos on the walls, shots of elaborate tattoos on arms, legs, chests, hips, asses…he peered closer. *Yup, that's a tattooed dick.* As determined as he was to win Rosie back, the thought of needles down there—*No. Just, no.*

The artist strode into the room, dropped into a leather armchair, and crossed her legs. "Rosie's trying to impress me with her cool, but she's clearly uncomfortable with this. What are you trying to accomplish here?"

Those ice-blue eyes reminded him of his own babka's unerring bullshit meter. She'd see right through any lies—and he was a shitty liar anyway. He sat across from her and clasped his hands between his knees. "A while ago, Rosie said this would make a great tattoo. But I laughed it off."

"Because you're scared of needles?"

He swiped a palm down his clammy face. "It shows, huh?"

Her throaty chuckle held a note of sympathy. "Looked like you were gonna vibrate through the floor."

"Anyway, we broke up last week. I want her back."

Magda tapped her long, pointy nails. "What if you get the tattoo and she doesn't take you back?"

He'd thought of that, of course. In fact, he lay awake all night chewing on the possibility his grand gesture might net him nothing but more pain. But talking hadn't worked, nor staring at her like a starved puppy, nor texting her, nor pleading with her best friend. Lana just fixed him with a freezing gaze. "Words don't count for shit, Eddie. You want Rosie back? You gotta earn it."

He shrugged. "She's already left a permanent mark on me. Might as well make it visible. If she won't take me back, at least I'll have a beautiful design from my family's history. And a reminder not to screw up next time."

She lifted her chin. "So the breakup was your fault."

"Totally."

"Another woman?"

He bolted upright, eyes wide. "No way. I could never—"

"All right, kiddo. Don't shit yourself." She rose. "I believe you. And as apologies go, this is pretty ultra." She held out her hand. "I'm Magda, by the way."

"Eddie."

"You want some ibuprofen before we start?"

"Already took four."

She tilted her head toward the studio. "Let's go."

* * *

Bad plan, point one: Eddie hadn't thought to wear a sleeveless undershirt. Sitting bare chested on what looked like a dentist's chair while Rosie's hot breath fanned over his skin had the predictable result. He shifted his discarded shirt to better cover his inconvenient erection. While she pressed the stencil to his shoulder, her boss turned away with a soft chuckle and fiddled with her equipment. His cheeks heated, even as goose bumps sprouted over his exposed skin.

Magda gathered her silver mane into a high ponytail, then leaned in to inspect Rosie's work. "Peel it off slowly, now."

Bad plan, point two: Of course Rosie wouldn't work on him without supervision, which meant he'd have no chance to tell her he broke the news to his parents and they didn't totally freak. Well, Mama did, but she was gradually thawing. And with her boss literally breathing down their necks, he damn sure couldn't tell Rosie how his body and soul and mind and heart ached with missing her.

Magda switched on her tattoo gun, which looked like a sci-fi movie prop and buzzed like a murder hornet. Gritting his teeth so hard his gums throbbed, Eddie gripped the arm rest.

"Relax your hand, hon." Magda gave his gnarled fist a gentle tap. "Now, the first few minutes are the worst. After that, your skin goes numb. Right, Rosie?"

If that was true, why did Rosie look so queasy? But she nodded. "No worse than a bee sting."

"I'm allergic to bees," he deadpanned, then forced a smile. If this was what it took to prove himself, she could peel off his skin like some medieval martyr, and he'd keep on grinning.

Bad plan, point three: *Fuckin' ouch!* He flinched as the needle bit into his skin, huffing and puffing like the world's wimpiest big bad wolf. *Just don't look.* He'd felt worse pain. Like that time in elementary school when a huge dog bit his scrawny leg. But that pain was quick and intense, whereas this sharp scraping sting went on and on, and that infernal buzzing...

He squinched his eyes shut. *Breathe in. Breathe out.* Should've asked for something smaller, like a tiny crab for his zodiac sign, or an R for Rosie. But that moment was seared in his memory—Rosie crouched between his spread thighs as she sketched his belt buckle. When this was over, he'd have a permanent record of that delicious night. Not that he'd ever forget.

The buzzing stopped. He opened his eyes and found Rosie hovering inches away, a crumpled paper towel in hand. "How you holding up?"

"Great," he lied.

Nibbling her lip, she gently blotted his forehead. "You look kinda shaky."

"I'm fine."

Magda pushed up from her wheeled stool. "Gonna take a quick stretch break." He thought he heard quiet laughter as she ambled away.

Rosie rolled her stool closer. Her eyes narrowed. "Why are you doing this, Eddie?"

"To prove to you I'm not afraid." He shifted his sore shoulder and winced. "I mean, I thought I was going to pass out at first, but I'm still here."

She grimaced and rubbed the back of her neck. "I never said you were a coward, Eddie."

"Yeah, you did, actually. And you were right. So thanks for pushing me in the right direction. I told them."

Her eyes widened. "Your parents?"

"All of it. Showed them my vision board, my business plan, everything."

"And?"

"There was some yelling. A little gnashing of teeth. But we're still speaking. And another thing—I'm moving out. Hard to claim my independence when I'm living rent-free above their garage."

"Where will you go?"

"Dawn's basement apartment. It's been sitting empty since River moved in with Charlie."

"Wow. That must've been hard."

"Not as hard as this." He glanced at his reddened shoulder. "How did you handle your first time?"

A smile flickered over her face, there and gone like a firefly's wink. "Not gracefully. But like Magda says, the pain dulls, and you start to feel kind of badass for handling it."

"Right. I look forward to that phase." He sat up, swung his legs over the side of the reclining seat, and reached for her hand. She stuffed her fists into her pockets.

"Look, Ro, I know you don't trust me. Some of that's because I was an ass at the wedding and at work. Some has to do with your past. But it's not like I'm asking you to move in with me—though that would be great. A dream come true. I'm just asking for the chance to show you who I really am."

Her brows drew together as her gaze dropped to the floor. "I don't know, Eddie. We're so different. Your type never sticks with a girl like me."

"Hey." He grasped her arm. "I'm not a type. I'm just me. And I'm in love with you."

A loud clatter rang out from the break room. Rosie jolted backward.

"Fuckin' coffee machine." Magda returned with a steaming mug but didn't sit on her weird backward stool. Instead, she handed her tattoo machine to Rosie. "You can do the upper lines of the wings. Check your needle depth."

The flash of panic in Rosie's eyes kicked his pulse into overdrive. She fiddled with the gun-shaped torture implement, making the needle protrude like a wasp's stinger. Cold sweat dotted his forehead. The edges of his vision dimmed. His stomach sank…

"Eddie?" Someone patted his cheek, over and over.

He groaned and tried to sit up, but something gripped his ankles, holding them high in the air. "Here he comes. Attaboy."

Rosie's face floated into view. "You passed out."

Magda released his feet onto the chair, now stretched out in full recline mode. "It was cute. Your eyes rolled up, and good-night."

Eyes wide, Rosie cupped his jaw. "You scared the shit out of me."

"Not your fault, hon," Magda assured her. "Lots of people faint, especially when they got a needle phobia." She clucked her tongue and handed him a paper cup of water. "Sip slowly. Don't need you puking on my equipment."

Just let me die. Never in the history of guys trying to impress women had a grand gesture gone so spectacularly wrong.

Rosie dabbed his forehead gently. "You want to stop?"

"Might as well finish it, right?" He glanced at Magda, whose mouth quirked in a wry grin.

"A lot easier than coming back and starting over, but it's your call."

An odd sense of lightness filled him, tugging the corners of his lips upward. The worst had already happened, so why not? "Let's do it."

"Are you sure?" Rosie asked, rumpling her forehead.

Magda smacked her arm. "He's trying to impress you. Let him."

Rosie bit her lip and dipped her needle into the ink.

He closed his eyes, sucked in a breath, and nodded. "I trust you."

The needle buzzed to life. It still hurt like a motherfucker, but the room didn't tilt, and neither did his stomach. And she was right—gradually, the pain dulled to mere irritation as Rosie worked her needle over the meaty part of his shoulder. When she finished, she switched seats with Magda, leaning close to watch her mentor's progress. He felt a soft touch on his hand—Rosie's fingers sliding through his. He gripped her tight.

"Hold still, unless you want a lopsided bird," Magda grumbled.

"Yes, ma'am." He kept his focus on Rosie. Watching her dark eyes follow the tattoo gun's motions was the perfect distraction.

Her gaze flicked to his, and her eyes crinkled at the corners. "I know this isn't your thing, Eddie. You're brave to do this."

This was his chance—the wall around her heart was cracking, just tiny fissures, but enough to let the light shine through. Everything depended on breaking through to that light.

He turned to Magda. "Gotta move, ma'am."

She lifted the needle from his arm, and he raised Rosie's knuckles to his lips. "Not gonna lie, Ro, this is hard. But I'll do whatever it takes."

Chapter Nineteen

Rosie sat in a booth with Lana, stringing paper hearts onto ribbon streamers to hang for Bangers' Anti-Valentine's Party that night. While Jojo hung a heart-shaped piñata above the stage, Kiara tested her playlist of breakup anthems. The J. Geils band belted out "Love Stinks," and Rosie's gaze flicked to the bar. No Eddie—must be in the back.

Lana snatched up a lavender heart that read *Love Sux*. "I mean, if getting a tattoo doesn't prove commitment, I don't know what does. Can't believe you didn't drag his ass home and bounce his bones into next week."

Oh, she'd wanted to, all right. But rushing into things caused their first crash and burn. This time, she'd step more carefully. "The timing wasn't right. First of all, he was in pain, and kinda green. Hard to feel romantic when you're trying not to puke."

"Uh-huh. A 7-Up would take care of that."

"And his apartment is all packed up. We'd have to bone on a stack of moving cartons."

245

"You could do it standing up." Lana flashed a wicked grin. "You're the same height, so that works perfectly."

Rosie huffed and rolled her eyes. "Sex with Eddie means something now. We've got some stuff to talk through before we jump back into bed." Not that she didn't crave his touch as much as ever, especially when he brushed past her at the bar and his woodsy scent triggered heady, horny memories.

For the past two nights she'd stayed up far too late, snuggling alone in her bed as Eddie's voice rumbled sweet nothings through her earbuds. But he hadn't made the move toward physical intimacy, and she was surprisingly okay with that. This time, they'd connect for more solid reasons than hormones and mistletoe.

Lana snatched up a hot-pink heart inscribed with *I Heart Me.* "I'm gonna wear this one tonight." She shuffled through the pile. "Sorry, Ro. Don't see one that says *I love Eddie.*"

Feeling her hackles rise, Rosie grabbed a paper heart with *You Wish* and stabbed the ribbon through the hole. "It's an anti-Valentine's party, in case you forgot."

"Yeah, well, I wouldn't be surprised if Eddie does some rom-com grand gesture tonight."

"Something even more dramatic than getting a tattoo?" She'd told Lana most of the story, omitting the part where he passed out.

Lana leaned closer and lowered her voice. "I never told you, but back in early January, he quizzed me about your favorite places in Tacoma, what you like to eat, your favorite music. Wrote it all down in his little notebook."

Rosie smacked her arm. "You didn't tell me?"

"He asked me not to. And I thought it was sweet."

A flush heated Rosie's cheeks. This new information further

cemented her plans for tonight—if she didn't chicken out.

The front door opened, and a stiff, frosty wind wafted in the scent of spray paint. Dressed in a pink hoodie screen-printed with Rosie's cupid design and *Love Shouldn't Hurt*, Dawn carried the wooden donation box they'd used at Christmastime, now sparkly pink and stenciled with *Support Tacoma Domestic Violence Shelter*. Eddie followed toting a carton of paint cans.

Lana snatched his sleeve as he passed. "Pick a heart, Eddie. We're all wearing one tonight."

His hand hovered over the pile, a hint of humor dancing in his luminous eyes. He plucked up a red heart that read *Bite me* and held it over his chest. A flirtatious smile ghosted over his lips. "Be gentle. I bruise easily."

"Eddie, need you back here," Dawn hollered from the dart area, transformed for the night into a shooting gallery where patrons could nail Cupid's ass with suction-cup arrows. Gus would hand out drink tokens to anyone who hit a bullseye.

As always, the Bangers crew had brainstormed competitions and events to draw in customers. Diego and Shelby invented tonight's food specials: Love Bites—jalapeno poppers with bacon and an extra-spicy dipping sauce, plus tots smothered in cheesy artichoke dip and garnished with bacon folded into hearts. Kiara and Eddie assembled an impressive list of drink specials: a Black Heart Cocktail made with fig vodka, a Bourbon Sour-on-Love, Dark 'n' Stormy, a rye-based Blue Valentine, and a vintage classic called the Suffering Bastard.

Rosie's contribution to tonight's charity event was a window mural with a dozen cupids battling it out. Trailing smoke, one spiraled down to earth like a WWI biplane. Another lay on the ground, feet in the air à la dead bug. Yet another snuck up on his rival, his spiky club poised for an attack. She'd had so much fun painting the silly scene, Dawn suggested she hire herself out to do window art for other businesses on Sixth Avenue.

Once the paper hearts were all strung and hung, Rosie and Lana put the finishing touches on the photo booth just in time for the first customers. While Beyoncé belted about single ladies, Rosie hustled drinks to thirsty patrons. Charlie's social media blitz had worked, judging by the packed tables and bouncing bodies on the impromptu dance floor. Bangers didn't usually offer dancing space, but when a table of forty-something women started bopping to Pink's "So What?", Jojo cleared a space to keep them from knocking into other tables.

The crowd's happy, snarky energy was contagious, tamping down Rosie's jittery nerves. She hated public speaking as much as the next person, but making things right with Eddie was worth the embarrassment.

She slid up to the server station and hip-bumped Charlie. "Ready for River to come back?"

Charlie tossed her ponytail and grinned. "Sooo ready. Once you get used to a warm man in your bed every night, it's hard to go without." She nudged Rosie with her elbow. "You know what I'm talking about."

Biting her lip, Rosie ignored the gibe and placed her drink order with Kiara. At the other end of the bar, Eddie juggled bottles like a pro, whipping out complicated drinks with grace and a smile. The girl he was serving giggled and simpered as he slid her order across the bar. "Hands off, princess," Rosie grumbled under her breath. "He's mine."

And the time to tell him was rapidly approaching. Every hour or so, Dawn mounted the stage, grabbed the mic, and announced the next competition, also urging the crowd to donate to the Domestic Violence Shelter. Now, as the clock ticked toward ten, the boss moved through the crowd, greeting customers with back slaps and hugs as she made her way to the stage.

She looked so happy up there, arms spread wide, freckled cheeks plumped in a broad smile, her short locs tipped with pink glitter—an irreverent, teasing mother hen presiding over a family party. Of all the bars up and down Sixth Ave., Dawn's was by far the homiest, welcoming everyone from college kids to old folks like Gus who'd been coming here for years. Bangers never took itself too seriously, never tried to be trendy, always welcomed locals and visitors with a warm, greasy, boozy hug.

No wonder Eddie wanted a place like this of his own. With his honest, open heart and his attention to detail, he'd create someplace just as welcoming—with dumplings!

Dawn tapped the mic and held up a clipboard. "For tonight's open mic, we challenged y'all to tell us about your worst date ever. We got some nice prizes for our brave storytellers." Fingers splayed over her chest, she winked. "Now, you know how shy I am, but I'll break the ice. So, my sister talked me into trying one of those online dating apps."

"Tinder?" someone yelled.

Dawn waggled her finger. "You hush. This is my story. Anyway, first date. It was April, and she showed up at my door with a huge bunch of lilacs from her backyard. I stuck my face in there for a big ol' sniff, and a bee stung me right here." She tapped her eyelid. "My eye swelled shut and turned purple. But she was cute and kept apologizing, so we went to the restaurant she picked out. The server waited until my date went to the can, then slipped me the number of a domestic violence hotline." A smattering of laughter and applause rang out. "Speaking of—donation box is on the bar, folks, or donate online." She rattled off the shelter's website, then called up the first storyteller.

Rosie chewed her nails through stories of slobbery kisses, projectile vomiting, unwelcome groping, and alarming allergic reactions. Customers hooted and applauded each presenter. At last, Dawn squinted at her sign up list. "Our last contestant is—looks like Ariana?"

"That's me." She raised her hand and, quivering with nerves, climbed onto the stage and took the mic.

Dawn's forehead rumpled.

"Ariana's my middle name," she whispered before facing the crowd, her heart thundering. "Hi, guys. So, I'm gonna break the rules tonight."

"Naughty girl," someone yelled.

"I promise it's for a good cause. Who was here at Christmastime?"

Scattered hoots and applause.

"You remember that mistletoe? Well, I gave in to temptation and kissed the wrong guy. Could not be a worse fit for me."

"Been there," a woman shouted. Her tablemates guffawed.

"That's what I thought at the time, anyway. Because of a bunch of dumb ideas I had about who I am and who he is, I never really gave him a chance, and, well—" She shrugged. "I'm no good with fancy words. I think in pictures, as you can see." She lifted her sleeves to show her arms, then tugged down her neckline to show her rose bouquet.

Whistles and applause rang out.

"Anyway, I was wrong about this guy. He's perfect for me, and I want to show him why. Jojo?"

Chapter Nineteen

Beaming from ear to ear, the big guy pulled her portfolio case from behind his stool. "Eddie's gonna shit himself," he whispered as he handed it over.

Her gaze flicked to the bar. Eddie stood frozen, mouth agape, clutching an empty glass in one hand and a bar towel in the other.

She unlatched the case and pulled out her first drawing.

"What's that, a turd?" Dawn asked.

"It's a chocolate salami."

"Eew!" a woman squealed.

"It's actually delicious. This guy surprises me all the time with good things I never would've known about if I hadn't kissed him."

Her next drawing: an open book with a quill pen. "He doesn't just lurch through life like me, he's a planner who thinks of every detail. He's got a list for everything."

"Sounds boring," a girl said.

"Not at all." She glanced at Eddie, whose face had gone neon red. "It's the reason he gets shit done. I admire that."

Her next drawing, a skinny superhero, fists on his hips, cape flaring behind him, an E across his chest. "Because he's brave. And reliable, and honorable, and determined. He really cares about doing the right thing."

Eyes wide, Eddie set down the glass and clutched the towel to his heart.

She held up a drawing of kissy lips. "He's an amazing kisser."

Wolf whistles from the audience.

Next came a heart with a line of birds perched on its swirling tail. Beneath, the word *Family* in looping script. "He's sweet and respectful to his family. He makes me want to be a better daughter and sister."

The crumpled towel now covered Eddie's mouth. His eyes gleamed.

"That's a tattoo design, by the way. So is this one." She held up a white starburst surrounded by rays of yellow, orange, red, and purple fading into blackness and stars.

"What is it?" A girl beside the stage asked.

"A supernova." She cupped the mic with her free hand and whispered, " 'Cause, you know, in bed…" Grinning, she spread her fingers to indicate an explosion. "But I shouldn't tell you that because you'll try and grab him for yourself." She glanced at Eddie, who was either laughing or choking behind his towel. "He's taken."

He nodded slowly.

Next she held up an eye, its iris reflecting the earth in brilliant blues and greens. "I love the way he looks at me like I'm all the beautiful things in one—an ocean sunset and a soaring eagle and a juicy sex goddess. He's a great listener too, but who wants a tattoo of an ear?" When the laughter died down, she added, "He takes me seriously, even though I'm not a very serious person. He treats me like my dreams and plans are important."

"Because they are," Eddie called, his voice gruff but strong.

The crowd turned as one to the bar. Eddie's gaze held hers, his chin lifted, his hand over his heart.

Rosie set aside her drawings. "This last one's not on paper, it's on me. Wanna see, Eddie?"

The crowd parted as he slowly moved toward the stage, stumbling like a sleepwalker.

She lifted the hem of her skirt above her thigh-high sock to reveal a fresh tattoo, still covered with cling film. The low stage put the design right at his eye level.

Chapter Nineteen

"What is it?" Lana called.

Eddie gently gripped her thigh, his thumb stroking her skin beside the medical tape. "It's a rose," he croaked. "With writing around it."

Rosie glided her fingers into his soft curls. "The word love in Greek and Cantonese, for my family, and Russian, for yours." Tears clogged her throat and blurred her vision until all she saw was his beautiful, stunned face gazing up at her. "Because your love made me bloom, Eddie."

Slowly, his arms circled her. With a shuddering sigh, he buried his face in her stomach.

She folded over and wrapped herself around him. "I love you, Eddie."

And then she squeaked as her feet left the floor. Eddie lifted her down, raked his fingers into her hair, and kissed her until champagne fizzed in her veins and stars flashed through her closed lids.

"Awww," someone cooed. "That's the best love story ever."

Rosie opened her eyes and realized the starlight was actually the flash of phone cameras. While the customers applauded, she and Eddie joined hands and pressed their foreheads together. "You forgive me for being an ass?" Eddie murmured.

"If you do the same."

"Done."

"Aww!" Lana launched herself at them, colliding with a solid thunk and wrapping her arms around them both. "I'm so glad you guys worked it out."

Jojo folded all three of them into his enormous arms. Next came Kiara and Charlie, surrounding them in a squishy group hug. Warmth spread through Rosie's chest as she nestled in the arms of her love and her work family, the people who held her up in good times and bad. She was so lucky to have them. And when Eddie finally opened his own bar, they'd build a found family of their own.

Chuckling, Dawn spoke into the mic. "I dunno what it is about this place. Can't seem to keep my employees' hands off each other."

"It's his fault," a deep voice called from the doorway.

They all glanced up to find a snow-dusted River pointing at the carved Cupid above the bar.

"River!" Charlie squealed and dashed into his arms. "Thought you weren't coming back till Tuesday."

"Couldn't miss Valentine's Day with you, babe."

And so, Bangers' Anti-Valentine's party turned into a big, mushy love fest. At closing time, when the piñata was smashed, the tots gobbled up, and the donation box stuffed, Dawn wished them all a happy Valentine's Day and shooed them out the door.

Well, not all. Once again, Rosie and Eddie found themselves alone beneath the kitschy disco ball, swaying to "When a Man Loves a Woman."

Eddie's lips brushed the sensitive spot behind her ear. "My boxes are mostly unpacked. Wanna come see my new place?"

She let her head loll back, inviting more delicious kisses. "I don't know, Eddie. It's way past my bedtime."

"I've got a bed." He feathered kisses down her throat. "And a fireplace." He nibbled the crook of her neck, drawing a cascade of shivers. "And hot chocolate." He rolled his hips, grinding his erection against her thigh.

Her pussy fluttered in response. "Is that a chocolate salami in your pocket?"

"No, love. I'm just really glad to see you."

She grabbed his hand and pulled him toward the back door. "Let's go."

Chapter Twenty

Something scratchy rasped Rosie's bare shoulder. Blinking the sleep from her eyes, she inhaled Eddie's familiar, woodsy scent. With a contented sigh, she pulled the quilt up to her chin and rolled onto her side, pressing her back to his toasty warmth. His arm banded her waist and squeezed gently.

"Good morning," he croaked. "Sleep well?"

"Absolutely." There was no denying she slept better in Eddie's arms. His quiet warmth stilled her restless limbs and calmed her buzzing brain. Of course, their bone-rattling sex helped too.

Wiggling her ass, she nestled into the cradle of his hips. Her reward, a hungry moan and a poke from his morning wood.

"Shame to let that go to waste." She twined her fingers through his and lifted them to her breast.

He shifted, spooning his warm, sleepy-soft body to hers. His erection slid against her pussy and rested there, pulsing softly. His breath tickled her nape. His grip on her breast slackened.

"Not fair," she protested. "Don't tease me and go back to sleep."

He gifted her one slow thrust, an exquisite whisper of pleasure. And then he nuzzled her ear and gave a loud, phony snore.

"Think again, mister." She angled her hips and slid more firmly against his shaft. Happy shivers danced up her spine.

"Lemme sleep," he groaned, but his cock thrust again, sliding deeper into her folds. His grip tightened on her breast.

"You are asleep." Reaching between her thighs, she grasped him and notched his plush crown at her entrance. "This is just a dream." She arched her back and coaxed him inside.

After last night's marathon fuck-fest, she expected to be sore, but this lazy tease felt so delicious. No urgency, just sweet waves of sensation building slowly. They had all the time in the world to enjoy each other.

Eddie's hands slid to her hips, kneading gently as she rocked him in deep, measured strokes. "Best dream ever," he murmured.

"Isn't it?" She coaxed his hand between her thighs, and he began to circle her clit with a fingertip, his movement feather light. Bright sparks of bliss had her whimpering into her pillow.

On and on, spooned together, they undulated beneath his phoenix quilt. She imagined how they must look from above, the great bird rhythmically flapping its wings below their bed-mussed heads.

Eddie's grip tightened. Deep inside her, his cock grew even harder. Knowing he was close to coming fired her blood. A glance over her shoulder showed how right she was—face flushed, eyes screwed tight, mouth softly open on a gasp. She drew her knees up and rolled onto all fours, taking him with her. "Fuck me, Eddie."

"Yes, my queen." His laughter dissolved into a groan as he plunged deep, the pleasure so sharp and bright she jolted. Murmuring sweet, filthy words, he pummeled her while two fingers firmly pressed her clit. His breath grew ragged and shallow. "Give it to me, Ro. Come on my cock."

"Almost...there..." Gasping, she threw back her head. His hot mouth closed on the sensitive juncture of her neck and shoulder. Like lighting a fuse, the scrape of his teeth skyrocketed her to the heavens. She burst into a million shimmering sparks, her pussy clenching his hardness in waves of bliss. He followed in a flood of heat.

Chest heaving, she collapsed onto the bed. Eddie fell with her, his weight welcome, delicious, the thunder of his heart echoing her own. They rested that way until his softening cock finally slid out of her. She buried her wide, happy grin into the pillow. "Good morning, love."

"Good morning to you, angel." His fingertips traced hypnotic whorls over her skin. When she finally opened her eyes, she found him gazing at her with an expression of awe. He pressed his forehead to hers. "Wow."

She winced. "Morning breath."

"Gotcha." He rolled to the nightstand and pulled out a roll of mints.

Laughing, she helped herself to two. "Always prepared."

"I try." After they'd both crunched up a few mints, he pulled her into his arms and kissed her breathless. "Thanks for staying, Ro."

She rose onto her elbows. "Didn't get a good look around last night." Bigger than his last place, this low-ceilinged basement apartment had a cozy, hobbit-hole feel. "I like it."

"Needs more color, I think." He kissed her shoulder. "Maybe a potted palm over there. Some of those dangly mirror things above the bed."

"Yeah?" She giggled as he nuzzled her neck.

"The light's not great, but we could put in a strong lamp. You know, in case someone wanted to draw something."

"Hmm—whoever could you mean?"

He rolled her onto her back and crouched over her on hands and knees. "I know it's too soon, Ro, but with your schedule and mine, the next few years are gonna be rough. I want you here, in my bed. I want to wake up to your beautiful face and your morning breath and your luscious body. And we could make an art space just for you in the living room. I'll put up screens and corkboard and—"

"Okay." She wound her arms around his neck and pulled him in for a kiss. "Yes. Let's do it."

"Really?" He blinked as if he'd run out of words. Which was fine. They didn't need words now. Well, maybe just a few more.

"I'm in. I love you, Eddie."

"Thank God." He peppered her face and chest with kisses. "I love you too, Ro." He sucked one nipple deep, then the other, before popping up. "So, I've got this idea." He lunged for the nightstand and pulled his little notebook from the drawer. "About my bar and your tattoo studio. Wanna see?"

Wrapped in Babka's quilt and each other's arms, they talked and laughed and spun plans—perfectly mismatched, perfectly happy, perfect together.

Epilogue

"You ready, babes?" Rosie held up the giant scissors they'd borrowed from the Chamber of Commerce. Outside, a crowd gathered on the sidewalk, waiting for them to cut the ribbon.

Eyes sparkling, Eddie grabbed her nape and kissed her silly. "I can't believe we're finally doing this." She'd never seen him this wiggly with excitement—and why not? He'd earned it.

She straightened his silk tie. "Five long years. We couldn't be more ready."

Thanks to Uncle Pete's help and a loan from the Seattle Russian-American Society, they'd secured the perfect spot in Tacoma's Lincoln District, sandwiched between a Korean grocery and a Mediterranean kebab place. With the help of family and friends, their adjoining businesses, Dacha Vodka Bar and Flaming Rose Tattoo Emporium, were finally ready to welcome their first customers.

Rosie gazed around Dacha's gleaming dark wood interior. Eddie's Dedka had supervised while Eddie and his dad and cousins transformed the dreary cement-and-linoleum interior, hung antique frosted glass lamps, installed black and white floor tiles, and filled the mirrored bar with over one hundred vodka varieties, including rarities hard to find outside the Old Country. Adding to the speakeasy vibe, a beaded curtain hung over the connecting door to her new domain, a three-station tattoo studio. Gloria, her very own apprentice-receptionist, waited at the desk to book appointments.

Rosie gave Eddie's ass a squeeze. He looked damned fine in the slate gray suit Uncle Pete gifted him for the occasion. The tie was her gift, printed with classic tattoo motifs.

He tugged the ribbon laces at the neck of her velvet mini dress. "You are stunning tonight, Ro." He ran his hand up her fishnet stockings. "Love the way these look over your ink."

"Too bad your suit hides yours." While still not a fan of needles, he'd let her adorn his arms with a Russian bear holding a vodka bottle, as well as a rose tattoo just like one on her thigh.

He gave her a wink. "I'll roll up my sleeves later."

"Swoon!" She fanned herself.

Shelby stepped out of the kitchen and wiped her hands on her apron. "Just say the word and I'll start the dumplings."

"C'mere, Shel." Rosie beckoned. "This is your day too. Let's go meet and greet."

Shelby blanched and tried to wriggle free. "No way. There's a reporter out there. TV cameras. No me gusta."

Eddie grasped her shoulders and fixed the jittery cook with a stern gaze. "You got this, Shel. You're an outstanding chef, and all of Tacoma's gonna know your name."

Shelby huffed a few breaths and rolled her head like a

prizefighter warming up. "Okay. But just five minutes."

Eddie turned to address the servers and bartenders. "You guys ready?"

Looking dapper in a crisp dress shirt with an old-fashioned arm garter hugging his giant biceps, Jojo's brother Kai nodded. "Bring it, boss."

Rosie hooked her arm through Eddie's, smooched his whiskered cheek, and called, "Drumroll, please!" While Kai and Theo, their head server, drummed on the bar, she and Eddie strode forward to greet their first customers.

Eddie flipped the sign from Closed to Open and flung open the doors, blinking into the barrage of camera flashes and cheers. He raised the giant scissors. "Ready, Ro?"

Tummy fluttering, she nodded.

Cheers erupted when he cut the red ribbon stretched across the doorway.

Clutching a bunch of mylar balloons, Dawn pushed through the crowd of well-wishers and wrapped Rosie and Eddie in a tight hug. "I'm so proud of you kids." She doffed her Seahawks cap and rubbed her misty eyes. "Now show me your bar."

Puffed like a proud rooster, Eddie hooked his arm through his mentor's and led her to the bar, where Dawn oohed and ahhed over the shiny brass fittings. Meanwhile, Theo deposited Shelby's first dumpling sampler platter on a long table they'd reserved for the Bangers crew.

Clucking like a fussy hen, River helped Charlie into a seat. Only seven months along, she looked like she was ready to pop. Rosie couldn't wait to meet her adoptive nephew—in fact, she was putting the finishing touches on a set of onesies painted with classic tattoo designs.

"Look at this spread." Charlie bit into a chicken-kimchee

pirozhki and moaned. "So good. Ooh!" She grabbed River's hand and pressed it to her bulging belly. "Junior likes these."

Kiara tried a traditional cabbage and onion steamed pelmeni. "I love it that you have vegetarian options. You know what this would be good with? A mustard dipping sauce."

Rosie squeezed her shoulder. "Go tell Shelby. Kitchen's that way."

Grinning, Kiara stuffed another dumpling in her mouth and trotted off.

Lana skipped up to their table, squeezed Rosie tight, then plopped into Kiara's empty seat. "Sorry we're late. Jojo's parking."

A moment later, the gentle giant strode through the door and spread his muscly arms wide. "Eddie! You did it!"

His arm around Anna, Diego gave Jojo a shove. "Don't block the door, meathead." Jostling and joking, they made their way to the table.

Eddie joined them a moment later with a tray holding chilled shot glasses, sparkling water for Charlie, and a cut-glass bottle. "A very special vodka from my family's hometown near Omsk. I've been saving this for tonight." He poured out a round, then raised his glass high. "Rosie and I toast all of you, the family of our hearts. Thanks for believing in us."

Rosie dabbed her eyes and added, "And for knocking our heads together until we finally figured out how well we fit. To family!"

They all clinked and downed their shots. All around the bar, customers joined in the inaugural toast. And hours later, when the dumplings were all eaten, Rosie's tattoo appointment book filled, and the last customers had trailed out, Eddie and Rosie swayed to a growly metal ballad, arms wrapped tight around each other.

Rosie gazed into Eddie's dark eyes, so warm and sparkling in the low, golden light. She pressed her brow to his. "You did it, babes."

"We did it." His lips feathered over hers. "Thank you, Ro. Now—" He waggled his eyebrows. "What say we lower the blinds and christen this bar properly?"

"You mean—?"

Walking backward, he tugged her toward the largest booth. "Salesman says these seats are stain-proof. Wanna try?"

She answered his devilish grin with one of her own. "You know I do."

"My hot-blooded Rosie." Nibbling the crook of her neck, he unlaced her dress.

Delicious shivers skated over her skin. "Eddie?"

"Hmm?" His hands slid down to cup her breasts.

"Tell me the truth?" She loosened his tie.

"Always."

"Did you put this on your list? In your notebook?"

He nipped her earlobe. "Of course."

"That's my Eddie. A man with a plan." Reaching out, she flicked the switch to lower the blinds.

THE END

Thank you for reading *Opposites Ignite*. If you enjoyed the story, please consider leaving a review on Bookbub or your favorite eBook retailer. For news about new releases, deals, giveaways, and some really bad romance jokes, consider signing up for my **Author Newsletter.** Read on for Valentine's Day cocktails from *Opposites Ignite!*

Valentine's Day Cocktails from Bangers Tavern

❦

Suffering Bastard

According to several sources, this tasty drink originated as a hangover cure invented during WWII by a bartender at Cairo's famous Shepheard's Hotel. Here's my simplified version. I was skeptical about the combination of bourbon and gin, but it's truly delish and very refreshing.

In a cocktail shaker, combine 1 ounce/30 milliliters of bourbon, 1 ounce of gin, 1 teaspoon fresh lime juice, a generous shake of Angostura bitters, and an orange wedge. Add as much ice as you like for one drink and shake vigorously. Pour into a lowball glass and top up with ginger ale or ginger beer. Garnish with mint, if you like. Serves one. Yum!

The Bangers Brawl

Have you noticed how often the Bangers bartenders take out their frustrations by muddling drink ingredients? This tasty concoction is Kiara's twist on a whiskey smash, a vintage cocktail dating back to the late 1800s.

Cut half a small blood orange into chunks. If it's a big orange, use a quarter. Add six fresh mint leaves and smash 'em good with a muddler or the back of a spoon. Doesn't that feel good? Add one ounce of simple syrup, or to taste. I like my drink a little less sweet. Add 2 ounces of good rye whiskey. Shake well with ice, then strain into a lowball glass, add crushed ice, and garnish with more fresh mint and a slice of blood orange.

*If you can't find blood oranges, use half a lemon and you've got a classic whiskey smash.

The Zipper

This refreshing cocktail is super-simple. In a highball/tall glass, muddle a few tablespoons of fresh or frozen black-berries, then add a shot of berry-flavored vodka, a shot of raspberry liqueur (such as Chambord), plus ice and lemon-lime soda or sparkling water—try berry-flavored seltzer with this one! Stir well, then garnish with fresh blackberries and mint.

Chocolate Salami

Yes, this is really a thing! This no-bake, fudgy Russian treat comes from the Soviet era and utilizes things people would've had on hand: butter, milk, cocoa powder, vanilla cookies, and nuts. The Food Network site has a fancy version, but you'll find plenty of simpler recipes online. Priyatnogo appetita!

Author's Note and Acknowledgments

Thanks so much for reading *Opposites Ignite*! If you enjoyed the story, please sign up for my monthly newsletter to hear about new releases, deals, giveaways, and some really bad romance jokes. Sign up at www.sadirastone.com.

Pretty please, if you enjoyed this story, consider leaving a review on Bookbub or your favorite eBook retailer or review site!

One of the many things I love about writing fiction is the chance to try out (virtually) the many careers I never got a chance to pursue in real life. So far, I've written about running a bookshop (*Runaway Love Story*), an ice cream shop (*Gelato Surprise*), being a photographer (*Runaway Love Story*), a graphic artist, a potter (*Love, Art, and Other Obstacles*), and now running a bar.

Thanks to my beta readers Laurie Ryan, Cari Davis, Marie Tuhart, Michelle McCraw, Jessica Buchanan Jang, and Carla Luna Cullen. A huge smooch to my editor Judi Mobley, AKA Music City Freelance Editor. Another smooch for Dar Albert of Wicked Smart Designs for her lovely cover.

Thanks to King's Books and Doyle's Public House for allowing me to mention them by name in this novel. If you find yourself in Tacoma, be sure to visit T-Town's best bookshop and Irish Pub!

And most of all, thanks to my husband for supporting me in my writing journey. You're the BHE!

Books by Sadira Stone

Through the Red Door: Book Nirvana 1

Letting him inside could be her salvation...or her undoing.

Clara Martelli clings to Book Nirvana, the Oregon bookshop
she and her late husband Jared built together. When rising
rents and corporate competition threaten its survival, her best
hope is their extensive erotica collection, locked behind a red
door. In dreams and signs, her dead husband tells her it's time
to open that door and move on. When a dark and handsome
stranger's powerful magnetism jolts her back to life and he
wants a look at the treasures of that secret room, she can't
help but want to show him more.

Professor Nick Papadopoulos is looking for historical erotica.
Book Nirvana's collection surpasses his wildest dreams, and
so does its lovely owner. A widower, he understands Clara's

battle with guilt, but their searing chemistry is too strong to resist. Besides, he will only be in town for two weeks, not long enough for her to see beyond the scandal that haunts his past.

Runaway Love Story: Book Nirvana 2

High school history teacher Doug Garvey is trying to enjoy his last few weeks of summer vacation, but receiving his final divorce decree hits him harder than expected. After a brief fling fizzles, he fears love just isn't in the cards for him. If only he could find someone who's real, someone interested in something beyond herself...maybe a new running partner who can keep up with his more carnal appetite. When sexy, straight-talking Laurel runs across his path, he dares to hope again.

Fired from an art gallery, Laurel Jepsen shelves her pursuit of an art career in San Francisco to help her beloved great aunt Maxie move into assisted living. While out on a morning run, she's harassed by a group of teens until a tall, broad-shouldered hottie steps in, pretending to be her boyfriend with a kiss that makes her wish it were true. But she's only passing through, not looking for a relationship.

Their fierce chemistry burns up the sheets—and the couch, the shower, the forest—but falling in love would ruin everything. Laurel can't stay in Eugene, and he can't leave. Doug's only hope is to convince her the glittery life she's after could blind her to the opportunities already in her path.

Books by Sadira Stone

Love, Art, and Other Obstacles: Book Nirvana 3

She's a free spirit. He's a one-woman man.

Rejected by her family for her bisexuality, graphic artist Margot DuPont yearns for a life with no fences, no limits, and no family ties. Between college, work at Book Nirvana, and an art competition, she barely has time for her part-time girlfriend, much less a flirtation with her competitor.

Dumped into the foster system at a young age, ceramics artist Elmer Byrne craves a big, loving family of the heart. His artist family almost fills that need, but something is missing...until Margot. But when he offers his heart, her thorny defenses shatter him.

Thrown together in an art competition that could jump-start one artist's career, but not both, their irresistible attraction forces them to reconsider the meaning of success.

Gelato Surprise

She came to the beach to find herself—and found him.

Forty-two-year-old divorcée Danielle Peters ends up alone on her family's annual beach vacation. Maybe time to herself is exactly what she needs. That and gelato from her favorite ice cream shop. But when the owner's intoxicating young nephew offers more than sweet treats, she's tempted to indulge in a hot summer fling before returning home.

Thirty-one-year-old Matteo Verducci craved a fresh start to mend his broken heart, and he's found almost perfection in Ocean View, where he scoops gelato by day and crafts furniture by night. But when a sexy older woman stops to sample his wares—Mamma mia! He only has two weeks to convince her their passion is more than a delicious surprise.

Christmas Rekindled: Bangers Tavern Romance 1

Bartender River Lundqvist has a damn good reason for hating Christmas. Bangers Tavern is the perfect place to lay low over the holidays—until Charlie walks in. His first encounter with the saucy server nine years ago was utter humiliation. Her reappearance stirs up powerful desires and hopes for a new start. But the timing is all wrong.

Back in Tacoma to care for her estranged dad over the holidays, freelance web designer Charlie Khoury braces herself for the suckiest Christmas ever. A temporary job at Bangers Tavern gives her a chance to escape Dad's criticism and blow off some steam. But why does the hunky bartender seem to hate her?

A pretend girlfriend is just what River needs to keep his family off his back—until a kiss under the mistletoe flares hot enough to melt the North Pole. When greedy developers threaten Bangers Tavern, River and Charlie must team up to save it. Their sizzling chemistry feels like the real thing—but everyone knows rebound relationships don't last.

Come to Bangers Tavern for an enemies-to-lovers tale of reconciliation, found family, holiday cocktails, and the steamiest Christmas miracle ever.

About the Author

Ever since her first kiss, Sadira's been spinning steamy tales in her head. After leaving her teaching career in Germany, she finally tried her hand at writing one. Now she's a happy citizen of Romancelandia, penning contemporary romance from her new home in Washington State, U.S.A. When not writing, which is seldom, she explores the Pacific Northwest with her charming husband, enjoys the local music scene, plays darts (pretty well), plays guitar (badly), and gobbles all the books.

Visit Sadira on All the Socials!

Author website: www.sadirastone.com. Don't forget to sign up for my monthly newsletter for news, freebies, and some really bad romance jokes!

Facebook: sadirastone

Twitter: @SadiraStone

Instagram: @sadirastone

Pinterest: www.pinterest.com/sadira0641/

Bookbub: www.bookbub.com/profile/sadira-stone

Made in the USA
Middletown, DE
15 September 2021

48363251R00170